The Lucid Veil

By: Richard A. Gutiérrez

• • •

The difficulty is in the details ~

Not in remembering them, but in their remembrance.

• • •

● ● ●

TABLE OF CONTENTS

DEDICATION

• • •

Dedicated to those who have helped me on my Spiritual Journey and to the ones I have yet to meet

• • •

Chapter I - Marissa

I sweetly enjoyed the smell of fresh-cut grass and the colorful flowers that my abuela had in their yard. She was already collecting leaves and plucking parts of some of her plants along the deciduous garden, while I stood gazing at a tree that grew near one of the corners of the fenced-in areas of their lush corner property. Its large dark pink flowers arranged in sets of five, nearly the size of a saucer and closely related to hibiscus, and their shiny green heart-shaped leaves were aesthetic and very pleasing to my senses. I felt comfort in the shade it gave me and the other surrounding plant-life. I only saw this tree around here as it was endemic to Puerto Rico. With a fist full of vegetation and herbs, she walked towards me in contemplation and focus.

"Flor de Maga," she said as she walked towards the side entrance of the house, and I followed. *The Maga flower.* A couple of small harmless lizards with long tails were above the doorway, waiting for their next meal of an insect, in the shade. In a white dish, on top of a small plastic table next to the washing machine, there was a dried plant with no dirt or water.

"Abuela, what is that plant called, in that bowl there?"

"Muere-Vivir," she blurted.

"Oh. Ok."

Abuelita always made sure I was never hungry, and I loved her cooking. My dad and I would visit his parents at least once a year, from New Jersey, as often as we could for a week at a time, and while he was in the parlor with abuelito watching television I sat on a stool by the kitchen counter watching her fry eggs and plátanos maduros for breakfast. Waiting, while dangling my legs from the high seat, I spun the wooden rack that contained about twenty different spices in plastic jars. There always seemed to be a gallon of cooking oil readily available, tucked away in a cabinet below, for safe and proper storage.

Sometimes she would light up a cigarette while she cooked and was often careful not to have any ashes fall on the food or floor. She would strike a *Three Stars* safety match when she turned on the gas stove to light a burner and then light her smoke with it. It would just dangle on the side of her mouth and if she needed to flick the burning ash, it would be in the sink and not in any visible ashtray. At the age of six, I already knew my grandmother was cool.

After breakfast, dad drove us in the rental car about ten minutes away to visit a dying family member in Aibonito. It was his oldest uncle, Miguel, who has lived to the age of seventy-two. Bedridden, he had almost lost his ability to fully control his bodily movements and just laid there – tired and anxious, wondering why he hadn't noticed or attempted to fix the small cracks in his bedroom ceiling. The oscillating fan moved from left to right at a medium speed, periodically allowing his eyes to move and not be fixated on one spot, or thought, as his mind wandered.

A small crowd of family members convened at their front door, some pointing at the foliage and tropical flowers displayed in the front jardín notating its scintillating colors and beauty, while others poised to fix their attire or even wipe the sweat from their foreheads with a handkerchief, caused by the stroll in the laboring heat. We drove up at the tail-end and parked in front of the one-story house when the front door opened, while his aunt Melita greeted everyone, waited for us and welcomed us all inside.

We quickly got reacquainted with each other and I was somewhat forced to break out of my shyness because I was the newest addition to the family whom some have never met. There was life to this gathering, with constant chatter and pleasantries. I sat on the end of the sofa to get away from all the attention. The plastic covering stuck to my legs, so I just sat there without moving or making any unnecessary noise. Titi offered coffee and water to the familial guests but she offered me a cold drink in a bottle.

I was enamored by the clean and shiny beige tile floors and her white doilies carefully placed on top of a few end tables. The house was neatly decorated inside and now we were invited to go outside and see the backyard. In the carport a long dark vehicle was covered in a protective cloth and walking by it I was greeted by a small Pekingese dog. I was startled at first but since it didn't lick or bite me, I was fine.

"That's Pumpkin," my father said to me. *Pumpkin the Pekingese – made sense.*

I nodded in affirmation.

Around the back was an entirely unexpected environment. They owned three bird cages full of parakeets and they were hung and protected under an extended awning. There must have been seven blue ones from the twenty small Aves and their cages were kept clean considering that they had plenty of food and water. Roaming on the grounds were several chickens accompanied by one black radiant rooster that had red feathers on his head and blue feathers on his tail end. His claws looked sharp and scary, so I avoided going near him at all costs. I stayed close to Pumpkin because I knew she wouldn't hurt me.

"Hola, Marissa," one of the ladies addressed my grandmother.

She just nudged her head and greeted her in return. Although my grandmother was family, she was seemingly being treated differently, judged, or perhaps the other way around; it was peculiar.

Titi came around with finger sandwiches that she made and offered me a small bag of plantain chips and even a banana and orange. She was such a hostess and tried to take care of everyone's immediate needs, partially out of gratitude that we had come over to visit. Some of my father's cousins had already went back inside to see Titi's husband, who wasn't feeling well. I noticed more lizards, on the white walls, imitating push-ups to attract others. Nonetheless, there was constant motion, mobility and energy throughout the property. I munched on chips and pork rinds with my Malta India beverage and stayed far away from the rooster.

After a couple of hours, they had all gone but the three of us remained. My father was talking to Titi Melita about fond memories they had while growing up, laughing and reminiscing. Abuelita motioned for me to come with her, to see my second uncle Miguel, in his bedroom.

"Hola, Miguelito. ¿Como estás?" she greeted him.

His head moved slightly jolted in surprise, hearing a familiar voice he hadn't heard in a while. She introduced me.

"Aquí está mi nieto."

His right forefinger twitched, and his glassy eyes started to fixate and focus on me, then on her. She held his hand, his trembling, while she placed her other on his head.

"¿Cómo te sientes?

She asked him how he was feeling and instructed me to have a seat. There was a chair near the right foot of the bed. The breeze from the fan intermittently hit me and slightly eased my sense of suffocation from the tropical heat and small dim-lit room.

He looked comfortable in his light blue pajama button-down shirt. His skin was not as tanned or olive as the inhabitants of most of the people in town, which could be said and determined that he hadn't been as exposed to the sun lately. The window shutters allowed a perpetual breeze and hints of daylight but not enough to make anyone squint from the bright rays. Confined to this house, and maybe solely to this room for a duration, his body was slowly lacking the nutrients and necessary elements of activity needed to thrive.

Abuelita fixed the sheet and moved it up to his waist, then sat on the side of the full mattress bed, facing him but not omitting me from the view. She wanted me to see. I heard my father murmuring and laughing from the kitchen area and continued his dialogue with Titi. My grandmother said something in Spanish, to her older brother as he laid there motionless, that I didn't understand. My mind drifted into nothing but the present, my eyes unable to blink, hanging on to every accented word, syllable, sound, astounded by the interaction and in that prolonged blink of an eye, he succumbed from all fear.

We left the room and Grandma Marissa told Melita and my father about Miguel's passing.

Distraught by grief, Titi felt some comfort in knowing that he was visited by family before his death and her conversations with my father helped her to previously lighten the mood. She notified the others and by the time some of them returned, we had already left to go back to the house. That was the first time I had ever witnessed anyone transition in front of me.

It was a solemn remainder of the day for me and I wasn't sure what to say or even feel, but not for my sake. I didn't know Uncle Miguel. I was more empathetic to my dad's and grandparents' feelings and how they were coping so I remained in my best behavior and continued to follow their leads. Surprisingly, abuela stayed busy by prepping dinner for the four of us, smoking a cigarette in intervals and she may have taken a shot of clear alcohol, tucked away in a top shelf in one of the cabinets. The food smelled good as it permeated throughout their one-story house, and she let me sample a spoonful of her beans that would deliciously compliment the white rice and fried bone-in pork chops. Once again, it was perfectly seasoned – just like grandma makes it.

After dinner, the guys went to the parlor to watch boxing on the television. While she washed the dishes, I cleaned off the round wooden table and wiped the plastic cover. I had ripped the paper towel I grabbed from the holder affixed underneath the last mustard yellow cabinet next to the refrigerator and used it to remove some grains of rice that fell off my fork and never made it to my mouth. I heard a match strike but instead of lighting up another smoke she lit a white candle and placed it on a saucer in the sink. She then walked over to the wooden hutch in the dining room and opened the left drawer, and there, inside, were two decks of cards but she pulled out the playing deck.

"Robar. Cuenta."

She wanted to play "Steal the Old Man's Pack" and for me to keep score, and it was probably better for me to tabulate the game to prevent possible cheating, which she always accused me of whenever I won.

She shuffled the deck a few times and asked me to cut it, then dealt out four cards each and closely monitored my hand. She was focused on every card I presented and really into it, almost as if she were playing another game.

"Sin trampa," she told me. I just smiled and tried to concentrate on not having her steal my pile. After a few hands, and before I could officially win, it was time to retire to sleep; it had been a long and exhausting day.

The hallway bathroom emanated a calming atmosphere, color-coordinated with a bold palette of blue hues. The tub area was decorated with an aquatic blue shower curtain with images of tropical fish, baby blue walls were painted in a flat matted finish, and the toilet had matching cobalt rugs both on the floor and toilet seat cover. I felt at ease and was even humming quietly while brushing my teeth at the blueish sink basin, and when I finished swishing and spitting the toothpaste, I looked for the dental floss. I opened the vanity mirror and there were two spools between a bottle of hydrogen peroxide and rubbing alcohol, which had me thinking about the removal of decay.

Before going to bed for the night and when I finished and entered the hallway, I passed my grandparents' bedroom and saw her through the doorway standing by a small table that had another lit candle accompanied by small figurines. She may have been praying, and as I crept and tip-toed into my room, I heard her door close shut behind me.

Chapter II – The Wake

I slowly opened my eyes, awakened from a deep meditation, unclasping my hands and lifting them up from the opened casket that contained the peaceful Mr. Gerald Kaminski. I had been kneeling in reverence and when I arose I looked around the room to gauge if I had unintentionally attracted much attention to myself and when I recognized that I hadn't inconvenienced anyone with my prolonged presence, I walked over to admire photographs the family affixed and pinned to a couple of cork boards to commemorate particular fond moments of his life. I was so surprised and thrilled that there was one where I was present, not that many would notice or see me since I wasn't a pronounced subject with the immediate family – I was the photographer. *I remember that day.*

My mother had notified me two days ago of his passing, when she read the news in the obituary column. Initially, I was in shock, not because I thought he would live forever, but from the casual reminder that I indeed knew and met him long ago, and that my mother remembered him, as well. He was there at my high school graduation and was a role model and male archetype as a commuting New York City professional. Mr. K was a great family man, or at least I revered him as such, and saw no other way that would reflect otherwise, and so my attention was drawn to his family in their moment of deep loss.

He was a church-going man who was balanced and fair, especially when I was dating his daughter. Mr. K, along with his wife Kristina, was open and patient with the notion of allowing me to spend time with his only child, and in return I exuded the most caring loving relationship with my first girlfriend – Jeanette. It was this integral reason that I had not only loved her, but also her family who had no reservations or qualms in accepting me on who I was and how I treated a special member of their family.

I wore one of my favorite dark gray suit jackets that I recently picked up from the dry cleaners days ago, and a dark tie with a subtle image of a computer mouse imprinted on it. He introduced me to the MAC computer in the late eighties and swore its allegiance over any other operating system. While Jeanette and I would watch a movie in their living room, he would often be working on certain tasks and projects on his bulky computer, his eyes affixed for lengthy portions of time staring at a monitor, and he taught me what I could handle on learning, while I was attending and studying the subject of Computer Science at my Prep school.

I arrived at the McLaughlin Funeral Parlor before the evening rush hour and hadn't communed with much of the visitors, family and friends. Jeanette's mother walked into the viewing room and I was elated and aquiver to see her again. She remembered me.

"Hi, Coronado. So nice to see you again."

"Hi, Mrs. K," I said as I hugged her.

"So sorry about Mr. K. My sincerest condolences to you and your family."

We gently held an endearing look and grin at each other, in a moment of silence.

"Thank you so much. Have you seen or spoken to Jeanette?"

"No, ma'am. I haven't heard from her in years."

"Well, she's on her way. Stay a while, won't you?"

"I will. Thank you, Mrs. K. Let me know if there's anything you need."

I walked over to the back row of cushioned wooden chairs to allow newcomers, especially family members, their space to congregate in closer proximity to the body. At times, random people would ask me for directions as if I were an employee there, and I would kindly direct them to wherever they needed to go, and because of my experience with so many wakes and funerals that, I, over time, developed and adapted enough self-awareness and self-confidence to fit the role of a care taker. A small group entered and came towards the side of my seating area.

Initially upon walking in the vestibule, there is a book that allows a guest to sign in so that the family knows who was in attendance. Leather bound and already opened to a fresh clean page so that the pen, attached to a silver chain to avoid mistakenly leaving the podium, marries its ink with the parchment, and could readily be used by the next willing soul. Pulling a black-ink fountain pen from my inner jacket pocket, I legibly handwrote my signature to log my name into its existence, creating the unspoken direction for the next participant, directing them to follow my lead and sign the ledger. I was the fifth person to check in, thirty minutes ago, only recognizing one other name above mine, whom I've only met once but heard about a multitude of times – Cheryl, one of Jeanette's best friends from long ago, so long she had yet to recognize me from the next room.

To the right, on the same podium, was a wooden tray compartment that held a couple of dozen 2.5" x 4.5" prayer cards displaying several different images to select from, and laminated to maintain and preserve, in loving memory, an excerpt in commemoration of the deceased. There were a few that captured my eye, but I chose the white dove that seemed to be floating effortlessly in a light blue and violet sky. Flipping it over, there was a small symbol of a cross on the top, followed by Gerald Kaminski's name in an italicized and bold heading, his birth and death date, with the funeral home's name at the very bottom. In between, there was a bible verse so endearing I read it twice. It spoke of comfort during grief, laughter and joy overcoming burden, and good times with good friends. It was a reminder that there was life after death, a faith held true by Christian beliefs. I placed both my pen and the card in my jacket pocket and took a deep breath.

With head bowed in reverence, I took notice in this alternate perspective. I saw the slow solemn parade of leather and canvas footwear. I saw them all: the new and spiffy, the polished and the scuffed, the worn and the torn. Each pair supported the weight of characters, each having their own recollection of moments, shared on earth, with the deceased.

Chapter III - Jeanette

Jeanette and I first met at a high school Dance in 1989. I had no idea what to expect since it was my first time visiting the inside of St. Dominic's Academy, an all-girls school, in Jersey City. I was attending St. Peter's Prep, an all-boys high school and sibling institution, and had known about the event from the flyers randomly displayed throughout our hallways, and from word of mouth. Attending a private and parochial school meant having to adhere to a dress code consisting of either a uniform or formal attire, for us – a jacket and tie, but this function allowed us to dress comfortably in a more casual attire.

As I entered the stairway downstairs to the dance floor, I couldn't help but to think that I was in someone's basement with gray painted pillars and checkered floor tile. I was nervous since my view was obstructed by the descending stairs and unable to see legs or feet on the way down. When I finally hit the ground floor, I was amazed that the ceilings were rather low, suffocating and confining, compared to other dance hall facilities I had frequented.

It was during my late elementary education and my four years in Preparatory school where I listened and lived to the music from the 80s. Many great artists from different genres immersed on my list of listening pleasures, and most have survived their popularities. It was partly a reason why I decided to become a disc jockey at an early age, slightly before my love for House, Club and Electronica. The eighties were a time for me to transition through my teenage years.

If it weren't for old 8mm films that my father took, reminding me of how my uncle Charlie danced like it was nobody's business, I probably wouldn't have the courage to do it today. He was calculating in being zany and free, and magnificent at it. He had fun and it made me smile just to watch him perform on being him. I was comfortable with watching people dance and with the progression of popular trends and styles, I felt that some techniques were timeless while some were less flattering. I used to be a wallflower at every school dance. It just seemed a little odd for me to move my body when everyone was looking and judging, and although I was a bit athletic I didn't feel as if I needed to work on my cardio while wiggling about to the beat of someone else's drum, but that was me talking myself out of it and creating excuses because of my fear of fallibility.

There were two girls chatting, not close to the realm of plotting devilish or heinous deeds although they could have been talking about anything, but they were too innocent for any of that. They were both pretty – one blonde and the other a brunette – and they were very different from each other, in addition to the hair color. The brunette was a bit shorter than me by about an inch, her straight hair down just above her shoulders and her turtleneck shirt and additional sweater hid her figure well, so I needed to explore her personality beyond the Preppie appearance and engage in active conversation. I waited for them to discontinue their alleged scheming then I approached her.

"Hi. Would you like to dance?" I asked without fear or hesitation, and without reciprocated fear or hesitation she responded with a

"No" then walked away. She was as guarded from me as the black wrought iron gate that protected the fine institute's front walls.

As an introvert and an extremely shy guy, I often find it challenging to want to connect with anyone because I am occupied with working within myself to become an evolving better person, however social interaction is a component of that growth. I am a Puerto Rican, considered a minority to most and was not from an affluent family but with some planning and saving, my parents were able to provide a better education for me and that was my focus and priority. It didn't matter to me how I looked because that was an outward appearance, but often I felt that I am judged by what wasn't aesthetically pleasing to society whether it was my hair style, the clothes that I wear, or even my height.

Born, raised, and growing up in the most diverse city in the world – Jersey City, I wasn't familiar or focused on the concept of racism. Living in a bustling city, I did not have time to even know it existed because I felt we were all in it together – surviving, living, and trying to advance with our goals. People would try to hustle, scam, or try to get over on you no matter what you looked like in this rat race, as with the opposite, so there was no real way that the brunette knew I was a particular nationality or race. I am certain I was just a boy who wasn't her type in a dance partner, that she was interested in.

Music was so influential to me while growing up and during the nineteen-eighties, that I continued buying record vinyl albums so that I could play them on my parents' record player. The first album I owned was Billy Joel's *Glass Houses* and there were so many different artists and great music coming out in the late eighties that I extended my album collection, and organized them in empty plastic milk crates that I borrowed from the front of the local corner grocery store. Some of my prevalent albums were the Beastie Boys *Licensed To Ill*, Run DMC's *Raising Hell* and Eric B & Rakim's *Paid In Full*, although I really enjoyed listening to Whitney Houston, Prince, Peter Gabriel, Madonna, Van Halen, John "Cougar" Mellencamp and so many others on the radio.

The Beatles had already been a staple in my musical repertoire that even after their breakup, whether you blamed Yoko Ono for it or not, I still followed their individual works and as a youth I enjoyed watching *The Yellow Submarine* movie even though none of their actual voices were used in it, so with that my favorite tune was "Nowhere Man". Perhaps it is fitting to begin to rationalize who I was and who I was to become at an early age with the influence of music.

I casually walked away listening to "The Promise" by *When in Rome* for only a few moments before I really saw my future dance partner surrounded in an aura filled with a light blue glow. The blonde friend was moving and dancing in place and caught my attention, in her elegant dress below her knees, her hair puffed up – permed and teased - and wearing light-color framed glasses. A feeling came over that made me anxious and nervous, interviewing for a job that I wanted as a career. I began to really see her and was instantly attracted to her presence, and I felt as if I needed to talk to her but if she rejected me it would be as if I missed the lottery by one number. Since she was already grooving to the song, I casually danced over to her and introduced myself.

"Hi. I'm Coronado. Mind if I join you?"

"Hi. I'm Jeanette. Keep up," she teased with a mysterious grin.

She was beautiful. Her dress twirled and flowed in every direction as we sashayed and danced the night away, having such a great time conversing and laughing.

"I'm in the school choir and we have our first recital soon, if you're interested."

"Yeah. Sounds great. You have a nice voice. I'd love to go."

We decided to see each other again and exchanged phone numbers.

We periodically hung out at her house, under respectful adult supervision. If I got lucky, I was able to get close enough to pull her long hair up and sneak a couple of nibbles and rub my nose behind her neck while on the couch. She smelled so good but wasn't an advocate for perfumes.

"Mmmm… what are you wearing?"

She giggled softly, "Dove soap."

"Sexy."

At times we wanted to explore and get away, so we decided to go for a ride. When I crossed the railroad tracks, on Morris Pesin Drive, I turned off my car radio so that we could further immerse ourselves into the sights and sounds of Liberty State Park. The clanking of rope against the row of over twenty flag poles along the way sounded like slow intermittent claps of applause as to be greeted into the welcomed gates of nature. The lined trees offered shade and we tried to remember the order and names of the different countries that were represented by their respective country's banners.

It was a great day to have and want a picnic, and early enough that the late March air would cool us off from short walks in the sun. The two or three jetties by the parking lot gave refuge to seagulls anxious to perch before venturing into the waters for their next meal. The geese felt more comfortable being inland where they could contribute to the composting of grass, leaving trails of waste in numbers. The Information Desk and Park Office was closed, along with the concession stand which would have been serving hot dogs, hamburgers, and other food items later that day, but luckily the restrooms were easily accessible, if necessary.

I rather appreciated the fact that we seemed to be the only ones there, although the steady wind and sounds of playful seabirds reminded me that we were not alone. The smell of the sea air awakened me like the smelling salt a trainer puts under a boxer's nose to wake up; I felt alive. I placed our brown bags of sandwiches and drinks on a wooden picnic bench and took a deep breath as we sat – admiring the Statue of Liberty from afar. We were teens living in the moment, feeling responsibly care-free and soaking in the energy of nature. The constant clamor from the thirteen flagpoles displaying the US flags near the center of the park, sounded off in a tribal rhythm preparing us for festivities of what was to come.

I took a picture, with an automatic Kodak *FunSaver* disposable camera, of her with sandwich in hand and a smile, then forwarded and advanced the film so it would be ready to take the next. The ratchet-sounding mechanism was necessary as my thumb did all the work, until it stopped. We threw out our trash in one of the few fifty-gallon drum barrels then strolled towards the set of swings at the playground area. She sat on the soft leather strap that was connected by a set of sturdy and safe chain links, and I gently pushed it when it came towards me. She laughed at the idea that I suggested that we wait longer after we ate, to be swinging to and from.

A guy walked over to us, introduced himself as being a photographer for the Jersey Journal newspaper, and felt obligated to show us his credentials. He wanted to capture us enjoying the first day of Spring, although I wasn't sure if it was the 20th or 21st day in March, at the park. We thought it was a great idea, one that would capture and personalize this day for us and was a precursor to great things to come that day. It didn't take long for him to truly capture, in a snapshot, what our intent was. Afterwards, we drove on Freedom Way towards the other side to the old Railroad Terminal to get ferry tickets to see Lady Liberty up close.

It was full speed ahead and the way the wind moved her hair as she leaned over the top balcony of the ferry was playful, allowing her blonde hair to periodically sparkle. *Click.* I took another photograph. Sea birds matched our periphery and glided in autonomous unison. We became adventurous explorers, docking on the island to experience and create history. There was no other place to be than to check her out up close.

She was magnificently epic, for being green, but nonetheless very symbolic. Her physical features are significant, as the broken shackles at her feet signify a breaking away from tyranny and oppression and the seven rays on her crown stand for the seven continents. Sculpted by Frédéric Auguste Bartholdi, the Statue of Liberty is a figure of a robed woman representing Libertas, a Roman liberty goddess, although she resembled the Greek god Helios, because of the seven rays of the sun darting from his crown.

We took a quick tour inside to see how she was built and before we knew it, we made it to the pedestal. I was almost dizzy looking up from that level, but it was a first for us.

"Did you want to keep going up? I bet we can reach the crown." I asked.

"Let's go." She was fearless.

What I didn't know was there was just one set of stairs going up and down, but there were people daring enough to make the trip, so we were encouraged by their vitality.

"Ladies first." I insisted with a huge grin.

Each step going up the spiral staircase was about two feet wide, extremely narrow for my comfort, and I didn't appreciate that I could look down through the holes of the step grates and the side rails were strong enough for me to clinch and white-knuckle during my ascent. That was the first time I experienced not only a taste of what it was to be claustrophobic but was also confronted with my fear of heights. I think it was more the idea or fear of falling over the side rail than the actual height, but when we climbed nearly half-way I had to stop.

"Are you ok? We made it half-way. I can't believe it. Half-way more to go!"

She was a powerhouse of strength and determination. I pulled myself together and looked at her. She reached out her hand and encouraged me to continue. We climbed over three-hundred steps to reach the apex, the crown.

I quickly and nonchalantly wiped the sweat off my forehead and there was another couple there, looking out one of the windows. There were two people too many with the amount of walking room up there, but I was grateful that we made it. The ceiling looked like an octopus and its legs holding up the inside of the tiara.

"Wow! What a view. Isn't is awesome?" I asked.

"Unbelievable."

"I have to take a picture of this. Smile." *Click.*

I was overwhelmed with the achievements of the day, the overcome of fear, and my willingness to walk up to Jeanette and to hold her hand once again this time looking into her eyes and engaging in our first kiss. *Magical.*

Music is universal and the catalyst for shared interest due to its many genres and invocations of feelings and emotions caused by a note or lyric. Our mutual love and appreciation of music allowed Jeannette and I to interact and come together in the late eighties more so because of the new and popular sounds of different genres and although I immersed myself in all of them, we stabilized more so with the growing popularity of glam rock and metal. She liked bands like *Skid Row*, *Poison*, and of course a Jersey favorite and local - *Bon Jovi*. With collaborations like *Run DMC* and *Aerosmith*, and *Lita Ford* with *Ozzy Osbourne*, it made it easy for us to crossover to appreciate other musical talents and groups. On June 25, 1989, I took Jeanette to see Ozzy perform live at the Meadowlands, in East Rutherford, for the *No Rest for The Wicked* Tour, while *Vixen* and *White Lion* opened. It was a tremendous show, even without "The Prince of Darkness" biting off the head of a bat.

One early evening on another date night, I pulled up and double-parked in front of Jeanette's house, shortly after the nine to fivers must have already arrived at their homes after a long day of answering phones, performing customer service duties, or whatever else happens during that time, and have filled all the legal parking spots in the area, especially on her block. I opened the green iron gate that separated the two nearly five-foot tall thick hedges. It squeaked a little and I left it opened since we would be leaving momentarily. Two rose bushes sprang up to the green bannister on their front porch.

I was overjoyed with her family allowing her to come out tonight. She was an only child raised by her mother and father and they lived upstairs in a brownstone building in the Heights section, while her grandparents resided downstairs. They being of Polish descent, it was refreshing and delightful to learn about their culture and their views on the world, but if her grandparents had a dog named Duke, stemming from John Wayne, what difference in American values could they really have?

At first, I rang the doorbell and requested her presence from her parents since they were the ones who walked down the stairs and answered the door. If one of them came down the other was sure to follow to verify the visitor and their intentions – it was one of their familial involvement and security mechanisms.

Mrs. K. told me that they were finishing up with dinner and that Jeanette would be joining me as soon as she finished with her chores and other responsibilities. I went back to my car to look for a spot but wound up circling a couple of times, once tempted to park in front of a fire hydrant but could not justify the consequences of either paying the exorbitant fine, or worse, blocking the fire department from access to the pump in the event that they would actually need it to extinguish a fire, and in the process damage my 1976 Chevy Nova.

The sky was nearing twilight and, fortunately, Congress Street was wide enough to double-park for a short duration with my flashers on. I turned on the *Bose* car stereo, along with my *Blaupunkt* gooseneck equalizer, and listened to one of the mixed tapes filled with House music and syncopated beats I made from the night before. I shut off the straight-six engine to conserve gasoline and reduce noise pollution out of respect for her neighbors, which is another reason I didn't just honk my horn when I pulled up, and after listening to a full side of the Maxell cassette and nearly thirty minutes later, her front door opened. I attempted to turn the keys already in the ignition, but it wouldn't start. The interior lights dimmed drastically when I tried to crank on the starter engine, and quickly realized that I had drained the life of the battery by running the car radio and leaving the hazard lights on to continuously blink.

I shut it all down and popped the hood as she met me at the front of the car. Her parents had walked out behind her to initially see her off then waved over to us from the porch. We didn't hug or show any public displays of affection, especially with her family looking. I lifted the hood, propped it open with the rod, and examined the battery enclosed on top of a rubiginous casing while she looked at the mechanical and diabolical schematics of a problem and my determination to come up with its solution. For safety reasons, the Kaminski family were genuinely concerned as they wouldn't want us to be stranded anywhere if something went unreliably wrong.

"Hey, Jen. Sorry. I think the battery is dead and its primary function is to turn on the alternator, which starts the car. I know it's not the starter because it makes that clicking noise when I turn the key." I looked up at her. "I left the blinkers on for too long. I'll figure it out soon." I smiled and waved over to her parents, to indicate that things were fine and not all that bad.

From under the hood I could see a car pulling up behind me and its driver-side door opened. It wasn't a big deal, except that he didn't put his blinkers on and could get rear-ended by an incoming vehicle because of sudden nightfall. A lanky guy with dirty blonde hair came on the scene and continued to approach me. I stood up and reached out my left arm to bring Jeanette closer to me, to shield her from a possible attack. Another guy flanked to our left – a stockier Hispanic male with a short haircut and a blue light jacket. The driver discreetly flashed me his law enforcement badge that was concealed by his waist-side, under an untucked plaid shirt.

"I need you to move this car."

"The battery died. I can't right now," I explained.

"Need to move it now. We're in the middle of an investigation," he demanded in a snarky manner.

I wasn't sure what they were investigating. It was more like aggravating. Mr. and Mrs. Kaminski were still on the enclosed porch, hidden and tucked away by the neighbor's mini pine tree and the bushes that lined the front of the property line.

"What's going on?" asked her dad.

I turned to the officer: "Give me a quick jump and I'll be out of your way."

"Move this piece of shit or I'll have it towed!" Jersey City's finest, Officer "Sphincter" said as he started walking back to his unmarked car.

"C'mon! It'll take two minutes. Help me push it down the block, at least?" I requested.

"My battery died," I yelled over to Mr. K. "Is there any way you can give me a jump? I have a set of jumper cables in my trunk." *How embarrassing.*

I returned to Jeanette, and she and her parents were fine with this slight hiccup. They just rolled with the punches. I waved to the undercover police, who looked like they were doing surveillance instead of investigating and using my circumstance as cover from the alleged perpetrators, and I might have been giving away their location and existence by drawing attention to myself and my flailing hand. I was assuring the dynamic duo that I was complying in hopes that I wouldn't get a ticket for whatever they deemed illegal. A couple of neighbors were walking their dogs while a pizza delivery vehicle pulled up and double-parked a block away, to deliver two pies.

It didn't take more than a few minutes to have Mrs. K. position their royal blue four-door Buick Park Avenue in front of mine, pop the hood, and hook up the corresponding positive and negative cable lines to each battery. Although it was against the one-way street direction, it didn't deter anyone from being able to drive around with ample room.

"Thank you, Mrs. Kaminski."

Within fifteen minutes total, my car was charged enough to leave the neighborhood, with just the right amount of time to make it to our planned outing, and as we were approaching the venue, we had already forgotten the snafu and all the adults we left behind.

Nothing compared to the energy we felt at the "And Justice for All" *Metallica* concert on July 22nd at the Meadowlands Arena. We had great seats, not too close to the infamous mosh pit, and although the concert goers in our row were hyped up and getting into the music, she did most of the head-banging that night. Her poofy hair shook front and back and floated at the same time, and it's probably why I carried a pack of aspirin with me. We rocked out that night, charged with the help of the current music, and had a phenomenal time while embracing our youth.

With the shift of this new music and another year, more friends and altering lifestyles entered her life. She started to hang out with this new friend from her school – Cheryl. Cheryl was Greek and had a Greek boyfriend named Savvas, but I never got to meet him since he was much older than us, possibly in his thirties and working at his father's garage in North Bergen. I met her a couple of times and she was cool. Her uniform skirt was a little above the knee, her curly dark hair was tall enough to reach my height, but she was a smoker and ultimately influenced Jeanette into a rocker lifestyle. It got dark but I didn't judge and watched her transform into whoever she wanted and needed to be, and instead of embracing her new circle of friends with willingness to get to know them better, I pushed them away as if we were in opposition or competition. I loved her unconditionally and I knew that I didn't own her; she wasn't "mine".

While it was healthy to include new acquaintances, it put a slight wedge in the time I was able to spend with her and even though I was getting caught up with my new "friends" – Tony, Louie, and Vinnie – I was rather curious on her whereabouts, in a loving jealous way. I had never felt jealousy before and so I was coping with that aspect in my young adult life. In the end, we were drifting apart and because of our disconnection, I broke our relationship off, and Nick eventually entered her remaining Metal years.

Months later, I took mild comfort in being able to visit her on her porch one day and while she told me that Nick wasn't as good as a friend as I was to her and weren't seeing much of each other, she did meet another guy who just happened to be walking in front of the house for their rendezvous. It was a bit awkward, but I did arrive sort of last minute, and I respected her decisions and her new life, but I was outraged – in primal survival between the male species and dominance. He entered the front gate and on to the front door where we were hanging out and talking. I was suppressing aggression and hostility. I could have just thrown him over the porch bannister into the rose bushes and hard ground, but I just smiled and said hello out of respect for her.

At the very least, she was brought out of the darkness and into the light. He had bleached straight white hair that came down just below his shoulders and his eyes were of a light tint, possibly from colored contact lenses, but he resembled more of an elvish androgynous male than a Bret Michaels from *Poison*. His pale complexion suggested he either applied makeup or didn't spend much time in the sun. Even his garb was not of a current urban lifestyle or look, but the clothes don't determine the man, and what did I know about fashion? He wore rings of different stones on both hands and a white crystal around his neck.

"He is a wizard in white magic," she casually stated.

"What is it, wizard?" I jested.

He was tall and had a thin frame. I don't remember if she told me his name, but I didn't care and I didn't have the sense to extend my hand in friendship, or allegiance. Being taught and brought up in Roman Catholicism throughout my youth, I never questioned its teachings and held firm beliefs in its dogma, so I was ignorant in the ways and rituals of other worldly religions. I was out of my depth and element with her new belief structures and let it go, but he was a guy – the other guy – and for that, I took off my rose-colored glasses.

"Oh. Ok. Cool. Well… I'll leave youse two alone. Nice meeting you. Take care, Jeanette."

We hugged goodbye and that was the last time we saw each other.

Chapter IV – Moved to Ears

My father quickly and quietly parked the rental car under the shade of the palm tree that was growing from the sidewalk in front of my grandparents' home. He always wished to come unannounced, and I guess it was a running gag even though we would come at least once a year, but I never minded the look on his parents' faces whenever we surprisingly showed up at the door. We would get as far as unlatching the black car port gate before it squeaked, and before opening the screen door, he would give a slight shout into the occupied home.

"La bendición," dad greeted.

Abuelita came with a surprised look, gave us each a hug and a kiss while abuelo sat on his reclining chair in the patio room watching a boxing match.

"Dios te bendiga... aye, mi madre," she said in a whimsical flurry of joy.

It was a charming home with a lot of love, and framed photos of all my aunts and uncles, and even myself and my sister, on the walls.

Every time I came over, I had my own room. It was the one between the kitchen and the bathroom. What more could I have asked for? The house was cool, since the town was at a refreshing altitude in the mountains, and after I placed my bags in my quarters near the closet doors, I walked over to the shutters and opened them slightly. It was a view from the left side of the house, but primarily it was next to the washing machine. On the floor next to the sewing table was a 36" x 24" glass-frame photo of my father and his two brothers. They had to have been in their very early twenties; they looked so young but mature. I sat on the bed for a while nostalgically thinking of my existence. From the other room I could hear abuelo talking to the television set yelling, "Toma... Toma" which meant "here you go," but he was replying to the punches and blows the other fighter was receiving. I never doubted his passion for the sport.

My father's bed was designated in the front patio room across the hall from my room, and to the right down the hall was the master bedroom in which they had their own bathroom. At the end of the hall, lived my younger aunt, Laura, but she had been visiting some friends in San Juan at the time. My grandmother called the two of us into the kitchen for an early dinner while she prepared and already served my grandfather who was being entertained by the sporting action on the tube. Her dining table was round and comfortably seated four. Chicken stew and rice were served in our plates along with a pasteles each on a separate side dish. It smelled great and one thing was always certain – my family was accustomed on making extra food in the event an unannounced guest arrived then they would have plenty of food to offer and if not, they would have given their portions to them.

The carport gate squeaked and alerted us that someone was approaching the door, and my grandfather surprisingly got up to answer it. It was my Uncle Justin, whom I hadn't seen in years, and here he was risen from the figurative dead. It was truly an exciting day for me, not only to see my grandparents but to see one of my father's brothers in the flesh. His birthday was one day after mine, on the twenty-eighth, and we were similar in most ways.

Although we were many years apart from each other, I looked up to him and saw many traits that I admired and took on. First, he was very charismatic and enjoyed life and its vices. He occasionally enjoyed a beer, or three, and would spin around and dance to a good tune on the radio – a partygoer. He was often quiet and kept to himself, but when he did speak people listened, and even his silence said a lot. Ultimately, he didn't care what people thought of him. He served his time in the US military and spent most of his time healing and doing inner work, for his own survival.

I had traded places with abuelo and while he and the rest of them were hanging out in the kitchen, laughing and reminiscing, I was watching episodes of a cartoon version of *The Beatles*, translated into Spanish, on the television. After singing along to many of the popular songs, I walked into the kitchen to get a drink of water. He was sitting at the table and from where I was halted, Uncle Justin appeared to be front and center between the hutch and under the hanging chandelier and was certainly my center of attention, but then he put me in the spotlight, in front of everyone.

"Hey, Corey! Can you move your ears like this?"

I looked right at him. I never tried it before in my life but in that instant, I moved my ears without touching them. I didn't know that it was possible, and I have no idea how I was able to do it, but it was truly fascinating. He willed it on me, and I give all credit to my ear-moving avuncular superpower to him. We were all delighted and astounded, so I poured two glasses of water – one for him and one for me. *Clink.*

"Corey, we were just talking about you and your sixth birthday. Remember this?"

He held up a piece of red wood which had been preserved by my grandmother all these years. It was the same splinter which had entered my knee that dreadful birthday. It was the little things that we remembered and cherished. I was in awe that such a small memento was kept, like a tooth collected by the tooth fairy to commemorate a point in time.

"Come here, nephew, and be with the family," he said as he extended his arms for a hug.

Those were one of the last times I saw my uncle alive. Years later, my parents took me to visit him at the Disabled American Veterans Hospital in East Orange, New Jersey; he served his time in the United States Marine Corps. He didn't have much to give and when he did, he gave it away. My mom and dad allowed me to talk with him one-on-one – uncle to nephew – for a good while. He looked so relaxed laying on the gurney in his hospital gown. Surprisingly, he handed me two things besides the sacred wisdom and knowledge he whispered before he reached under his pillow.

"I got this from the treasure box of goodies they have here. I want you to have it."

He reached over and I grabbed a model kit for a classic car – the '56 Chevy. It was cool, a nice project to work on, and whenever I would get around to constructing it, I could have it displayed and always remember him.

"Come here. You're in school and you'll be going to college soon. Learn as much as you can. Here is a book of one of my favorite authors."

He handed me a hardcover early edition work of *Edgar Allan Poe*. I held on tightly to the book and cherished it because it was endearingly personal and sentimentally priceless.

"Thank you, Tio."

The following day, I was awoken by my father's other brother who received word from the hospital, then yelled out and cried upon hearing about the passing of my Uncle Justin. His words were inaudible when he was grieving with my father in my parent's bedroom. My room was next door, and all I could really hear was the word *why* over and over. I wasn't as distraught or shook up by the news but more focused on being able to comfort the family during their times of emotional struggle, confusion, and sadness as I was able to say good-bye to him the night before. My mother walked in my room.

"Uncle Justin passed away early this morning. I'm sorry."

"Thanks, mom, for telling me. Please let me know what I can do to help."

I slept with the book he gave me and only read a couple of chapters of "The Fall of the House of Usher" before sticking a semi-crumpled dollar bill in between the pages where I left off. I brought the literary work downstairs and placed it with the other classic works in my father's library, near the top shelf. He always believed in me and had high expectations for me. I miss my Uncle Justin, and I never forgot his birthday. He died during my sophomore year in high school, on April 17th, 1988.

The funeral parlor was just as I remembered it from the couple of times in my life that I visited a deceased friend or family member. My parents are always punctual and arrived early mostly in part to ensure a good parking space, ahead of a crowd. Parking was limited but, somehow, we managed to parallel park on a quiet street off Brunswick Street as we came to see my uncle Justin one last time. The façade of the business resembled a Romanesque theme with a black slated accented sign with the name *Introcaso-Angelo Funeral Home* in non-conventional font gold letters and the top border appeared to have symbols of column tops. An awning offered shelter from rain or overhead pigeons, from the door to the end of the sidewalk curb.

I was pleased for the chance to all see us all together again, this time celebrating in his honor – a party without streamers, balloons, or candles but with flowers and heartfelt stories with every participant respectively dressed in dark shades of black to represent their mourning and sadness. The narrow hallway was carpeted and lead to different chapels and gathering rooms. It was eerily quiet like entering a cave looking for Jesus himself, not knowing what to find or if he was even here. The time for denial was nearing an end.

The room was empty except for him and the three older women that somehow always seem to be at these private, yet public, functions whenever I am here. I'm not sure if they are part of a union or a prayer group club, but every Puerto Rican wake I have attended they are always there reciting prayers one rosary bead after another and after a while it resonated into a unified hum or dialed-in frequency and a precursor to a lullaby to somehow put me in a slight sleep or trance. Light shrouds covered their heads, each one of their thumbs bent at the first digit to signify which bead they were on, and while two were knelt at the side of the shiny black coffin the third lady stood behind them to maintain the unified cadence, more disciplined than a metronome. I sat in one of the back rows – listening, observing, entranced in the ritual. When they finished, they nonchalantly walked out in single file, and my mother thanked them for coming and for their services.

According to the Bible, in 1 Corinthians 6:19-20, Catholics take care to honor and bury the dead because it is said that we are temples of the Holy Ghost, and that God lives in our very bodies and therefore we should honor God with them, and that honoring the body doesn't stop after the person has died. In Catholic Mass we profess our belief in the resurrection of the body when we say the Nicene Creed, 'We look for the resurrection of the dead, and the life of the world to come' and just as Jesus' body was raised and ascended into heaven, we also believe our bodies will be returned to us when Jesus returns. Burying the bodies of the dead reminds us of this hope and is not simply a disposing of the body but caring for that person. Even though our body and soul separate at death, the body still belongs to that person and it will be returned to them.

Death is a part of life. Not everyone goes to wakes or funerals, and sometimes people only show up to those occasions to show their last respect for the deceased. I walked over to my mother.

"The only time you get to see family the most are for funerals and weddings," I mentioned.

"If you're invited or told about it, otherwise you'd need to periodically check the newspaper for wedding announcements or the obituary columns," she said.

"Yeah, if you're invited - but family is family, ok, so that's really the only time to see everyone. Do you remember your first time at a funeral?"

"No, I do not. My first time, no. Actually... thinking about it, I do. It was my baby cousin and I must have been seven or eight – George's sister. She was just months old, and she was born sick. That's the first one I ever went to, but I never thought about it because I was so little that I never thought about those things. Back then, it was like a shock, but now I remember."

"What was it like, in Puerto Rico, to attend a wake back then?" I questioned further.

"Well, back then it wasn't in a funeral parlor. What was that? It was in the homes. It was in a house. That was a main reason why there are so many flowers – to get rid of and neutralize the smell of the decaying body. My paternal grandparents, I don't remember, because they brought us to the States, then they went back and then they passed away. We were younger, I was in the seventh grade, and we couldn't afford to go back and forth. My maternal grandparents, we did go to theirs because they died sometime later, and that was at their home. Back then there were no cars riding behind a hearse."

"Interesting, mom."

"In PR, they always served hot chocolate. There were no refrescos – no soda, and they had the little Ritz crackers with guava and the cheese that was given to everybody, passed around on a tray. After that, it was placed on a table and we just grabbed a toothpick and helped ourselves to another."

"Thanks! I had no idea." I started to walk away.

"Coronado… don't forget to sign in," she called out to me.

Many of my father's side of the family were expected to come shortly, some I have never met but knew I would be introduced to all of them before the evening was out, so I quickly wrote my name in the guest book. It wasn't long before I went to the restroom to wash my hands which I found at the end of the hallway. The rushing water from the faucet was the only sound I could hear. I looked in the mirror to make sure my dark blue tie was on straight, fixed my hair, and took a deep breath.

I remembered how it was, going to my pediatrician's office for the annual checkup and wondering if I was scheduled to get a vaccination or a shot from a needle. Usually, whenever my parents drove past the Jersey City line on JFK Boulevard towards Union City, it was an indication that we were off a beaten path, in unchartered territory. Leaving our city limits was a field trip since everything we needed was within our bubble. The moment we pass Manhattan Avenue and the Leonard Gordon Park, where a buffalo roamed, is when I start getting tense and my stomach starts to churn. I dreaded being driven to the entering parking lot of the doctor's office, not being told of an appointment my parents had made to suffice requirements for school or just a regular medical checkup to take advantage of the medical insurance proclivities. I would eventually get better after leaving Dr. Arkis and Hamilton's office, and likewise knew I would heal once I left the funeral parlor, but that wouldn't be for another three hours.

By the time I reentered the viewing room, there was a line forming from outside and I could breathe in and smell second-hand smoke from the small packs of cigarette smokers convened out front. I was emotionless when I walked to the entranceway of our chapel gathering and its seating area. Gloria held a seat for me as I walked towards her, my mother tugged at my arm.

"You remember Sammy and Kim?" she asked me but as a quick introduction so I would already know their names.

"Hi."

"That's your son? Wow. I haven't seen him since he was *this* little. You were still in your crib. Such a long time ago," Kim expressed.

"Good seeing you again," I said as I inched towards my sister. The room was getting full and the back room behind us was also filling up with mourners, but it became more of the chatting section the way some of the conversations veered. I finally sat down.

"You wouldn't believe it, Susie. My company really sucks, and the phones keep ringing. They need to hire more people, because I don't know how much more I can handle," a woman ranted.

"Aye, Marta. And I was just worried about doing laundry and what shoes to wear…"

A couple of kids were stomping and getting restless behind me and one of them was whining.

"You get up off that floor and stop crying or I'll give you something to cry about!"

I just remained looking forward and focused on why we were here. I turned to Gloria.

"How's dad doing?"

"He's ok. He's over there with mom and abuelita."

Gloria pointed to the front of the room in between a big display of white lilies on a stand and a wreath of white and yellow chrysanthemums. My parents were being sociable and greeted many of the guests, but my mom did most of the talking. It helped that she kept dialogue going to also distract my dad from thinking and looking at the casket. My mother eventually left to have a cigarette with two of the guests, leaving my father alone with my grandmother in a room that fit from seventy-five to a hundred guests, but then he suddenly left towards the restroom door.

It was very warm, and I could hear sobbing and crying not too far behind me. I tried not to listen. I tried not to absorb the inclination to feel what they were feeling. I took a couple of deep breaths. Some others began to let their emotions go. It started to get even warmer in the room. I looked around to see if I could find the thermostat on the wall to lower the temperature but all I saw were rows of more people piling in, and the volume of conversations getting a little louder. To my left along the wall was a nightstand, a small wooden table with four legs, with a box of tissues on it. I grabbed a couple to put my already hard and worn out chewed gum in it. The flavor lost its zeal long ago but chewing it also helped to distract and deter my thoughts of emotional distress. I discarded the piece of Chiclet and asked my sister for another.

"Is it warm in here or is it me?" I asked her as I reached for the pack of gum and made all these crackling noises trying to open it.

"It is a little stuffy."

The strongest woman in the building entered the room. She was the only one I knew who could pull off wearing a white dress at such an occasion and not have anyone question it. Wearing white was a fashion faux pas to perhaps days following Labor Day or at a wedding when you are not the bride, but certainly not to a function as it relates to death. No one noticed her astutely slipping through the density of conversation and solemnity as she approached the casket. They were all preoccupied with their own issues, more demanding and outlasting the short span that was devoted to the reflection of my uncle Justin's span on this earth.

My eyes were fixed on her every step, stride, and calculated delay. She took her time, savored every second, but was focused on her intent, until she reached the opened casket, stood right beside him and began to speak to him aloud.

"Hello, Justin. You look so handsome, my son." She gently put her hand on his upper chest, then lightly waved her hand down to his stomach, fixing and slightly tugging on the lapel of his suit jacket. My ears automatically pierced back on their own to deflect the emotional connection I had during her conversation. Her voice carried above all the others as I was honing on each word, but she eventually slipped into whisper mode. I heard similar fragments of words, familiar to those when her brother Miguel transitioned. The distracted lull of the room subsided, and all eyes were affixed as she reached in and gave him a hug, a kiss, and then calmly rested on his body. *Peace.*

That was the moment when I held my breath, and my eyes scurried throughout the front of the room – anywhere but at them. I clenched my teeth but couldn't hold back my ears any longer and let them go. A vision of a Renaissance sculpture by Michelangelo Buonarroti, *Pietà,* flashed in front of my semi-weltering eyes. The tender work of art that is housed in St. Peter's Basilica, in Vatican City, captured the loving bond these two had together – mother and son. This was the first time a deluge of tears ran down my cheeks, not stemmed from the act of death itself but from immense love as a casualty. I quickly wiped them with a left-over gum tissue I never discarded. I got up, discreetly marched past the crying kids behind us, and disappeared out the front door into the billows and a thick plume of cigarette smoke.

Chapter V – The Fine Print

Ever since my mother went to Ferris High School, in Jersey City, and started reading the Jersey Journal, she would immerse herself in current events and the local news. Separated by sections, she dissected and broke down what captivated her interests then moved on to the next article that seemed somewhat interesting.

"Mom, what's black and white and red all over?" I asked her once while she flipped through pages.

"I don't know. What?"

"A newspaper," I laughed jokingly, at the age of six, and waited for her approval. Because the newspaper took her attention away from me, I comprehended that whatever she was looking at was of more importance enough to take away from my current existence.

Dear Abby became a compelling column that offered compassionate advice, opinion, and a straightforward rhetoric that one would appreciate coming from a good friend. Luckily, I wasn't privy to the drama, stress, and relationship issues when I first heard the author's name and the questions asked of her but even though the columnist didn't know the questioner personally, answers were given in the best diplomatic positions with conjecture and well intentions. Either way, my mother always gave her thoughts aloud or through facial expression, comparable to the weakest poker player in a tournament of high stakes. If my mother wants me to know something, she would not hesitate to tell me, and that would be from her fiery side – Sagittarius. *Dear Abby* prepared me on being a better diplomat, and to give the most appeasing answers for all sides.

Mom zipped through the comics section, not relating to any of them, and for the most part I hadn't either, except for the Peanuts strip. My favorite is Snoopy portraying the Red Baron, with Charlie Brown coming in a strong second place, but my favorite depictions of them come from their television specials during the holiday season. I started to collect comic books around this time beginning with Archie then The Amazing Spiderman. Stan Lee did a great job illustrating and holding my attention to the Marvel publication and held down its integrity of comics for me because of his amazing artwork.

In the back pages there is a list of winning lottery numbers from the night before, hosted by the New Jersey State Lottery commission, and the mission of the New Jersey Lottery is to "raise revenue for maximum contribution to education and institutions benefiting the citizens of New Jersey through the responsible sale of Lottery products." They accomplish this by "providing entertaining products through a dynamic public business enterprise built upon honesty, integrity, customer satisfaction, teamwork, and public/private partnerships." The numbers are usually drawn on television shortly before eight in the evening and portions of the winnings are designated for either education or to pay the government its share in taxes. I was too young to gamble legally but pleased to hear that schools would have adequate supplies and teachers would be fairly compensated with all the funding they would be receiving through this racket and scheme.

My further involvement with the newspaper came when I participated in horse-track betting and the street numbers which were an entire game altogether. It coincided with the horse track and its total haul. Whatever the Meadowlands Racetrack in Secaucus took in for the entire bets for the day, that number was reported, and the local newspapers would include that figure in their papers the following day, up to the penny. Bets opened midday and results would be posted the following day, but the results that were of only true importance to the gambler were the last three dollar amounts of the total take. If the Track collected $1,234,567.89 on a Wednesday and you bet, on Wednesday, that 567 would come out, you would find out on Thursday, preferably by way of The Daily News newspaper. This New York paper somehow had this daily result highlighted and made it easier for those who were looking for it to see. For a mere fifty cents, you could pick a three-digit number to come out "straight", or exactly the way you called it, and for another fifty cents, you could pick it so that your three-digit number comes out "boxed", or in any combination. Say the number was 418, as was mine, and one dollar was paid for that number to come out straight, the payout was one thousand bucks. If 148 or any other combination, but 418, comes out, for that same dollar, the payout was two hundred bucks. It was an underground lottery for those who didn't feel compelled to report or pay taxes on their winnings.

I had taken a more active interest in newspapers beginning in the eighth grade where I picked up a paper route in my neighborhood. Understanding my sales product and its contents, I was comfortable with delivering the local newspapers to their subscribers and placing them specifically to their needs whether it was in the mailbox, under their front door mat, or in the side door. Tips were greatly appreciated, and the business began to shape and guide me towards a more dependable and reliable work ethic. It taught me microeconomics through the value of supply and demand – the amount of a commodity, product, or service available and the desire of buyers for it, and how they are all considered as factors for regulating price.

The horoscopes are when I first discovered astrology as it related to the twelve zodiac signs. Depending on the day I was born, I am a specific sign of the Zodiac, and since it was February 27th, I am considered a Pisces. According to its philosophy, being a Pisces male means that I am very interested in mysticism and the spiritual unknown. My spiritual life allows me to escape the mundane and my creativity often leads to being highly artistic and altruistic, and in whole, feeling more connected to the universe. I am incredibly self-sacrificing when I'm in love, and some may mistake my self-sacrificing nature as weakness. The symbol for Pisces represents two fish tied together and swimming in opposite directions.

The daily horoscopes, according to what I read in the Jersey Journal, laid out the blueprint of what that eventful day had in store for each sign, and I didn't really much care about any of the others but mine so it became a brief excerpt and a quick flip of the page. Due to the minimal stresses I had, I could not relate to most of what was being prophesized, but it didn't deter my curiosities especially upon knowing that it was for entertainment purposes only. Horoscopes are an outlet to help guide those who are lost on their paths – a beacon, guidepost, or a heads-up to help avoid conflict or drama, but I wasn't much of an erudite student on the topic so this is what I thought in the beginning. It was mystical guidance from the wizards that could foretell hidden messages and truths simply by understanding the exact positions and placements of stars and its constellations.

Lastly, because no one in our family was interested in sports, we ended our curiosities by viewing the pages that listed those who were no longer with us on this physical plane – that visible reality of space and time, energy and matter at the end of its existence. She scanned the black and white photographs then, from top to bottom, internally read the names of the deceased in the Obituary column. That was when and where my mother recognized and was alerted of the death of Mr. Gerald Kaminski. She read the short account of his life and information of the upcoming funeral. He was survived by Jeanette Kaminski and that was the nail on the coffin that confirmed to her who he really was.

Chapter VI – Charting the Course

It wasn't the first time she experienced a traumatic death in her family. Her relationship ran deep – she was raised by him, they lived together until she moved out during her college years and had been close and retained a healthy father-daughter relationship. The loss of a family member can be difficult to overcome, and although she was in mourning, she would hold the appearance of remaining strong and maintaining a sense of calm.

I only saw her lose her cool once, and not in a screaming fit or an attack with a deadly weapon type of rage, but more of a distressful and slight loss of emotional control. Years after our breakup, after reserving a table for two, we met up and went out for dinner at the *Chart House*, in Weehawken. I wanted to make it a memorable evening, one that we could never forget, since I had missed her so much and I valued our friendship. The panoramic views of the glittering New York City skyline offered a classy and romantic backdrop along the Hudson River.

She was in her third year of college so she already reached a requirement to consume alcohol in New Jersey, the determined age of twenty-one, allowing us to share our first official glasses of wine together, although we may have had a few wine coolers way before, in our hay days. I started to learn about wine and food pairing when I began my interactions with fine dining at fancy restaurants, and as a rule of thumb for me, white wine would be the better recommendation with seafood. We ordered a couple of appetizers including the calamari and even though I was leaning more towards a seafood entrée, we decided to start with two glasses of red.

Although soft white-noised chatter and ambient piano music accompanied our views of the gentle-waiving waters beneath us, and the horizontal white and red headlights slowly scanning along the streets of a bustling city, it was just the two of us. In anticipation of a possible ensuing headache from the wine, I popped two Advil and took a drink from the iced water the waitress had served us. She was just as I remembered, from the moment I first gazed into her eyes at the high school dance. Time stood still. I was in love again.

A toast was in order.

"To our youth. To our health," I declared. *Clink.*

"I think the last time we had a drink together was at my Senior Prom, when we drank champagne in the limo," I reminisced.

"That night was so much fun. And the ferry ride…"

A tear began to shed from her right blue eye when she took a sip, although her smile fought hard to neutralize any sadness. She quickly wiped it away with one finessed stroke of her forefinger.

"Hey. It's so good to see you again. Are you ok?"

"Yes. I'm fine," she chuckled," It's really nice to see you too."

After a lot of small talk and complimenting gestures, she began to catch me up on her life. We talked so much that we hadn't entirely finished our salads or soaked up all the fried calamari with the marinara sauce well into thirty minutes after ordering our main dishes, and I noticed that the wait staff was actually waiting for us to finish first before serving the next course. I appreciated that we were not rushed, and how they allowed us to continue in our meaningful conversation. I was elated to continue being there with her. Her logorrhea energy left me engaged because she kept it true, real, and personal and I wanted to know everything about her. Jeanette was captivating and cheerful and when she started to tear again, she started to lose her vitality. I waived the servers to come with our next dishes.

"Sounds wonderful, Jen. It's just me… Corey."

The table was cleared of the old dishes, and they brought out her herb crusted and slow roasted prime rib and my Ahi Tuna with fresh vegetables, but I was sure they were held at warm temperatures since they were cooked a while ago. We were asked if we would like more wine, but we politely waived it off, like a Jedi, and instead insisted on refills of water. I've always appreciated the sound of iced water pouring from its carafe into a glass, the clinks they make, and the popping noises as they react to warmer temperatures in its stages of melting. *Clink. Clink. Pop.*

She hesitated to talk about it first but then she allowed herself to open-up a little more, lowering her walls of vulnerability and I was extremely grateful that she let me in to listen. My mind began to bombinate soon after she mentioned she had a boyfriend in college. It was numb and garbled as if I jumped into the deep end of a pool, scrambling in a slight panic to reach the surface, and when I did, her words were beginning to become audible again. It was then, she told me she was pregnant.

She and my sister were the same age, and Gloria was pregnant with my first nephew when she was eighteen, so it didn't really freak me out about having a baby so young. I'm sure it was my "guy" instincts kicking in, alerting me that Jeanette had a lover in her life, good enough to have a child with, but I initially and selfishly made this information about myself when she was clearly concerned about something, and that something had nothing to do with me.

"Pregnant. Wow. Congratulations."

She sobbed a little and I handed her a clean clothed napkin from the table. I looked around but no one was making it obvious that we were being casually observed while involved in a deep and emotional conversation. I took the last swig of my wine and took another bite of the salted crisp asparagus accompanied by a sliver of the tuna.

"We are not together. I only knew him for a short time, and he was a controlling prick."

"So sorry to hear. Are you ok?"

"My parents don't even know. Please don't tell them."

"I won't tell anyone."

I wanted to help but I didn't know how, except to just listen and comfort my first girlfriend. I felt guilty – guilty for leaving her years ago in the first place. If she and I had stayed together then she wouldn't have met this other guy and she wouldn't have gotten pregnant. If she was fated to be pregnant, then it might have been me instead of another, but who was to really say?

I never told her the real reason why I called it off between us and often I go back and forth on its validity and if I made the right decision, but I did give her the lamest excuse – "I was going to college and I would be meeting new people." It was such a cliché that didn't deserve to be used on her, but it was the quickest out for me. It was partly true since I would be entering my first year of college and although I was accepted to attend Princeton, I chose to go to Seton Hall University in South Orange, NJ, instead, plus she would have been a junior in high school and still considered a minor.

Another reason I chose to leave was because I started to get involved with a group of guys from the neighborhood and I didn't want her to get indirectly involved or know about my involvement in an alleged life of crime. As far as anyone knew, I worked at a warehouse facility but had not revealed that I was also into racketeering, gambling or anything else deemed illegal according to the RICO Act. I pushed her away in order to protect her.

The ultimate real reason I left was due to my commitment issues. Profoundly or stupidly, I felt that I did not want to end up with my high school sweetheart, my first love, and not be able to live and explore life and its many other opportunities. I started to understand the progressive stages in a relationship that would ultimately lead to marriage, then children, and I wasn't ready for that mind set at such an early age. These were preconceived notions I brought on to myself, supported by the fact that both of our parents married at a young age and were still happily married, although it seemed I wasn't ready for that tradition. I was afraid because of the love I felt and the closeness I had with her would restrict the possibilities from dating other people for the sake of self-growth. If I could separate and find my purpose in life and come back later, then there wouldn't be any resentment for not trying new and wild things. In the *Forrest Gump*[1] film, I was Jenny.

I took a gulp of water, long enough for the ice to numb my upper lip just a little.

"I was scared, and I didn't really know him that well."

She was now here with me. She confided in me. The other guy doesn't matter anymore. They are not together. For the first time in my life, the concept of raising another man's child had surfaced as a passing thought, and I wondered if I could go past the idea that I was not the biological father to a child I would be loving and caring for. I loved Jeanette unconditionally and she was not a stranger to me or my family. It would be ok and acceptable. I opened myself up to her.

"It's all right, Jeanette. Is there anything I can do to help?"

She began to cry. Sitting across from her, I held her cold and shaky hands and started to rub them.

"I'm sad because I got an abortion. No, I am outraged at myself for getting rid of it!"

I was in utter shock and those words deafened my senses for a while. I wasn't sure if she said if their one-time sexual act was consensual or not, or if it was planned or not, or about any of those details because I was focused on the strong emotional energies being discharged towards my empathetic soul. Thoughts escaped me as I focused on her well-being and concentrated on this latest turn of events.

---

[1] *Forrest Gump*, 1994 American comedy-drama film, directed by Robert Zemeckis

"Because of the operation, I may not be able to have children again. I was so scared and felt I didn't have anyone to talk to, or go to, about it."

After realizing that I would have stepped up to the stepfather plate, the plate was taken away and smashed, and possibly never to be replaced. She and I wouldn't be able to have our own biological children and we never mentioned getting back together. I wasn't judgmental or criticizing her actions. It was done, and I calmed her down with my attentiveness and understanding. She was very heartbroken, to say the least, and traumatized by her decisions but was a step closer to forgiving herself, by allowing to talk to someone and releasing some of her burdens and mental anguish. That was the last time I saw her. *I miss you.*

Chapter VII – Customs

As I walked off the aircraft and unto the jet way, it became a reality that I was in trouble. Even if I wanted to take the flight back to Newark it wouldn't be until early morning. The last flight to Ottawa meant that, at the very least, I would have to pay the twenty-four-dollar departure tax just for a short visit.

I'm sure the rest of the other passengers had their E311 Declaration cards filled and ready for presentation, and I marked down the last piece of information - the date: 031111. I had Tuesdays and Wednesdays off, great days to fly while on standby, and I was on an adventure. I reached into my duffel bag and pulled out my passport and clasped it with my Declaration paperwork. Alas, the short two lines only posed the threat of being singled out. A woman behind me sneezed. "Bless you," I automatically said when I twisted my body towards her a quarter turn. If there was a larger number of deplaning passengers, I would have had a chance of being lost in the crowd. *What do I say? Do I smile? Crap! I'm next.*

As I handed the female Customs Agent my papers, she took a glance at me with a provincial grin.

"Bonjour. Bienvenue."

"Hello." I responded.

I could have greeted her in the same French, but by speaking English there was no guesswork that the conversation should continue in English, for my sake. If I had spoken in French, perhaps she would have continued in her proud language and I would have just embarrassed myself. She procedurally sifted through my responses and rifled through my slightly bent passport. I've only used my passport to go on previous Cruises to the Caribbean, but because I carried it in my shirt pockets and maybe occasionally in my left rear pants pocket when I sat, it was a bit warped.

"Are you here on business or pleasure?"

"Pleasure." I had a slight grin to make it seem like I was happy to be there, and that I am not hostile but I'm not entirely sure that it worked.

"Where will you be staying?"

"At a friend's house. They live near Elgin Street."

"Where did you meet these friends?"

"In Minneapolis at a convention."

The Customs Agent, I looked for her name on her badge, Sharon, was typing this information into her data base, then she came with a swarm of questions.

"What type of convention? And what was the address?"

I don't even remember my answers.

"What is your friend's address?"

I handed the jotted-down address to her and she continued to type. She then looked at me, gave me back my passport and asked me to follow the *Red Line* that was marked on the tiled floor, so I followed it into a Customs holding area. I was in a slight panic, but I knew I had to keep it together and gain my composure since federal agents are trained to sniff out fear and detect abnormalities through body language, tone, and sweat. I wiped my forehead and brow with the palm of my hand.

One of the two serious-looking Agents called me over and asked for my passport. He looked at it and did some processing, didn't appreciate the bent condition I gave it to him, looked at me in disgust and threw it on the ground next to my feet. I could have reached over the counter-top and choked the shit out of him for disrespecting an official U.S. document of verification, if it weren't for his firearm, but I just looked him in the eyes and smiled.

"What is this? Looks like you need a new one."

"Yes, sir. It must have gotten bent in my shirt pocket." I gestured to my pocket as I said that, but he didn't like my sudden hand movements.

"We'll need to check your bag."

"Sure. Sure. My dirty clothes are for the way back." I guess they are all trained not to have a sense of humor.

I walked over to the next room to the right and it was an illuminating bright white. It posed as their examination room and it was there that I propped my blue duffel bag on top of a fold-out table. As one of the Agents unzipped the bag he asked if I had packed it myself and if there was anything in it that we should be concerned about.

"We're good," I said.

I couldn't think of anything that would get me into trouble. I just had clothes, car and house keys, some paint brushes because they're my favorite and cost too much to buy again, but maybe it was a rogue nail clipper. I looked at my watch and started to realize that this may take longer than expected.

The Customs Agent pulled out my oil paints from the bottom of the bag.

"Do you normally pack paint in your bags? These are flammable and potentially hazardous in certain quantities."

"I didn't want to buy new ones. They are expensive, but I will need to buy canvas here because of the size."

He placed everything back in the bag, with a smirk look, and advised me to enjoy my stay. I zipped that bag up fast and headed passed the entire bag carousel area where I showed another Agent my bag tags for verification, submitted my Declarations Card, and went outside the Customs doors to the general airport area. I felt inconvenienced but satisfied that due diligence was administered, like having a guest take off their shoes before they entered and walked on a clean white rug in an abode.

The doors opened automatically, and I can feel the cooler air touching my face. I looked around. No one on the other side of the door was familiar. No one was there at all. The interrogation must have taken that long. I walked towards the currency conversion booth, taking roughly a couple of shuffling steps, when I saw her. She was leaning on a barricade in a red wool coat with a warm smile that made me feel as if I were welcomed home.

Chapter VIII - Minneapolis

I first met Paula at a convention in Minneapolis, MN, on September 18, 2003. She was helping with the registration process for a Canadian organization, being hosted at a hotel near the University of Minnesota. I was primarily there to support my friend Mark, who was a member and advocate for a similar cause, here in the States. He was dedicated to a safe world, in an organization of diverse individuals, committed through research, education, advocacy and activism to the prevention, treatment and elimination of all forms of sexual victimization. We had just flown in from EWR and were setting up our own Registration tables for day one of five. I already shipped my reproductions and paintings a couple of days earlier so that my submitted artwork for the contest would make it for the judged display already, and that my reproductions would already have been at the hotel. Mark first mentioned the trip to me back in early March when he also told me about an annual art contest that the organization sponsors. He liked my art at the time and thought it would be a great idea to go out and promote it, and I specifically painted two paintings to go with their theme: "Recognizing Strength and Resilience".

As I repeatedly walked down the corridor to setup, I noticed how busy everyone was to get efficiently situated so that the registrants were able to smoothly enjoy the process. That's when I saw this confident young woman assisting and directing every question asked of her. She wore a long dark dress and light-framed glasses, and her dark brown hair came down to the bottom of her scapula. I found a strategic corner, one that everyone would need to pass in order to get to one of the lecture halls. I used a couple of small easels I brought and displayed two of my works, and when I was finished, I walked over to the Canada table and generally asked if anyone needed help. I turned to her and asked, "Have I missed the battle?" whereby she responded with a flawless, "You have missed the war!" [2] We both smiled and went back to our tables. They assured me that they were fine.

It seemed, as though, they had everything under control and things had slowed down and simmered. I started to wonder what my function was since I was somewhat involved in something greater than myself but wasn't quite affiliated with their causes. I would have felt out of place if it weren't for Mark's reassurance that everything was fine, and now with her friendly presence, I felt more at ease and comfort. When the registration process was over, there was a considerable gap for a lunch break, so we convened in front of the hotel, towards Applebee's, until the next round of scheduled classes.

I took an open seat at one of the outside tables and the women were talking about spiritual growth and personal development.
"Hi, ladies," I said as a courtesy since I was extremely shy and an introvert, but also because I was interested in meeting new people, and there they were. Paula introduced me to Sarah, who sat between us, and to JJ who pleasantly sat across from us next to Melinda.

---

[2] *Gladiator*, a Ridley Scott film in 2000, whereby Commodus asks Marcus Aurelius, "Did I miss it? Did I miss the battle?" while Lucilla waits behind.

"Coronado is an artist and one of his works is currently being displayed at the University in an art gallery," she politely said on my behalf.

"How wonderful! We should all go and see it before we leave. Are those your art pieces displayed on the easels upstairs?" JJ asked me.

"Yes. They're reprints of my originals. They're of the Twin Towers, my first subject when I decided to start painting in oils on canvas. They were my view every day since I lived across the Hudson River in New Jersey."

"Ah, Jersey, huh? We'll go and look at those as well. They are so colorful and interesting."

"Thank you so much. Yes, I'd love to show them to you," I said with a happy grin. JJ was an older woman in her late forties with short brown hair, wearing a violet cotton sweater and a necklace with colorful stones on them. She was friendly and genuinely satisfied with her position in life; she was happy to be there. She was also intuitive and may have picked up on something I said, or how I said it, so she took out one of her business cards and wrote on the back of it.

"I want you to get these three books. They will help you on your journey," she told me as if she had the answers to questions that I didn't know I had yet. I read them and flipped the card over to read her information on the front and put it away in a fold in my wallet, for safe keeping.

"Thank you, JJ!"

The ladies went on to their previous discussion before I interrupted, and I ordered an appetizer, listening attentively to the delicate minds of women masterminds. Mark came soon after and called me away to help him with some furniture moving, which I obliged to assist in any way that I could.

The following day, after Friday convention tasks were completed, Mark and other members of the Board were planning to go to the Paul Whitney Larson Art Gallery at the University of Minnesota to view the submissions and artwork winners of the sponsored art contest. I couldn't think of anything else that I would like to do, and I was extremely eager and anxious to chill out and head to the gallery, especially one that I was a participant in. I mentioned it to Paula, and she was pleased to join us. Kate and Sarah were unable to attend that evening but promised to go tomorrow. Paula brought a small umbrella because there was a possible threat of rain on its way.

We took a bus from SE Washington Ave and it took us about thirty minutes to get there. I wasn't sure what to expect since this was the first time I had ever been shown outside a local café or even outside my city. We were all excited to be in an environment where we could wind down from the tensions and stress from the convention, and without the influence of alcohol this was a nice alternative.

The lobby entrance was warm, fun and inviting. We walked on multi-colored brick face that met the carpet to the left of the main doors. Its lounge area had a few art-deco styled tables and chairs while its walls were primary red. The light oak doors themselves matched the long wooden boards on the ceiling and the primary yellow wall on the left also brightened my mood. I was at the right place; I was at my "Yellow Brick Road"[3].

The Larson Gallery was spacious and was well-curated. We reached the section dedicated to the recognition of strength and resilience, and as with art, it was subjective. There were many different compositions and subjects, mostly abstract and some even avant-garde. Mark and Peter paired off and were studying some of the submissions, while I scanned the limited space and analyzed the competitor's styles and techniques. I looked over to my far right, in a lit corner with a few other paintings, and saw Paula staring at my painting. She found it before I did. *What was she thinking?* I walked over and she turned around to look at me, then back at the painting.

"Nice self-portrait."

"Thank you. There's a tri-fold mirror depicting the different sides of me," subjectively speaking.

"'Honorable Mention'. Great job! You have a great gift."

I was embarrassed and wasn't used to being complimented for my efforts and talent. It was kind for her to say those words. Mark and Peter made their way to us.

"Found it, guys." I said excitedly.

"Congratulations on that Honorable Mention ribbon. Fantastic!" Peter cited.

"Thank you."

"We saw the first-place winner's painting. It's over there. Yours is way better." Mark pointed to it at some distance away.

---

[3] *The Wizard of Oz*, filmed in 1939

"Thanks, Mark. Thank you, all, for being here and celebrating this moment with me. 'Honorable Mention' is nothing to be upset about. I am grateful for the opportunity. Thank you so much!"

I walked over to the long 3'x6' canvas, mainly painted in alizarin crimson red, with a quarter-sized black circle, slightly in the upper left side, and thought how odd it was to have selected this piece over mine. Perhaps it was the emotion that the judges felt when in its presence. Nonetheless, it was chosen, and I accepted the decision.

Paula stood beside me and asked me to talk about my painting to her and what the meaning was behind it. Afterwards, I used the restroom before I could withstand the bus ride back and met up with the rest of the crew in the front. It was raining, harder than a drizzle, but Paula opened her umbrella and allowed me to share its protection with her. The bus came and it was packed for a Friday night and since it was standing-room only, we strap-hanged the entire ride to the hotel, a little wet and misty, continuing the journey of unknown circumstances. We literally and figuratively were closer that day; the bond we shared was friendly and genuine, but we had another long day at the convention, so we turned in early and met up the following afternoon.

It's not every day I get to fly into the Minneapolis-St. Paul (MSP) Airport, even to ride the small roller-coaster or check out all the Peanuts characters at the Mall of America, so I wanted to venture out and explore the Twin Cities neighborhoods, beyond campus grounds, but the University was too big to escape that climate. While everyone else was deeply involved in their work, it being the last full day of classes and pocket-seminars, I went to visit the second-longest river on the North American continent – the Mississippi River. It was a nice walk with blue skies and the air was crisp. There were no clear indications that it even rained the night before.

I walked along SE Washington Ave and before I approached the bridge, like a fish being lured by a shining object, I followed a path to a peculiar silver and shiny building to my left. The Frederick R. Weisman Art Museum is a modern stainless steel and brick building that houses American and contemporary paintings. The first thing that popped into my mind was its modernity and how it just surpassed my image of the Solomon R. Guggenheim Museum, and my outlook on the architectural concept behind the uniqueness and simplicity of curvature. It certainly caught my attention, especially the darting rays of the sun bouncing off and reflecting, but I was more interested in reaching new boundaries.

I started to cross the bridge, above the Mississippi River, and felt this surging energy the more I reached the middle. In this moment of greatness and solitude, I took out my Qualcomm phone and dialed. It rang and rang until the answering machine picked up, and after the beep I left a message.

"Hi, Mom and Dad! It's been a while since I've called you. I'm in Minneapolis, in Minnesota, and everything is fine." Startlingly, I began to feel a bit overwhelmed with loving emotion.

"I won 'Honorable Mention' in an art competition, and…" I began to tear and cry, overcome by intense abundance of emptiness then love. I had created something out of nothing and manifested a positive result. "I wanted to share that with you. Love you, guys!" I hung up and crossed to the other side of the bridge, looking back at the shiny castle from a distance.

It didn't take long before I walked back to a convention room and made it to the tail-end of a documentary featuring aboriginal socialization. When it was over, the crowd emptied the room and I sat at a round table, alone with my thoughts. Paula walked in, and she sat across from me. She was silent for a few seconds, but I felt it too.

"Hi. Is there something going on between us?" she stunned me with that question.

"Yes," I feared, but in a barrier-breaking circumstance where the other side was unknown, and the wall needed to be removed. I asked Paula if she wanted to go for a walk, and she obliged mentioning that she also wanted to check out this store that contained old and rare books.

Book House in Dinkytown, was not a far walk and easy to find despite it being in between other bricked-building stores, plus she asked a couple of people along the way and they all pointed us in the right direction. I just looked around and was amazed at the quantity of hardbound books that were on the shelves, but I wasn't looking for anything specific. She, on the other hand, found a few books from the second floor, and she was pleased. As the smell of old paper dissipated, and we hit the streets now looking for a place to grab a bite, I whistled to Bob Dylan's *Positively 4th Street*, for just a stanza.

Upon the recommendations from JJ and Sarah, who were currently on their way to the art gallery, Paula suggested we try out this café not far from there. It wasn't crowded at all, spacious with an open-floor concept, and felt somewhat hip with art hanging on the minimal wall-space and chess boards on a couple of the empty tables. We sat at a high-chaired table by the window, at the *Purple Onion Café*, and it was a comfortable coffeeshop to hang out and chat, because of the dim-lit atmosphere. It was reminiscent of a dive establishment, with retro cafeteria furniture that hadn't been upgraded or well taken care of because it was so busy that business could not stop to replace anything, somewhat of an outdoor patio feel, yet covered without any air conditioning.

That wasn't the only thing that appealed to me. Other than the French toast I ordered, because breakfast was served all day on Saturdays, I also enjoyed a freshly roasted "Cup of the Day", and she spiced it up with an Apple Cider to go with her Maple Dijon Salad. We spoke extensively on what we were currently working on in life, and where we were headed. I told her that I worked for a major airline in Newark and was able to fly anywhere in the world. Sitting across from her, and really listening, gave me a different perspective and I began to see her differently as I enjoyed her presence and company, getting to know her a little more and understanding that she was an interesting woman, and that I realized that I found her to be somewhat amazing.

The told her about my adventure walk earlier that day and I wanted to show her the river. After coffee and chit-chat, we walked along East River Pkwy towards SE Washington Ave, and before we reached the Weisman Museum, we stopped to look at the mighty Mississippi behind a black metal boundary fence. The energy was tingling and trickled into a small surge; I couldn't explain what was happening, but I knew.

"My flight leaves early tomorrow morning back to Ottawa, eh."

"What time *aboot*?" I chuckled.

My heart raced. It was unbearably too much. The rush of pressure overpowered my senses, dulling any other thought than to just concentrate on breathing. I grabbed the rung of her pant waist with my right forefinger and pulled her close to me, while I embraced her even closer with my other hand, hips touching and steady. I leaned in to kiss her – we kissed gently, her lips soft and tender as her heart, and when we opened our eyes, she stared into mine. We held hands as we slowly walked among the emanating rays of the moon, back to the hotel.

As the team from Canada were assembling in the lobby the following morning, I met with the driver and tipped him twenty bucks to help make sure they arrived safely to the airport. I said my goodbyes to Kate, Sarah, the general others, and then I spoke with Paula.

"I took care of the driver already. You should be fine on your way to the airport."

We hugged.

"Thank you. That was nice of you."

Departing is bitter-sweet and sometimes filled with awkward pleasantries. Not only was it courteous to see her off, but I wanted to see her again.

"It was nice meeting you. Let's keep in touch. Don't be a stranger," I said with a smile.

She handed me her business card and hand-wrote her phone number on the back.

"Tres bien."

Chapter IX – Ottawa

We gave each other that same smile as I walked towards her and gave her a firm hug.

"Sorry I took so long. I was held up by Customs."

"I wasn't sure if I would make it on time. I took the bus from work. I'm glad you're here. Bienvenue. Welcome to Canada! How was your flight?" she excitedly asked me.

"Really short. As soon as we reached our highest altitude, it was time to come back down already. I barely had time to finish the Customs Declarations paperwork," I explained.

"C'mon. Let's get you some Loonies and catch the next bus." After the currency exchange I grabbed a bus schedule from the Information booth and asked her when the next bus was due. She said that she did not know but that we should wait outside for it so that we don't miss it.

"How cold is it?"

"Negative eight," She casually responded.

"Celsius conversion to Fahrenheit puts it between 15 and 20 degrees?"

"We'll have a smoke while we wait."

"Oh yeah. We can do that."

We lit up our smokes, her – a Marlboro light, while I switched from Newport to Benson & Hedges menthol the previous week, and we went out to the corner bus stop to wait for the 97 Kanata bus. It was out of the norm for me to enjoy a smoke within the confines of freezing conditions, but somehow it seemed legitimate and proper as if it was a necessary custom.

I smoked tobacco off and on for nearly ten years, more so out of boredom or as a social occurrence, especially if I had a beer or three. I only inhaled and polluted my lungs with nicotine for six months out of the year, or during the Spring and Summer months (whichever was longer) because it was too ridiculous to corrupt my body when it was cold outside, especially with the frigid temperatures in the Northeast during the brisk Fall and Winter snow months. The quality of the cigarette is different, especially the taste, on windy occasions as if sucking in cold air chemically changed the experience for me.

When the bus pulled up, the driver parked it and joined us for a few minutes. *Smoke break.* Seemed we all needed a break from the bustle, and when we were all satisfied with our cravings, he opened the doors and cranked on the heat for our voyage. It was the first time I had ever been on a bus that had an extension to it; it was nearly sixty feet in length. She took me to her favorite seating area since we were the only ones onboard and after she took her seat, she signaled for me to sit next to her. I placed my luggage in front of me and was curious about the twist and turns the driver had to maneuver, but luckily the route was straight-forward with minimal ninety-degree turns.

"This is a *New Flyer* model. They're fairly new," she explained.

"I'm checking out this articulation joint and wondering if anyone had ever been injured when the floor moves." She was a very knowledgeable and informative tour guide, and for the next forty-minutes or so we engaged in other small talk, but I also really tried to observe the city as we were being driven through it at night.

"There are a couple of safety concerns you should know about."

"Safety?" I asked, "This is Canada. Nothing bad happens here," I dispelled.

"No. No. There are two areas along this route that had been sources of security concerns lately. There have been incidents of swarming and other incidents mostly at transit stations, especially between Bayshore Station and Lincoln Fields Station."

"Swarming? What is that? Some type of bee thing?"

"It's when a group of people suddenly gather and then create a crime like a robbery or an assault."

"Oh. Ok. I think we're fine." I assured her.

I was ready for anything.

When we made it to our final stop, I stepped off mentally preparing for the brutal cold I was to walk into, but it wasn't bad at all. The November night air was still, and without any wind I felt as if I were overdressed with my scarf and gloves. People walked the streets in garb more designed for warmth than fashion. No one cared what they looked like as long as they were warm.

"If you wear the right clothes, it doesn't even affect you. We're used to it by now. Preparation and adaptation are key," Paula said while wearing her earmuffs and a smile.

Amidst walking a few blocks along Bank Street, we stopped at a *Tim Horton's* and afterwards I saw an occasional single article of clothing: a glove on the ground, a hat somewhere else, a scarf in the street.

"I'm going to write a book about stories and the conversations of people missing one of these items. I mean, do they go back and retrace their steps to look for it? Do they even know they're missing? Do they have another pair and wear those? Or, is it intended for those who don't have it and need it while they're walking the streets? Who picks it up and throws it away? Would you take it home, wash it and wear it? It'll be a coffee table book," I ranted in a stream of immediate ideas.

"Hahaha. You should. It happens all the time." I appreciated that instead of dismissing those ideas, she supported it as if to accept and not judge my views.

She took me to her one-bedroom apartment, which really had a nice view of Ottawa from the eighth-floor building. Her cat, Clyde, laid comfortably on the top of a blue and white-tiled quilt on her gray couch, unbothered that I was new to their domain. Her living room was cozy with an entertainment center and television, a coffee table, and a few shelves for her books. She even had a four-shelved stand, by the window, that housed ten of her plants. At the end of the nickel-tour she showed me her bedroom which had a Queen-sized mattress on the floor and told me it was great for her back. Her bed was made with a couple of fluffed white-cased pillows and the sheets were tucked. A brown decorative pillowcase matched the sheets and a couple of blankets were nicely laid on top. The two small teddy bears sat softly on top, and a lamp also illuminated a four-drawer white dresser.

On top of another dresser, in a large clear glass dish, she lit two candles – one tall white one and the smaller one pink, enclosed in glass to prevent its wax from losing its contained shape. The dish also stored Canadian paper money, a couple of stamps and her keys so I emptied my pockets and put both my currencies, keys and other coins that may have mixed in with a "loonie" or "toonie", and my Passport. I felt lighter and less constricted, but also like an equal.

I was wondering where I would be resting my head to sleep, hoping that Clyde wouldn't mind. The room looked bigger without a bed frame and the box spring. Even the walls were bare except for a necklace of the "Evil Eye" hanging on a string on a nail next to the bedroom door. She instructed me to place my bag next to the dresser and when I did, I unzipped the bag and took out a gift I made for her that was wrapped in a clean t-shirt. I took it out of the shirt and handed it to her.

"This is for you."

She looked at me and was surprised, and when she carefully unwrapped the white paper and tape, she was in awe.

"No one has ever painted a portrait of me. This is me. You captured me. I love it!"

She held on to it for a while noticing all the details and quirks that I recognized as unique and her.

I painted her portrait on a 12"x16" canvas in oil, of how I remembered her in my mind, from sitting across and enjoying our time together in Minneapolis. I titled it "The Purple Onion" but the only thing that was purple, really a few shades lighter to violet, was the background. Her head slightly tilted to her left, with no facial features except for the glasses, hanging without a nose. She immediately hung it on her bedroom wall, above the "dresser of equality".

"You're such an artist. Thank you for being so thoughtful," she complimented and gave me a hug.

"I'm glad you like it. I brought my paints, which is partly why I was late at Customs. All I need is blank canvas. Maybe we can go to an art store tomorrow?" I asked.

"Sure. There's a place right down the street. We'll go after breakfast tomorrow morning."

"Yeah. Yeah," I responded.

"If you'd like to wash up or take a shower, be my guest. I'm going to make us some pizza."

"Sounds good. Thank you."

I traded my afternoon detail for the morning shift at the airport cargo facility and afterwards went straight to the airport terminal to catch this flight. With all the traveling grime from multitudes of domestic and international fellow-passenger hands and fingers, I felt a little dirty so a shower would help cleanse and wash away all those transgressions.

"There's a fresh towel and bar of soap in there." she said.

Her bathroom was tidy and organized. It felt good to take off my clothes and have that warm water hit my body from the showerhead. The water pressure was constant and rinsed away most of the lather, and since I never used *Dove* soap before, moisture remained on my skin, but it smelled good and reminded me of a time long ago – an age of innocence, as certain scents will.

As I walked out of the steam-filled bathroom, dressed in fresh clean clothes and ready to unwind for the evening, the smell of oven pizza filled my lungs. We must have come out of the heat at the same time and we were ready. Paula poured us each a glass of red wine, took a moderate drink, gave me a kiss, then was on her way to hop in the shower while I sat on the far-left side of the love seat.

"Make yourself comfortable. Do you like 70's or 2,000 porn?" she directed nonchalantly as she took a couple of steps to leave the room.

"Two-thousand," I hesitantly responded, but only for a mere second.

Off she went and then I put the oil paints, and some of my favorite brushes, in the room behind the couch to set up for tomorrow and emptied my travel bag back in her bedroom. I was admiring the view through the glass doors to her balcony, and listened to The Tea Party, the *Splendor Solis* album, but I wasn't ready for it. From the opening riff of *The River* I was hooked, and by the time *Winter Solstice* came on I heard the bathroom door open, the vent fan shut off, and soon after she walked in with black sweatpants and a green shirt; she looked comfortable.

"Nice tunes! Who are they?" I asked.

"The Tea Party. They're Canadian," she proudly responded.

"Freakin' awesome. Good choice. How was your shower?"

She grabbed her glass, took a swig, walked towards me and sat crossing her legs next to me, barefoot with blue-painted toenails. *Sexy.*

"Great," she softly spoke into my right ear, then gently nibbled my lobe.

"I broke my ankle years ago and sometimes it hurts so just be careful with it, ok?" she mentioned.

"Ok. I won't 'sweep the leg'[4]. What happened?"

She briefly told me the story and when she finished, I turned towards her and softly kissed her on her lips. My left hand automatically ran through her hair and I cradled the back of her neck while I sucked on her bottom lip. She quickly threw her leg over and sat on me, her hands on my shoulders and mine on her hips. She was so flexible and frisky, but we were slightly mindful of her left foot she hurt long ago, so I gently rubbed the bottom of it with my thumb without tickling her. After a long passionate kiss, she slowly disengaged and stood up and strolled away, looking for her lighter that she placed on the coffee table. She lit an incense in a distance.

"Are you ready for tonight's feature film?" she opened the glass door that housed her video and cd collection. There was no choice, option, or say in the mysterious movie we were able to watch, and conveniently, possibly due to lack of room and counter space in the kitchen, she tossed in a bag of popcorn in the microwave that was also in the living room.

"Dinner and a movie? Bonus!" I expressed in excitement.

I was quiet for most of the film. I never had a creepy sense of delight in a film such as in *The Wicker Man*. It was brilliant. It reminded me of my upbringing in the 70s and contradicted my beliefs in Roman Catholicism. My ship steered in an opposite direction that moment as I came to my own understanding, greater

---

[4] *The Karate Kid*, filmed in 1984, climactic action reference

than not having landed on the moon in the sixties or the earth being flat, or even being told that Santa Claus did not exist. Except now that he did exist but was a Pagan god. I genuinely felt uneasy, as if I missed out on the pagan way of thought for too long. *I questioned everything*. It was my epiphany, my awakening, and caused me to press *pause* and think.

I recognized Christopher Lee from many of the movies my father used to watch. I expected him to be a villain or some sort of scary character, but my imagination and expectation got the best of me. The acoustic and druid-like soundtrack was in a genre, or special category, that sounded different to me comparatively like listening to *The Monkees*, in American pop-culture. The thing I appreciated most was the flick's love for nature; I almost believed that I *could* sacrifice myself and reincarnate into nature. Thoughts of being buried and confined in a coffin became a lonely aftermath. It was completely spell-binding and unconventional. The *Maypole Song* challenged me to think that it was all connected.

In the woods there grew a tree and a fine, fine tree was he
And on that tree there was a limb, and on that limb there was a branch, and on that branch there was a nest, and in that nest there was an egg, and in that egg there was a bird, and from that bird a feather came, and of that feather was a bed.

And on that bed there was a girl, and on that girl there was a man, and on that man there was a seed, and from that seed there was a boy, and from that boy there was a man, and for that man there was a grave, and from that grave there grew a tree.[5]

After it was over, we went to her room and I expressed how I felt about the movie. I suppose not everyone would have appreciated the artistic and creative value it had, but I did. She valued my input and insight then she took off her shirt and slipped into bed.

"You can sleep on the couch if it makes you feel more comfortable. There's a blanket and pillows over there already, or you can sleep here next to me."

She took off her pants while under the sheets and put her articles of clothing on the foot of the bed.

"Either way, I'm going to sleep." Paula confirmed.

This was the first time I was experiencing this type of straightforwardness and approach in what seemed to be leading up to an intimate situation. Being shy, I questioned its potential and possibility, and feared making the wrong decision. *Was it a trick? A test?* Usually there was a playfulness leading up to a possible encounter and different steps and games were initiated, but it was right there, willingly presented to me and I was willing. She was gorgeous.

"Good night, Paula."

"Shut the lights off."

I got up, turned off the lamp, and left her room. I looked at Clyde, who was perched comfortably on his pillow near the love seat, and I

---

[5] *Maypole Song*, a song of fertility, The Wicker Man (1973)

unfurled the blanket. I turned off the remaining lights. The moon light peered into the apartment through the balcony doors and was enough to shed some light unto the situation. I undressed myself and took a deep breath, looking at Clyde then at the opened folding door that lead to the head end of her room.

She wasn't startled when I gently lifted the sheet and laid down next to her, her smooth back to me on her right side. I placed my hand on her strong left shoulder, lifted her long silky hair, and kissed the nape of her neck. She turned around and climbed on top of me. The moon glow partially revealed her dark side to me as she rested her hands on my chest, coming down to meet my lips.

"Hi," she whispered with a grin as she drew closer. I reached out to her and softly pulled her close.

"Bonjour."

I ran my fingers through her hair as we kissed sensually and uninhibitedly. Our breaths remained casual, our lips slowly kissing each other's lips, my hands caressing her back from top to bottom. I gently shifted our weights so I could wrap around her and have her laying on her back, mindful of her foot and how she wanted me to be careful with it. Our foreplay was extraordinary.

Her breasts were perfectly natural and average, but then, I'm an ass man and I don't whole-heartedly focus on breasts. I did, however, pass by and tease her nipple a few times before I pinched it gently. As I slowly kissed her belly and worked my way down, I grabbed her other nipple and gave them both a simultaneous pinch and rub.

"Two-thousand porn," she said in heavier breath and a giggle. "I left a little on the top."

She shaved for me, according to my preference and desire, and she was extremely warm and soft in my mouth as I started to suck on her clit. My tongue rolled around slowly, unpredictable and at quick intervals, firm with added pressure. After she orgasmed and remained stimulated, she threw me on my back and did the same thing to me. I thoroughly enjoyed it. I never experienced oral sex as sensual, erotic, and stimulating as I did with her. She took me to a height of awareness I didn't know existed. We simply connected on all levels, our bodies spoke, and the language was of fire and water. *Steamy*.

I opened the wrapper she handed me, took out the condom, and put it on. *Safety first.* I was gentle, took my time, and we were ready. "Thoomp," she said in onomatopoeia jest to describe the sheathing of a sword. We had passionate sex that was beyond casual, but playfully honest and real. She had a strong back and I rubbed from the base of her neck, down her spine and was further aroused by gripping her hourglass-shaped pelvic hips. I thoroughly enjoyed this new position that she favored, and it made a difference in sensation, so it was a learning experience of intimate self-exploration.

"Your back is so strong and sensual."

"I'm getting it tattooed soon so touch it now before it's sore later."

The respect and connectivity we had for each other's minds, bodies and souls were apparent on that arena of lust and love. No one was hurt during the magic of our lovemaking, I was ultimately satisfied in my decision for not choosing the couch, and that mattress did wonders for my back.

The next morning, she awoke me with a kiss. Her naked body was warm and smooth.

"Good morning. Hi," she greeted me with a smirky smile.

She rested her head on my chest and deeply breathed in.

"You smell like benzoin. So natural, so good."

I thought I might have smelled like *Dove*, sex, or something worse, but she liked it. It was a new dawn and I felt awakened, alive – overjoyed and connected with a burst of loving energy. There were no regrets or uneasiness.

We went out for breakfast to the Elgin Street Diner, by early afternoon. We certainly worked up our appetites, and the walk was short and pleasant. When I visit a new place, I tend to order the local item, especially a Signature dish that sets it apart from anything I can get anywhere else. Being from Jersey I am a fan of the diner experience, so it was just a matter of adding poutine, or not.

One of the beauties of a twenty-four-hour diner is the ability to order breakfast any time of the day, and my go-to order is usually French Toast, but I hadn't considered it this morning solely because it had the word "French" in it; I just wanted to try their real maple syrup with it.

We sat at a table instead of a booth, and overlooking the delectable dishes from another table, it appeared that the fries were a crowd favorite.

"Good morning. Welcome. What can I get for you to drink?" the waitress asked us.

"Hello, good morning. I'll have a tall glass of water for now."

"And for you?" she asked me.

"A cup of coffee please."

"Pardon?"

I can be a little soft-spoken at times, so I repeated myself, just a bit louder.

"A cup of coffee." I repeated.

The waitress didn't understand so Paula ordered a cup of coffee for me without the alleged heavy Jersey accent I had. I guess I was saying "caw-fee" instead. I laughed at myself because I didn't realize that I had an accent, and it wasn't a big deal at all.

She said that I could share her poutine – fresh-cut fries, gravy and cheese curds – to try it out, and when she returned with our drinks, we were ready to order.

"I'll have the *Breakfast Special* with sausage, poutine instead of the home fries, and scrambled eggs and please make sure the eggs are 'shoe-leather dry'".

"...Shoe leather dry. And for you?" she asked me after she finished writing in her little book pad.

"I'll try the French Toast with sliced bananas please," I said with a smile.

"Thank you," Melanie, our waitress, responded. I tend to read the names of anyone who wears a name tag. It makes it more personal, and I'm grateful to those who are helpful to me.

"I don't like eggs that are runny. They need to be as dry as possible," Paula explained to me but didn't need to. She pleasantly knew what she liked and felt confident in her decisions.

I don't know whether it was because it was the "morning after" but everything tasted great and I really enjoyed the atmosphere within the diner. I practically ate all her fries, some with my fingers, and even the bananas tasted fresh and ripe. The couple next to us ordered vanilla shakes with chocolate chip pancakes and the other blueberry pancakes, the guy at the counter had his share of poutine topped with smoked meat, and I had real maple syrup with my French toast.

Chapter X – Art Peace

It was a nice day to walk off a meal. We headed to an art store in The Glebe. There, I picked up several 11"x14" blank canvas, a palette knife, palette, and a sketch pad. I was all set to create, and on the way back, we stopped by an art gallery, on Bank Street, to check out the works of a local artist – RG, but the gallery hadn't yet opened on this weekday - Thursday.

Apart from working for a major airline, I started by own business representing local artists. Artists create art, and most do not know or have time for the marketing side of their talent, so I ventured into becoming their agent, so their works do not get buried in a closet somewhere and never get shown. Prior to coming, I already had two painters and one poet, all whom were extremely talented. I wanted to connect with the art and artists here, and to possibly showcase them in the States, produce a film documentary of the process, and encourage the local community to embrace an art niche in this government city. Those were high aspirations recognizing full potential, but I was bold and willing to make greatness happen.

"That's an interesting balcony," I pointed to a corner building, on rue Bank St. & av. Patterson Ave., that had a single door on the second floor with an iron balcony with seven potted plants on it. It was so small that only three people could comfortably stand side by side on it. Some of the graffiti artists must have thought that location was such an attraction that they coat-tailed its notoriety and scribbled some illegible nonsense on the bottom floor with spray paint.

In the spirit of expression and art, I drew my inspiration from being with her, so it was fitting that the first quick sketch I did, back at her apartment, was of her portrait, smoking a cigarette, with only eyebrows and glasses on her face. "Study of Dulcinea" 11-20-03. She was reading a book, while having a smoke, on the other side of the love seat and we coexisted and respected each other's space, more so me, since it was her apartment. I showed her the rendition.

"Dulcinea? Is that your girlfriend?" she jokingly asked.

"Yeah. But don't tell my girlfriend. That's my pet name for you now, like an anagram, because it has the letters in your name." I joked back.

"There are only three letters in my name in Dulcinea."

"Come here, beautiful. 'Dulce' in Spanish means 'sweet', and you're the sweetest thing. Do you like it?" I gave her a hug to affirm that I meant no harm or disrespect.

"I'm just going to draw some more sketches and start painting tomorrow. I'll set up a little area, out of the way."

"You won't be in the way. Wherever you want. You know honey is sweet too, just like you."

"We're saps," and with a kiss on her nose we hugged again.

She suggested we go get some minor provisions like fresh fruits and vegetables at a local market, and off we went. She led me through the streets and knew all the shortcuts. Unexpectedly, I walked by a sculpture of a Triceratops outside the *Canadian Museum of Nature.*

"Can we get some real maple syrup?" I asked.

"The freshest local products," she emphasized.

I felt safe in her presence. Paula was a confident and intelligent woman who knew when to take charge and when to relinquish that control, in order to balance our relationship and its maturity. Another sense of security came over me when I noticed the Embassy of the United States of America, and the American flag peering above the tall tree line. I reached into my back pocket to confirm that I still had my Passport on me, in the event I might have needed it for immediate disposal. That building itself looked quite new and guarded with proper fence-protection, but it looked desolate, there were no signs of guards or defending military personnel outside, especially for an edifice that appeared to have a multitude of glass protecting the outside walls.

The federal government office next door, the Agence Revenu Canada building, looked more like a fortress than the US Embassy, even though the Canada Revenue Agency administers tax laws for the Government of Canada and for most provinces and territories, and administers various social and economic benefit and incentive programs delivered through the tax system.

"What are you in the mood for, for dinner?" I asked her.

"If you're still hungry we can grab a bite to eat at the market, for lunch, otherwise I have a surprise for you, but first I'd like to get a book from the store just down the road."

"Sure. Yeah, yeah." I assured.

We continued to walk along Mackenzie Avenue until we nearly approached the Notre-Dame Cathedral Basilica in the near distance but first an architectural landscape caught my attention in the center of St. Patrick Street and Murray Street where they meet Mackenzie

Drive and Sussex Drive. RECONCILIATION is written twice on a monument wall commemorating Canada's role in international peacekeeping and the soldiers, both living and dead, who have participated and are currently participating. *The Peacekeeping Monument* is just south of the National Gallery of Canada and just north of the American Embassy and Major's Hill Park. The monument was completed in 1992 and depicts three peacekeeping soldiers — two men and a woman standing on two ridges of stone which cut through the broken debris of war and converge at a high point.

As the largest and oldest standing church in Ottawa, the Notre Dame Basilica stands majestically tall and has undergone many modifications and changes in construction. A wooden statue of the Virgin Mary, ten-feet high and covered with gold leaf, stands between two stainless steel steeples. The evening sun magnified its brilliance and I admired its exterior while walking on Murray Street.

"It's hard to believe that I was just in another country days ago and now I'm in this treasure trove of a capitol city with you. Everything is so beautiful, stable, and alluring." I commented.

"You must be on the right path," she countered.

I ran my fingers through her long dark chestnut hair and rested my hand on her shoulder as we walked off towards the bookstore.

When I walked into *Sunnyside Bookshop*, I couldn't fully comprehend the number of books stored and shelved. Their logo was a crescent moon on the bottom with a sun filling in the void, to complete the circle. They each had a face and rays projected outward in illumination. A young teenager walked out with several thin books, perhaps a compilation of short stories, and I recognized that the one on top was from an American author whom I was familiar with from my Prep school days. If he was able to find Nathaniel Hawthorne's *Young Goodman Brown*, then I had faith that she could find whatever she was looking for.

Every space was taken, as if wallpapered in its entirety and walking room was limited due to long tables dividing whatever floor space was available. Attendants carried boxes of more books to and from, each destined in their place waiting for their reader and new owner, except that we weren't in search for them – books find people. There was order throughout the perceived chaos. The multi-floored sanctuary for literary enthusiasts housed many, if not all, genres and each department was labeled with paper signs for more efficient searches. I asked an employee where the religious and spiritual books were but the young lady pointed me towards the ascending flight of stairs, so up I went mindfully staying to my right so as not to bump into anyone or anything, while Paula had already went in search for her items.

I was rather impressed that so many people were still interested in reading, perhaps expanding their collection, or motivated to learn something new, as literature was not a novelty. Even though I felt corralled, the lighting and temperature were very comfortable within and my eyes kept wandering from top to bottom of every row and from bottom back up, scanning for a topic that would catch my interest enough to make a purchase. It was a step above looking for a couch to sit on while she shopped at a department store since I wasn't bored or tired at all. Stacks of publications were on tops of tables, and bookshelves were to my left and right when a family came towards me, walking from the opposite direction. We smiled and gave each other the courtesy and room to get by without impeding or imposing on another's personal space, and in order to avoid the last member I scooted to the left, but my hip bumped into a table and it hit a connecting shelf. A book must have jostled because it fell flat from about four feet above and unto the table.

I immediately reached into my back pocket and retrieved my wallet. Inside the fold I pulled out a business card that was given to me by a person I met a while ago in Minnesota. I turned it around – *The Alchemist* by Paulo Coelho. That was one of the books on the list. I snatched and held on to it tightly then made my way around to find her. I was confident and shocked that it found its way into my life, although I did not know its premise or why it was even suggested for me to read, but I was excited and eager to discover the message within so that it could assist me on my journey. I met up with her and upon our purchases and exiting, I placed it inside my camera bag and zipped it up for safe keeping, for myself.

Along the way back to her apartment, we stopped by a vendor's tent that sells incense and oils. The ByWard Market (Marché By) is one of Canada's oldest and largest public markets, and provides a much welcomed connection between rural and urban life. With open-air stalls staging fresh local fruits, vegetables, flowers, and other keen products, the opportunity to indulge in a healthy lifestyle was but a grasp away. I was familiar with patchouli because of the popularity in the sixties and seventies and on how many of my hippie friends from those eras wore its oils as perfumes and as an all-purpose insect repellent. She looked around at the various forms of incense and found a couple that interested her. She even replenished her dwindling supply of sage and sweetgrass.

"Do they smell good?" I asked.

"The sage has a pungent smell but the sweetgrass neutralizes it afterwards. I'm running low."

Not far from the jasmine pack of incense that she procured, I noticed a small bag of benzoin that contained twenty cones. Slightly distracted, in the distance I heard one of my favorite Avril Lavigne tunes, and although "Complicated" was a big hit I liked listening to "I'm With You". Upon reading the fine print of the label, it was manufactured by NUR in Montreal, but I was attracted to the green leafy logo on the front of the packaging. I opened the bag and took in a steady whiff to learn that it had a smoky, woodsy scent. If this is what I naturally smell like to her, I'm ok with that. The small arsenal of natural fragrances we purchased were far better than any chemical spray used to eliminate odors around the abode.

I carried a couple of bags of fresh produce she purchased, and we strolled back to her neighborhood taking in the architectural sights and listening to people occasionally speaking in French and English, sometimes both. *Is "Frenglish" even a word comparable to when I sometimes speak "Spanglish?"*

Sunset would be coming a little after eight, so we had time to unload our weight, feed Clyde, freshen up, and attend dinner together at a local Korean restaurant on Bank Street. I was open on trying new foods and new places, interested in different cultures, and thrilled to just experience local nuances. We only needed to walk a block away from the apartment, as a matter of logistical convenience. There were so many great eateries along that street that it should be called the "Rue Roux", as in the mixture to make sauces, but with my Canadian French humor it probably translates to "Red Street".

The restaurant was appealing, and the different scents of spices appealed to my nose and taste buds, and I hadn't even taken a seat. We ordered drinks and cared about nothing else than being in the moment, across from one another, locked in and being happy. There was no doubt that we had a connection, emotional and physical, that built on gaining familiarity, comfortability, and trust. The sun was going down, but not our spirits, as we continued to laugh and smile at each other and ourselves.

It was so relaxing to spend the rest of my better day in nature, away from the office bustle and city traffic that was my daily routine, to a soothing and more ambient atmosphere with a woman who paid so much attention to my care and well-being and attentively listened even though I didn't say much. I was just as engaging to her wants, needs, and desires but more importantly it wasn't out of duty or expectation. We treated each other with such care because that was who we were taught or learned to be, plus we took a very active interest in each other. The Korean cuisine was a delicious recommendation and afterwards we set off to unwind.

Astrologically speaking, being a Pisces male, and she a Cancer sign, we naturally connected as we are both water signs. The female crab and the male fish are automatically attracted to each other, and in terms of compatibility, I felt we are emotionally, psychically, spiritually, and intimately attuned to one another. Ours is a bond that transcends the physical as we are on the same wavelength, upholding the strengths of one another, and the harmony between us is so peaceful and flows so well that this relationship could last a lifetime.

On one of her entertainment shelves, next to her television, was a wooden box with two golden latches on it. She pulled it out and placed it in front of her next to the lighter. In it were charcoal tablets and separate bags of incense crystals. She lowered the music a couple of notches before she grabbed a crimson red sculpture, about 4.5" tall, that posed as a base to put the charcoal on top of and placed it on an end table, on top of a doily handkerchief, near the balcony doors. It almost resembled an altar. She lit the charcoal and tiny sparks burned throughout, eventually turning it hot and white. I hadn't really noticed before but on the table was a wooden fertility goddess, two long thin green candles, and what looked to be a cup or a chalice. I just sat there letting her do her thing, setting up an atmosphere and mood, while I indulged and drank more wine.

Jasmine is considered one of the most powerful flowers used in spell work and magic. The sensuous scent of the Jasmine flower is highly recognizable and very popular among perfumers and there are many ways to incorporate Jasmine into rituals and spells. She used it in cone form and intended to burn it, in a white ashtray near the stereo system, to attract love and to induce dreams of a prophetic nature, purification, wisdom and astral projection. Over dinner, she mentioned relaxing techniques and meditations, specifically guided meditations, and I was open to the concept of freeing my mind to allow source energy to communicate to me. What she was about to perform was in no way an ambush or forcing me into doing something I didn't already agree to, but I had no idea what to expect. The smell of the jasmine incense was delightful and pleasing, and so was she.

The spiritual meanings of fragrances and magical properties of incense will help focus the mind on achieving specific goals. Burning incense has a symbolic meaning that helps pagans focus their attention on the purpose of a ritual or magical working. On the already hot charcoal, she sprinkled benzoin resin and desired to burn it for purification, astral projection, and clearing negative energy.

"I'm glad they had the book I was looking for. It has some fascinating guided meditations. Just relax, Hon. I've done these before with amazing results," she assured me.

"Yeah, yeah."

The incense was permeating the room and it aided in my relaxation. The book in her hand was smaller than *The Little Giant Encyclopedia of Runes* publication next to the remote control on the coffee table. She placed her gray Bic lighter on *The Alchemist* and instructed me to take a deep breath, then to exhale. Paula insisted I listened to her commands as she would guide me on this meditation. I took another deep breath, exhaled, and did it a couple of more times each moment concentrating on her voice and my breathing.

"Breathe in. Now hold it. Exhale."

The last thing I consciously remembered was walking through a field and coming across a hanged man, upside down and tied to one of his ankles, and that's when I fell into a sleep and dreamt.

"Wow. Sorry. I fell asleep, but the strange thing is that I remember it and it's weird." I said.

"What did you see?"

"Well, I remember you talking then you stopped for about a minute or two. I thought you left the room, but that book must have timed the directions of when to speak. Anyway, I was in front of my parents' house, double-parked at night, in the driver's seat of a car. A woman came up to the window and yelled at me to 'Get out!' There were two children in the backseat, and as I now stood behind the car, she drove off with them. Weird. I don't have any children."

"Mysteries of the Divine," she uttered, "I've never had a response like that from anyone before."

"What else you got?" I asked her.

I was mentally stimulated by the esoteric and the non-conventional ways of thought conflicting with what I was traditionally brought up with and taught, but I wasn't afraid of it. She pulled out a Rider-Waite Tarot deck and took the cards and the booklet out of the box.

"Now think of a question and focus on it. All right?"

That was simple; in my mind I asked about our relationship and our future together since I couldn't come up with a real question that I wanted to ask. It seemed appropriate. After cutting the deck, she laid the cards out one by one in the Celtic Cross format.

"How odd! I've never drawn these many Major Arcana cards in one spread reading. Out of the ten cards laid out, you have six. There is something powerful within you. You are about to experience some serious life lessons. You are connected and you don't even know it. What was your question?" She was flummoxed.

"I asked about my love life, of course."

"That's great, Hon, because the Sun is the outcome. Ok, so you have the Hanged Man…"

"Yeah, the Hanged Man from the meditation, right? Upside down by one ankle and leg crossed."

"Yes. Him. You also have the Devil, Justice, the Tower, and Death." I wasn't altogether familiar with this deck, except for her tutorial and explanations, but she told me that it was popular and first published in 1909. Paula was quite serious about her beliefs in esotericism and identified herself as being Pagan and was also into the Kabbalah. She showed me a diagram of the "Tree of Life" and how it was structured to manifest things into your life.

There are three things I don't normally talk about: politics, sex and religion. It's kind of difficult to not have a sensible discussion about politics since we were in Ottawa, the capital city of Canada, and the Parliament was but a few miles away. It was partly the reason why I didn't witness many opened art galleries or local artisans openly displaying their works. Such free-thinking in a government town was probably not the norm, or hardly accepted, but my admiration of the contrasting color bursting amidst the dull shades of government grey facades instilled in me.

Paula is of Dutch descent, living in Canada, now hosting a man of Puerto Rican descent whom she met in Minnesota but who lives in New Jersey. There are going to be differences in the way we view the world, and that's part of understanding each other and ourselves.

I was more aware and opened to her beliefs and the others I hadn't explored yet, and it initiated and peaked my interests in studying comparative religions. Ultimately, I am responsible for my own beliefs and actions, since good and evil are abstractions and are subjective.

The following day I started on five different paintings. I was into it, inspired and high on life and odorless paint thinner by the time I brushed the last stroke. The first one I worked on was in acrylic, just to get into the groove and get the juices flowing back again. I painted the "Eye of Protection", a Turkish evil eye amulet that does not have any religious connection but offers protection from anyone who does not have genuine good intentions. It safeguards against envious and deceitful people, and she had one of them already hanging in her bedroom. Since it is typically displayed with a couple of different shades of blue, I painted the background its complimentary color – orange, and instead of it a circle, I did it in a shape of a heart. I enjoyed artistic freedom and liberties.

The second acrylic I started and completed was a landscape, imaginary and totally made up, of mountains, trees, a field and land in the foreground that turned into a body of water. It was very colorful and primary with slight deviations, while the third one was a portrait of her and Clyde, on the couch laying down next to each other, her arm cradling his relaxed body. The last acrylic I attempted was that of a pan flute. I was curious of any musical talents or instruments that she may have had but all I found was a pan flute, so I painted another blue and orange complimentary still life of it.

After washing the palette and brushes with warm water, I looked down at the sketch book from yesterday and I decided to oil paint a still life on a new canvas. On the following page of sketches, I had drawn a quick rendition of three people wearing animal masks – fox, cat, hare – but it seemed too involved for now so I started to paint one titled "The Secret", of a wine bottle with two glasses filled with red wine, and an ashtray. It was a study of circular, and ovular, tops and shadows. After applying the first coat I walked over to her with paint brush in mouth and pencil and pad in hand and started to sketch "Study of Dulcinea II".

"Perfect," I stated as I finished and dated it. I walked back to the make-shift studio space behind the couch and by her older collection of books on a tall bookshelf, where she allowed me to display the already-dried masterpieces, and I attempted to continue the oil rendition.

Oil paintings required patience and a different method of brush work and cleaning. As such, I knew I wouldn't be able to finish it that day, but I took my time to convey the vision.

"Hey, there's a cool concert on tv. Can you see it from there? Let's watch it together." She invited me to take a break and hang out on the couch with her.

"Wow! Yeah. Definitely." I was excited so I cleaned up as much as I could and let the paint dry on the canvas and joined in on the fun. What I didn't realize was that she was drawing sketches of me while I was focused on painting. One was of me painting a landscape with two hovering birds, in my shorts, and the other was of me sleeping by a tree while an angelic female creature in a robe and wings watched over me. I didn't know she sketched, and I was extremely flattered of the attention and detail she captured with mere graphite, paper, and thought.

I just made it. The crowd cheered and the musician ran to the front of the stage, thanking them. After the drummer clanked his sticks, the singer banged on the piano keys and the green laser lights darted its rays. A taping of their July's performance in Sydney was airing now and Coldplay was jamming out to "Clocks". We noticed some writing on his hands written in black ink – "Make Trade Fair". I moved to the music, my head bobbed front and back to the tempo and she also moved her body to the rhythm; her hand tapping her knee. It was such a catchy tune, and I seldom listen to lyrics, but towards the end is when I tuned in and tweaked my hearing just a notch. *Home. Home. Where I wanted to go.* Chris Martin sang those lyrics several times, but I didn't want to go home. Then the house phone rang.

Paula looked at the Caller ID and then looked up at me with a disturbed concern.

"This number has been leaving messages all day," she calmly and casually stated.

I looked down at the house phone and the number as it rang again and ignored it until it stopped. The caller was relentless and was determined to get a hold of its recipient, as a collector would with a debt, so it started to ring again after a minute had gone by. I shook my head to waive off any involvement.

"You need to answer it," she insisted.

We both knew who it was… my wife.

"Hello."

"Hello, my husband. How are you?"

My husband. She's never called me that.

"I'm fine."

"Where are you staying?"

"At my friend Clyde's house."

Paula gave me a look of condemnation since she was a strong advocate for the truth. The stretching of the facts was unacceptable and mainly the reason why I couldn't dance around the issue or lie.

"I was worried about you. You didn't call, so I called every hotel in Ottawa looking for you."

"Everything is fine. No need to worry."

"The phone bill came in and it was four-hundred dollars higher because you were dialing this number in Canada. Whose woman's voice is that on the answering machine?"

"That's his wife's. They're married. We'll talk about it when I get home. I don't know why you're calling here," I said defensively.

"I'm glad you're ok, my husband. See you when you get home."

I had been married for four years and it was an interesting concept, but I allegedly made a commitment and I broke a vow of fidelity – she just didn't officially know it. I was truthful to Paula two months ago in Minneapolis about my marriage, so she knew, and now I needed to deal with some harsh realities, although I wasn't feeling altogether remorseful or guilty. I was more concerned about Paula's views since there wasn't any hard evidence that I did anything wrong, but she had her morals and code to follow.

"If your wife calls and asks me, I will tell her the truth. I will not live in lies."

I couldn't get upset with Paula. It was quite admirable and respectable that she would uphold those truths deemed necessary to live life with a clear conscience. This was about my character and my decisions, and I needed to recognize and take responsibility for them. Besides, what does Paula, or anyone lose by remaining true in any circumstance? I was at a loss for words.

"This is your 'Tower' moment and your life will change from this point forward."

There was no use on dwelling and stressing about the issue, right then; I would deal with it when I got back. For now, I was processing what I was doing in real time and what I really wanted out of life. I lit a benzoin cone to help me relax, and Paula rubbed my tense shoulders from behind the couch.

Chapter XI – The Fallout

I knew I made it back to EWR when I heard people cursing and the bustle and rudeness of getting ahead meant carelessly bumping into another to accommodate self-preservations and racing amongst rats. From Terminal C, I took a bus to the cargo building. Traveling light meant I didn't have to wait endless time for my luggage, whether it was lost, not a priority by the ramp personnel, or if one of the carousels was broken or temporarily jammed. I made it to work just in time to swipe in and attend the shift briefing.

An hour in I was already strategizing manifests, crossing-checking weights and piece counts, and coordinating time-sensitive and hazardous materials with load planners and Operations managers. Our Communications desk left her post and walked over to me.

"You have a phone call."

"Hey, 'Z', who is it?"

"No sé. It's a woman. She said she was your wife."

I was very professional and private. For anyone to learn anything about me other than cargo and freight was beyond comprehension. No one outside the workplace knew what my occupation was or where I worked, other than my immediate family. It made me more human and prone to mistakes to have a personal life. I always followed the rules and never deviated from the policies that were expected of me, and I never allowed my personal life to conflict or impede with my work life. Some of the staff were curious.

"Good afternoon. Coronado speaking. How may I help you?"

"Hello, husband."

My shoulders tensed up and I closed my eyes.

"What's up?"

"Glad you made it back. How was the flight, my husband?"

At this point I knew something was severely wrong. She didn't sound like herself and she was slurring some of her words as if she were intoxicated.

"Thanks. We'll talk about it when I get home. I gotta go."

"Ok, my husband."

It sounded annoying, it got into my head a little, and it may have affected my job performance. When some of the Export department crew wanted Chinese for lunch, I only ordered a Wonton soup, and for those who really knew me, anything less than four wings with pork fried rice was alarming. My appetite was skewed.

By the time I reached the apartment after my shift was over it was nearly 11pm. Outside, I walked up the first flight of steps that lead to the front door and looking through the small glass windows that surrounded it, I could see that the hallway light was off, to conserve and reduce electricity provided by the landlord who lived on the first floor. We lived on the second floor, so I needed to walk up another flight and when I switched on the light it must have signaled to her that I made it home because I heard steps and scurrying from above. I held on to the wooden bannister.

The fifteen stairs, or so, turned to the right and when I reached the top step, I saw an envelope taped to the apartment door with a letter in it:

To my husband,

Please read before you come in. Do not get upset or angry!

Thank you, Your wife

Rebecca opened the door and she was intoxicated.

"Hello, my husband. Did you read the note? Please don't be angry."

What was I to be angry about? I tried to walk through the doorway, but she stepped in front of me blocking my direct path, so I stopped. I could smell the wine on her heavy breath as she put her hands on my chest, my personal space, to thwart me from proceeding until I abided by the rules of the game she set up. I thought maybe she had arranged an intervention, but it was worse.

"What's going on? I can't promise not to be mad if I don't know what's going on."

I side-stepped her and made my way in through the doorway. The living room looked different, not from any new or rearranged furniture but it looked bigger. The light green walls were bare and the paintings I won on *Ebay* were missing. I walked towards the kitchen and the hung autographed photo of me and the CEO of the airline wasn't there. When I entered the second bedroom that served as our office, I observed that my easel, pictures and paintings, all my belongings on the right side of the closet were gone.

That is when the prevailing darkness rolled in, shivers ran down my spine, a deep cold and eerie gust of evil entered my being as if confronted with death itself, not because the gods and the heavens were handing out karma that day but because she initiated judgement and cast her stone.

"Where are all of my things?!" I asked in disbelief.

She didn't answer right away.

"Rebecca, where are my things?"

"There was a robbery?" she said.

"A robbery? We live on the second floor! Where did they come in from?" I quickly walked through and scanned the two-bedroom apartment to look for signs of a forced-entry, but there wasn't any.

"Did you file a police report? Do I need to get the landlord involved? Where are my things?"

"I told you. They were stolen."

They were stolen all right. I needed to leave to get some air and to think. All my material possessions: childhood photo albums, thousands of my original photographs and negatives, original paintings, everything I owned – gone, or stolen as she put it. You would not have known that I took a single photograph, brushed a single painting, or have even existed. Traces of my existence were quickly vanishing. Then I remembered how I never built the '56 Chevy model car my uncle Justin gave me on his deathbed, and now it was gone. It had been a long day and I was hungry, and I feared that fueling tensions could progress further, so I kept my remarks as anodyne as possible. Sometimes she would cook or I would check the fridge for leftovers, but there was no dinner on the stove and the only thing on the kitchen table was an empty wine bottle of *Yellow Tail*.

Her assumptions and jealous rage had gotten the best of her. There was no empirical evidence that I did anything wrong, other than conceal the facts of my sleeping arrangements, and even that didn't constitute theft or this severe violation of material trust. Compromise was out the window, along with the rest of my possessions, and I needed to leave but she wouldn't let me. There was no room for negotiations – nothing.

"Get out of my way," I demanded.

"Let's talk about this. Sit down."

"Sit down? What's there to talk about? The time to talk 'about this' was way before this happened. I guess we're lucky there's a couch and a tv. I need to go. I'm hungry. It's been a long day."

She persisted to stand in front of me, blocking me, bracing my arms to hold me back, but I shook them off and with the scuffle, heavy foot movements, and screaming, the landlord's door opened downstairs.

"Rebecca, let me go! I just want to leave. I have to go."

"You're not going anywhere," she yelled.

I made it to the hallway stairs, and she grabbed me from behind, her hand clutched on to my shoulder and with my forward movement she tripped down a few steps. The landlord's daughter was at the bottom step looking at us, listening, and frightened by the melee. Her parents stood watching by their doorway, not intervening, then heard the slamming of the front door as I escaped.

At eleven-thirty pm, there are no restaurants that are opened so I either had to go to a diner or a fast food joint. I drove around with the window down to get some air. My hunger vanished from my mind and all I could think about were all those things I owned and collected throughout my life. I didn't have much but what I did have were precious to me – they were mine. She forfeited her rights to all bargaining chips or compromises. She wiped me out, so all deals were off. She was a thief.

From the Greenville section of Jersey City, I drove on 440 to 1&9 south, and decided to maybe stop by my uncle's place that night to stay over, in Elizabeth. It was only fifteen minutes away but when I got close to the Burger King I pulled through the drive-thru and ordered a Whopper with cheese combo. I talked myself out of visiting him because I didn't ultimately want to involve him or any other family member, so I drove to Warinanco Park, in neighboring Roselle, to eat.

I prayed to St. Anthony, my patron saint and heavenly advocate for lost things, to show me where all my belongings went. Ninety-nine percent of all the times I asked and prayed to him for guidance of things I had misplaced, I have been presented with either a quick vision, a valid best idea, or intuitively and divinely guided to it within minutes of my request. He was my last resort. I didn't automatically depend on him for help, but this was a huge favor. Contemplating further, it seemed that I could depend on the spiritual side more than I could of human nature and its reactions to rejection or hurt, but I saw and felt nothing.

After thirty minutes had gone by, I drove back home hoping things cooled off enough to be able to sleep and figure things out in the morning, and when I got there the bedroom door was locked. I slept on the couch in the living room and roughly an hour or two later, she walked in with my uncle and aunt from Elizabeth and her mother, but I pretended to stay asleep. My relatives walked into the office then left but when she and her mother unlocked the door to the bedroom, she decided to lash out.

"I hope you had fun with your whore! You better not be here in the morning. The cops are looking for you and you will be arrested!"

She locked the door behind them.

In fear that I would go to the police station to file a Police Report for my missing things, she decided to beat me to the punch and declared that I assaulted her in a domestic violence dispute. She went to the hospital to care for her alleged bruises, and me wrangling away from her at the bottom of the stairs was corroborated by the landlord's daughter who didn't know what she saw but was later identified as me striking and assaulting Rebecca. I don't even think they tested her for alcohol consumption. I was livid at the allegations and what she would do to cover up her evildoings for the sake of self-preservation.

My aunt and uncle were there to confirm that my things were not there because I removed them myself so that I could move in with another woman, is what her story was to whoever would listen. My possessions were not stolen, but rather, I left the premises, in an attempt, to abandon her, is what she stated to law enforcement. Early morning, she opened the bedroom door and continued to yell at me, while I was laying down on the couch.

"I hope your whore was worth it! Lucifer is who she is!"

Her mother gathered some of her things during the tirade, without getting completely involved, and left the apartment through the front door. I quickly left soon after and saw her mother waking down the block, as I drove off. I called my attorney and told him my version, and when he returned my call, he advised me to turn myself in because the Warrant Squad would be on their way.

"Go to the precinct on Summit Avenue and turn yourself in. It'll be better for you." He advised.

"For what? What did I do?"

"Apparently, you assaulted her and that's considered domestic violence," he tried to explain. "Call me when you get there."

"Yeah. Ok."

At what point in time was it all right and acceptable to gather your spouse's belongings and get rid of them, such as in the movies portraying women throwing stuff out the window? Is this what the foregone conclusion is to assumed infidelity? Ironically, Rebecca contacted my twenty-year-old cousin, who was also my Webmaster for my artist agency business, so that she could shut down my website. She did under Rebecca's advisement without alerting me, and blindly took her position in this whole scandal. My cousin apparently conducted a Tarot reading and the conclusion pointed towards a third-party situation. Apparently, the esoteric interjected into our lives to inject major change.

I reached the Municipal Court House on 365 Summit Avenue and cleared security and asked the officer where the processing office was, and after direction I went in and took a seat. I recognized the clerk to be one of my neighbors from across the street. She asked me what I was doing there, and I told her that my attorney advised me to turn myself in for a domestic violence violation. She was assisted by a tall officer possibly in his late fifties or early sixties assigned to desk duty, who she referred to as Thomas. She was running my information through their computer.

"What are you doing here?" he asked me.

"I'm not really sure. I do what I'm told, and my lawyer told me to come here."

I gave him my name after he requested it and sat quietly for a duration. Two other guys came in from a side entrance and told Thomas that they were on their way looking for a "Coronado" who beat up on his wife. I recognized one of them – Officer "Sphincter" from over a decade ago.

Officer Thomas turned and pointed at me: "Well there he is. He came in on his own recognizance."

The undercover cops looked at me and the blonde one with scruffy hair gave me his two cents.

"You're lucky you came in. We were ready to bust you up for beating up on a woman," he said with a brusque sternness.

"Here I am," I said.

"Has he been processed yet?" he asked Thomas.

"No. We were waiting to hear from either the lawyer or from a Supervisor."

"Well, process him and do his paperwork. Process him."

The goon squad left, and Thomas asked me to stand up and turn around.

"I retire from the force in two months and I never made an arrest in my career of thirty years."

"Well, honored to be your first collar, Officer."

I turned around and put my hands behind my back, as I had been instructed. *Click.*

I was taken to a basement level – a sub level, via an elevator, where I was photographed, fingerprinted and held in a cell, along with other innocent criminals in our system. The depth of escaping illuminance increased. My energy was quickly draining, and I became in a logy state of physical and mental being. How could there ever be forgiveness for this? Rebecca stole my possessions, yelled at me during a heated argument and touched my body to emphasize a point when she was angry. I died in that apartment, but reborn into my next phase of endurance and preparedness for whatever is to come. Those actions were deliberately misrepresented in a way that resulted in me being removed from my home because of her statement and police report. There was no empirical evidence that I did anything and was in no way comeuppance if there were. The system failed and tainted me – forever. That was my thought process over and over while in my cell. Think of it this way – even if "I did not have sexual relations with that woman" this could still have happened. *Let that sink in.*

Chapter XII – The Pen & The Sword

A relationship grows stronger when there is an acknowledgement that it exists. Many factors aided in the contributions and acceptance of keeping us together, and I would be amiss if I didn't recognize one of her best friends as being a life force to our union. Paula spoke of her friend, Roxanne Duke, and how she was an aspiring artist who really enjoyed painting. Prior to coming to Ottawa for the first time in November, I reached out to Roxanne, on the 18th, in hopes to not only gain further insight into Paula but to also encourage her and perhaps give some of my inside tips and advice on painting.

Hi, Roxanne...

Have a great time at dinner, well, I mean, I have dinner every day and I'm sure you do too, but Paula tells me you're going out for Aboriginal food. I only tried Buffalo wings myself and they're finger-lickin' good. Speaking of fingers... did you get the size?

How's the artwork coming along? Sometimes I have anxiety attacks of all the feelings and emotions that I want to capture on canvas. Lately, since I haven't been painting, I find myself expressing myself to Paula.

Gosh, drifted off. Enough about me. How are your creations coming along? I really liked your paintings. Don't stop now. If you can create one a week, that would be wonderful. Hey, how about a small painting for me. That'll get the mind flowing... Either way, have a great day and I'll talk to you soon.

-Coronado

We have had several correspondences beforehand, but this one was written the day before my first excursion North. It is important, however necessary, to gain favor and support from the third-party friend because they are the ones who are not blinded by the emotional, physical and psychological barriers that may inhibit common sense and logic when it comes to matters of the heart. They are the outsiders looking in, seeing beyond the proverbial trees, casting judgement from a non-partisan perspective. She was the one who is trusted as a confidante and keeper of her secrets, and ultimately is the one who really knows her more than me, at the current moment. With her continued endorsement and sustenance, I felt vindication that we were behaving and treating each other with positive acceptance.

Hello Dearest Coronado:

Well, I haven't found out the size yet, but I am going to tonight on my way to meet the Missus.

Yesterday, the water in my building that I work in was out, so we all got to go home at 11:00 a.m. I was so excited I wanted to yell at people on the street "I get to go home early and paint!!!!"

Last week I started a painting and wanted to use some texture, so I used crumpled-up newsprint and got a very cool effect. Again, this one is in blues with the texture running from the bottom up the right-hand side to the top. But that's where it ended. I couldn't move on it and I was very frustrated. Then, it came to me yesterday. As I was on my way home I was thinking about Robert Trujillo – bassist for Metallica. I like to think about him from time to time. So, I remember reading something about him loving to surf. So, I painted him naked on a surfboard cresting the wave. I LOVE it. I also seem to be very apt at painting the human form so I think I will actually take a drawing course and I think this will help with my painting of human forms.

Anyway, it made me very, very happy. I wish we could talk more about this in depth because I could just go on and on. I know EXACTLY what you mean about anxiety attacks over painting. I almost hyperventilated over this idea yesterday I was so excited.

So, I am looking into putting some things in place so that I can quit working in the 9-5 world and free up my days for painting. A lot of money can be made bartending, so I am thinking I already live on the fringe of society, why not move outside the perimeter? I love the idea of sleeping when everyone else is working and working when everyone is out to play. So, these are just some of my thoughts.

I hope to paint one a week. This is not difficult when I usually paint all day Saturday and all-day Sunday. As far as painting one for you – that will be $275.00 US please! No – just kidding. I would be happy to create something just for you. But you can't have my naked surfer – that's just for me. Oh, I have taken a few umm, liberties shall we say with is appendage. WooHoo!!!

I will be sure to email you tomorrow with the size of the ring. Which finger is this for? Do you know about the webbing issue with her hands? Has she complained that she can't find her mittens to you? God!

Have a wonderful evening, and I will email you tomorrow.
Ciao Bello!
R.

Ottawa is a city of tremendous talent, but being an artist there isn't easy because you can't make a living from the art alone. With very little low-cost studio spaces for rent, artists cannot practice their art because they can't afford to and would do well with the needed support and encouragement from other artists. The City had yet to recognize and structure an arts and entertainment district, so it was interesting to brainstorm at this possible cusp for change.

Roxanne was a strong, charismatic, and determined woman who wore her natural red hair down to her shoulders and a constant smile. Curious, she was eager to learn and take advantage of life in her optimism and critical thinking. Conflicted and constantly walking the line – the line between coloring within them or not, she lived in a city that was structured with governing laws and principles, and as a young woman upholding those rules and regulations she waited for the moment to show herself, and the world, that it's ok to feel and move beyond the gray areas. Roxanne was not only inspired to make a big shift and difference within the community to promote the Arts, with me, but she was also my friend.

It was December, and Paula and I periodically corresponded via email and at times, very quickly, on the phone. I had already explained to her the aftermath of what occurred when I returned, and that I was living in my parents' basement until after the court date and other possible legal proceedings. We left further retrospection for when we would rejoin in person, and until then we kept in touch. Sometimes she would leave thought-provoking messages:

Hi,

I was on Powell's and found this synopsis for the 'Story of B'. I think you and your dad would find it interesting…

She copied and pasted a synopsis of Daniel Quinn's novel, and it sounded like an adventure of the mind and spirit, yet I contemplated when I would be able to find the time to read it. We talked about seeing each other again to spend quality time together, and for me to work with Roxanne on advancing and creating a very doable art involvement there. I reached out to her:

Roxanne,

Well, hello….

How was the show at Richard's? I thought the doors were pretty cool, and I enjoyed the Ice Cream painting.

Alex's stone slates (stained-glass art) were really cool.

And your weekend, Miss? Didn't go over-board on Saturday night, I trust.

Any who, just wanted to drop you a note – do re mi.

- Coronado

She responded the next day, and I appreciated that she liked to write and share herself in her words and creativity.

Hola Coronado!

The show at RG gallery was mind-blowing. It was a very surreal and emotional experience for me. And we were NOT making googly eyes at each other!! Last week, as I was surfing the web trying to find a website for Richard's work, I came across an article about a spoken-word poet/photographer named Jean. I read actually two articles: one was a review of his photography which was on display at Richard's, and the other was a review of his poetry. I was very intrigued and then I had this thought of certainty that I would meet him on Friday night. Well, who do you think is the first person I met right outside the gallery before we went in? That's right – Jean. We stood there and spoke with him for about half an hour before we went in. Cool, huh? I might be a witch after all.

I love the show and yes, Alex's work was interesting for sure. Isn't Richard the easiest person to talk to in the world? He is also interesting. It was like I was in a trance and he made me feel so good about me!! I am going to see him on Thursday to talk to him about a potential partnership (meaning: me working for him (and possibly you) even if it is on a volunteer basis at first.)

You know, Coronado, I will be finished my contract here in a few months, and I don't know if I can honestly continue to work in this kind of environment. I Literally feel like it is sucking the life and soul from me. It's not the people, because I love them very much, it's the nature of the work and the paper and the fluorescent lighting that is making me stupid. And the more I paint and learn about myself the more certain I am that I can no longer continue this, at least on a full-time basis. I don't know. I'll have to figure it out. Hopefully my meeting with Richard will help me to better plan my future.

And I did not go all crazy and puke on Saturday night – unlike some people we know (haha). Poor girl. She didn't seem that bad to me when she left. We had a fine time although since I am very emotional and militant about a certain subject and may have gotten into it with one of the ladies, that's all anyone will remember. That I'm angry. Oh well. Too bad for them.

K – email back if you get a chance.

Thanks,

Roxanne

P.S. – I cannot wait until Lord of the Rings!!!

Chapter XIII- Return of the King

We were fans of J.R.R. Tolkien although Paula is probably the only one I knew who read all of his books, especially *The Hobbit* and *The Lord of the Rings,* so when it was announced that *The Return of the King* was being released on film we just had to go see it on opening day, on the 17th – my mother's birthday. Sarah, whom I met in Minneapolis, was organizing a Christmas soirée at her place on December 21st at 6:30pm and Paula invited me to go as her guest. That was the week to take advantage of festive opportunities with my friends in Ottawa once again, so I booked my itinerary for Monday, the 15th.

I flew to YOW to meet up with Roxanne to discuss logistics and gallery spaces, and to be with Paula, and since I would be arriving at an earlier time – taking the first flight out of Newark, Paula asked me to meet her in town because of her work schedule. When I arrived at Customs, I was asked the same general five questions" *What is the purpose of your trip? How long do you intend to stay? Where will you be staying? What is your occupation? Do you have anything to declare?* The Agent stared at the screen and, surprisingly, although I should have probably expected it, I was asked a couple of additional questions relating to assault and desires to commit acts of violence. The false domestic incident hit federal status, and although the case was dropped in Court, it remained as a smudge and blemish on an international level.

"Why don't you just admit that you're visiting a girlfriend?" he casually mentioned.

I just kept my already-permanent grin as not to give away my hand in a poker game. My respect for my local law enforcement was deteriorating, especially since the arrest, and I wasn't sure how extensive the level of trust went. People were manipulating truths to benefit their angles, but I wasn't allowing it to damper my mood and trip. I smiled and just thought about how great the sound of him thumping and stamping my passport would be. He advised me to request a Disposition Form to carry with me to avoid lengthy interrogations in the future. He let me in, and I regained some faith in justice, however this thing was far from over since I dispelled forgiveness.

Even though Rebecca and I were undergoing unreconcilable differences and in a status of separation, I pushed forward with my love for Paula and Ottawa. Since I already did the time, I may as well continue the crime, and in that crime of passion, I was shedding my old skin and creating another version of myself. I had nothing to lose since I already lost it all, and there was bound to be a logical and bigger reason for it to happen the way it did, but only time would tell, through retrospect and foreshadowing. In time, I would be able to reconstruct the zeitgeist events through the lens of glass and scopes in order to dissect and understand its true purpose and meaning.

"Thank you, sir."

I cleared Customs, took the 97 from the airport to the Slater/Bank bus stop and called Paula from my cell phone, but she was getting new eyeglass frames during her lunch break. Having learned that calling Canada direct from my New Jersey phone number was ridiculously expensive, I invested in an international calling card and paid for the usage of minutes. Most of the bodegas by me sold these cards for calls to Central or South America, and even the Caribbean, so it was a challenge to find one marketing our neighbors to the North. Had I initially intended to hurt anyone in this entire process, I would have been less inept on covering my tracks for anyone to find out, especially from a spiked cost in the phone bill.

When I arrived at the eye doctor's, there she sat wearing blue jeans and a brown and white quilted-pattern short-sleeved shirt, and a smile. *I loved her smile.*

"I don't know about your vision, but you look great," I told her after a big embracing hug. We didn't mind being seen in public, as a couple, and besides, I was in an entire country where I didn't have to worry about being judged by anyone I knew. We felt free and young even though we were in our thirties, she – older by a few years. We held hands as we trekked through promenades to her place of employment since she had to be back to work soon.

At the steps, before my vision of her faded behind the two double doors, I asked for a favor.

"Can you please print me out an application for dual citizenship? I want to open a bank account here and see what I can do to possibly live here too. Is it easy to do?"

"I don't know. You might lose primary US status. Being able to print it out is the easiest answer I can give you."

"Great. Thanks! Besides, it has better artwork on the cover and on the inside, and mine is bent."

I had already told her that I would be going to the supermarket to get groceries for the chicken and rice dinner tonight, so she smiled, gave me a copy of the keys to her place, and gave me a kiss.

From our periodic strolls and ventures I remembered passing a supermarket not far from the YMCA building and across the highway. I entered on Isabella Street and was fascinated by the selection of produce and different products, even the cookies and packaging of snacks and treats. I tried to pick up some of the French language whether on the packaging or through other customers conversing to one another as I wanted to blend in and coexist. I picked up a small basket and went down every aisle, and by the time I was finished I purchased familiar supplies and had everything I needed to bake a whole chicken in the oven, whether she already had the ingredients at her place or not.

Once there, I made coffee using her French-press and smoked a menthol while I started my preparation. Her apparatus was staged on the countertop and ultimately was one of my favorite ways to brew coffee ever since I watched her do it for the first time. Clyde hung out by the balcony soaking in the sun. He rolled from one side to the other in one movement and remained there somewhat working on evening his tan. It was comforting feeling welcomed and loved and relaxed. I was in a happy place, away from unnecessary drama or demanding expectations. As I cleaned, rinsed and marinated the five-pounder and got more acquainted with her kitchen, I thought of Paula and being able to see her again but not until she finished for the day.

She wanted to go to the mall and check out a movie after work and I accepted the suggestion with alacrity, so we headed to the Rideau Centre. It housed a lot of stores and there was much to see, especially during this holiday season and we stopped at an art gallery on the first floor. I enjoyed the different displays of local Canadian themes showcasing their flag, but I think what most attracted me was the red against the white, and sometimes baby-blue-colored, snow. Upstairs, using the escalator, we arrived at the theater and grabbed our tickets along with some popcorn and drinks to watch "The Last Samurai" featuring Tom Cruise and Ken Watanabe.

Ultimately, I felt a strange, poignant connection while leaving the theater thinking how this US Army captain was in a different country learning their customs and nuances of life, battling his own demons and coming together with his new ways. Perhaps it was because it was a battle film where you decide which side of the opposing forces you are on, and sometimes it is not easy to choose between who, or what, is right and wrong.

When we left the Mall, we were outside by the exit doors and she commented again on how we should be vigilant because, the week before, there was a swarming incident around where we were standing at the bus stop, and it was hectic and bad.

"I don't fear any man. When I look around, I see peace, and besides, this is Canada. To me, other than Switzerland, this country is neutral. If anything happens to me, I just need to make one phone call and my crew will come up here in six hours and wipe them all out. I've seen crime. I can't imagine any of it here. Plus, I wouldn't let anything bad happen to you. I'd fight to the death – the last samurai."

Maybe it was the effects of the movie, but I meant it; she didn't scare me. I was fearless.

We made it back safely to her place. She lit up some incense and played some music and when she was comfortable enough knowing I wouldn't burn the place down and saw that I might somewhat know what I was doing in her kitchen, she called me over to her bedroom.

"Hon, I emptied out this drawer. You can put your things in it – your clothes or whatever."

That was a very nice gesture from her, as I had been sorting out my things from a carry-on suitcase and bag, and without being alarmed, I felt more welcomed and somewhat at home. She jumped in the shower and when she finished, she changed into grey sweatpants and a maroon long-sleeved cotton shirt, and even though it was warm in the kitchen, it was still December in Canada. I preheated the oven and when the oven beeped it let me know that it hit my desired temperature. I sealed it with aluminum foil so that it would cook inside more thoroughly, to hold in the moisture from the heat. I couldn't think of any stresses from work, the invoices from my creditors, or even the responsibilities imposed to me by the world. I washed the dishes and cutlery as I went along, to make room in the sink and to keep active.

She popped in once-in-a-while to check in on me while I carefully stirred the white rice and heated up a pot of beans with potatoes and my special Puerto Rican ingredients that I smuggled in my luggage. I was assiduous with meal preparations, and I wasn't sure if they carried Goya products, so I brought my own small packets of Sazón and Adobo. I threw in a couple of green olives and let it simmer.

"Smells good, hon. I'll make dessert. Does apple pie sound good?"

"Oh yeah. Perfect. I'll let you know when I'm finished with the oven."

After about forty-minutes I removed the foil, reduced the heat and let it cook for another thirty minutes until the skin got crispy. When it was all ready, she set the living room table, not with Styrofoam or plastic plates or even the good china either, but white plates that wouldn't slice open when cutting into the chicken, even though it was already soft and tender. Two glasses of wine later, we were enjoying each other's companionship once again. A mixed selection of her music softly played in the background, some songs I had never heard of like the one I poked fun of, out of sheer ignorance.

"Gypsies, tramps and thieves? What kind of music is that?" I asked as I mimicked the lyrics.

"Don't make fun of *Cher*! This is a good song!" she snapped.

"Yeah. Yeah. Ok. I didn't know," I chuckled. "I'll give it a chance."

The baked apple pie was warm and delicious. She made it from scratch and used fresh ingredients. I had two servings before I couldn't take enough; it was solid on the outside and smooth in the middle. I had an in-depth conversation with her about my experiences with Rebecca and how she didn't wait for the courts to decide to take everything away from me. It didn't deter me from wanting to build a life with Paula, but these things required patience and time.

We started to make love on the couch, but she was overly conscious of the view everyone would be having through the balcony glass doors. I did too, to some extent, but we left the shades drawn in a voyeurism spirit of expressing ourselves. It was when she went on all fours, her hands leaning on the top of the love seat, and her knees touching together on the cushions, when I saw the four beautifully colored butterfly tattoos on her back.

"Surprise! Do you like them?" she asked mid gasp.

Above her sexy grabbable waistline, symmetrical to her spine, was the first symbol of metamorphosis. The lower part of its sun-kissed orange and sea blue wings was in a shape of an upside-down crescent moon while the upper portion pointed outward like a bat's wings; its edges were sharp and well-defined. The Monarch directly above was slightly off-center to the left, facing left, and appeared to be floating with its deep orange and bordering black wings. It was most familiar to me since its migration usually passes in the northeast and tends to often visit my mother's garden, during Springtime. The next butterfly was in the aligned center of her back and if her hair were brushed straight back, it would just about cover its abdomen. Its mauve and violet colors were as soothing as its round contours, displaying a strong body and antennae, while the last was off-center to the right, facing the right. It was like the Monarch but was dazzling a cobalt blue color, which to me was a symbol of joy and happiness and of the Spirit transforming and changing.

I was admiring her strength and beauty, her courage and fortitude, and her willingness to embrace change. I dared not touch them, in fear of smearing their majestic symbolism.

"I love them!"

She then turned around and grabbed to pull me on top of her then laid back on the couch.

"Thoomp."

Our eyes locked in each other's gaze, sweat dripping from my forehead landing on the top of her bosom engaged in a connection that ran deep inside. I felt every part of her while she slowly then quickly felt very inch of me as I was in tune to her immediate needs and sensations, speaking and communicating so that I could fulfill her desire and climatic pulses.

A couple of days later, the time had come for all of us to witness the epic tale of elves, orcs, hobbits and Man in the *Lord of the Rings: Return of the King*[6], on opening day, and although we were not in full costume in honor of the characters and the film, we each had the spirit of Tolkien within ourselves. The first time I was introduced to a Hobbit was back in the late seventies, maybe as a holiday feature aired on television in November, and as an elementary school feature film in the cafeteria; the adventures held my attention still to this day. We were all eager and excited to continue the journey – together, and when our quest ended, Paula wasn't fully pleased with the overall conclusion.

---

[6] *The Lord of the Rings: The Return of the King*, a 2003 epic fantasy adventure film directed by Peter Jackson, based on the third volume of J. R. R. Tolkien's *The Lord of the Rings*.

"They missed an interesting and important character. I wished they expanded on some of the other characters like the dwarves," she addressed to Penelope and Monica. This was an example of the book being better than the movie but since I hadn't read the books, I could not relate to who or what was missing; I never thought to ask her, but I suspected that it was Beorn because of her interests in men with hair and the idea of nurturing nature and being self-sufficient, not to mention that she calls me "honey". Despite him taking the shape of a bear, Beorn appears to be an animal-loving vegetarian who lives on bread and honey, which he collects from his hives of giant bees.

To end this eventful cold and snowy week in December, we found time to celebrate the holiday season together. As soon as she pressed the button for the tenth floor to go up and the elevator doors closed, I put our goodie bag on the floor, wrapped my arms around her, and gave her a big kiss. We were alone in these closed quarters and even if there was a security camera, I wouldn't have cared. We made out for a couple of seconds, maybe bypassed a few floors already, and found adequate time to fix ourselves to appear presentable to the folks awaiting us upstairs.

"How's my hair?" I asked while combing it back with my fingers.

"You're fine. How's mine?"

"Beautiful. Perfect."

I ran my hand through her hair one last time for good measure and gave her one last kiss to help soothe the mild bite I recently snuck in, to her bottom lip. She rubbed my chin with her thumb and admired my recently trimmed and groomed goatee for a split second.

"Remember... we can't have physical contact. This is a work function, so I need to be professional. Ok?"

"Yeah. Yeah."

"Yeah. Yeah," she repeated playfully.

I was thrilled that she not only invited me to her work event, but to their Christmas holiday party, hosted by her friend and coworker – Sarah, whom I sat next to and met in Minneapolis. She greeted us when she opened the door and we were all so happy to see each other again.

"Hey, guys! Come on in."

It was a potluck and Paula had baked a pie and I made a dish of some yellow rice with pigeon peas, and they were properly stacked and kept warm in the cotton bag I was carrying with my left hand.

"Sarah, you remember Coronado, right?"

"Yes, of course. Great to see you again."

She gave us each a hug and I felt so welcomed.

"We brought some homemade food."

Paula took the bag from me and gave it to our gracious host.

"Wonderful. Make yourselves at home."

"Thank you so much, Sarah," I responded.

Guests were already being entertained with jazzy festive music and a nice spread of appetizers consisting of gourmet cold cuts and a variety of cheeses, chips with a side dish of French onion dip, and other delectable assortments of finger foods. Although non-alcoholic drinks were provided, we were encouraged to BYOB if we so chose to.

My decisions to change was all my doing, and although there were so many influences in either direction, they were all of mine to decipher and decide. Paula never demanded or asked me to convert anything about myself. She only presented her thoughts and beliefs and never dictated how I should live my life. She did mention how I should probably trim my goatee, prior to the party, since I had let it grow wild and bushy, and that was small and understandably considerate since I was due for a shape-up and grooming and about to meet her professional team.

The objective was to have lots of holiday fun, and I was getting into the spirit of it rather quickly. A few of the guests wore black while a husband and wife team wore red sweaters. Their son, a young man in his early teens, wore a red sweater with a horizontal black line and white borders, along his chest. He was the tiebreaker and middle ground to our checkerboard. Paula was mesmerizing in her thin black V-neck sweater and her gray and black striped pants that accentuated her firm hips. I fit and complimented her with my black slacks and short-sleeved black and gray shirt that fit well enough to show my upper physique, and be able to have a couple of servings and samplings of the tasty treats and morsels we all brought for the meal.

The living room was a primary red color and by the balcony window gallantly stood the decorated Christmas tree. The apex had a crimson bow with streamers coming down about midway, and the ornaments of different shiny balls and candy canes were placed in a fantastic colorful array. Behind the tree, looking out the glass, I could see a great view of some of the city, including the Rideau River and beyond towards the horizon.

It seemed easy and natural to converse and mingle with Evelyn, Thomas, and Mr. and Mrs. Campbell, since they were all so cordial and interesting. Although it seemed that these guests knew more about the US government than I did, I was ready to turn any conversation into an erudite discussion but what fascinated me was their ability to not be trite and keep topics flowing with interest.

"According to the Mayan Calendar, the world will have a significant change exactly nine years from now, in 2012," Thomas stated.

I wasn't sure whether to believe him or doubt it, but the others engaged, and before their theories and hypotheses would disembogue and flow with innumerable possibilities as to how it would affect the world, I excused myself and went to the kitchen to get a refill of soda and met up with Paula by the shrimp cocktail.

"Hey, honey."

"Hi," I said in my deep sexy voice.

I was just about to naturally put my arm around her when her boss walked into the room.

"Hey, guys, keep it clean. There's no touching allowed."

"Hey, Rick. It's good to see you again." We shook hands. "How are you?"

I met him in Minnesota at the convention and we had some good conversations and shared moves on playing chess, as he is a fan of the strategy game as I am.

"Good, Coronado. Pleasure to see you as well. So glad you could make it. How was the trip?"

"Great. I love it here. Thank you."

"We haven't scared him off yet," Paula stated.

"Well good. I'm going to grab some of these chocolate cookies that Evelyn made. See you two later."

I'm not sure what they know or what Paula told the office personnel about me, if at all, but they certainly played it cool and made me feel welcomed. I looked over to her and gave a happy grin to assure her that we didn't get in trouble during our brief water cooler moment with Rick. Everyone was so polite and propitious that they instantly gained and earned my respect. I tried one of Evelyn's cookies and it was so moist and delicious I had to smuggle another.

"Hey, Paula, I can't wait until we spend the rest of the Christmas holiday and New Year's together in Jersey. Hey, Winter Solstice is tomorrow."

She quickly looked around, threw her arms around me, and snuck in a quick kiss.

Chapter XIV – Reflection

She called me while double-checking her list of travel necessities, we were discussing last-minute preparations and where I was going to meet her at the airport. She shared her itinerary with me since she purchased her own ticket, otherwise I would have escorted and flown with her on an international buddy-pass. She also asked me if there was a current song on the radio that I liked.

"I'm not sure. Hmmm, you know I'm a huge Beatles fan, but I like all types of music. Not sure I have a current favorite."

It was thoughtful that she tried to get to know me better by asking me a question like that, and after careful consideration one came to mind.

"*Times Like These*, by Foo Fighters. That jam rocks."

"Thanks, Babe. I'll check it out. I'll see you soon."

She sent me an email of the current song she liked on the radio, and it was from someone I never heard of. Paula likes to multi-task.

I'm on the phone – with you…
Here are the lyrics – not sure about the third line…

She copied and pasted the lyrics of Fefe Dobson's "Take Me Away" and although I am not a lyrics guy, I'm more into the music, and after reading it I was interested in how it would sound.

After my morning shift was over, I took an Employee shuttle bus to the airport and anxiously waited for her arrival from the Air Canada flight from Ottawa. I was so thrilled to be able to see her again in the States, especially since I hadn't held her in my arms in a little over a week's time, and when we saw each other at Terminal A, we kissed and embraced like there was no tomorrow.

"Hi, honey!"

"Bonjour. Bienvenue au New Jersey!"

I picked her up and twirled her around a couple of times while she just giggled, and then when I let her down, I grabbed her luggage and we skedaddled to the nearest exit.

"Are you hungry? Did you eat on the plane?"

"No. Not yet, but I will be soon."

"Great! Let's drop your stuff off at the room and we'll go grab something."

I booked a room at the Ramada for a week since I was currently living with my parents through my ordeal, and it probably wasn't ideal to have her stay with me there. It was directly across the highway from my job which made it easy to commute to and from, but I had a car and we could go anywhere we wanted to. We took the shuttle to the employee parking lot, drove the eight minutes to the hotel to drop off her luggage and freshen up, then took her out to *Zesti's*, a small quant Italian restaurant by the water in Paulus Hook.

We first stopped off at the corner liquor store to get a bottle of red wine with our meals, and when we arrived, our *Reserved* table was available for immediate seating. Paula was telling me all about her week – work, her walks and mini-adventures along Bank Street and The Glebe, and I heard about all the little things that made her smile and laugh. I was intrigued and listened attentively while enjoying my Shrimp Fra Diavolo, with a side appetizer of calamari with marinara sauce, which are my absolute favorites when I come here. She savored the Chicken Francese, or as I pronounced it – "Française", with the mozzarella and sundried tomatoes.

"It's so good to see you again. I can't believe you're here. I'm so glad you are."

I raised my glass and toasted with her.

"We'll head back early tonight and rest up for tomorrow's trip," I said.

"Should be fun."

"But first... dessert!"

This wasn't the first time I flew into DCA, in Arlington, VA, and every time the aircraft descends towards the landing strip at Ronald Reagan Washington National Airport, I am always excited to see some of the historical landmarks from the small window. The ERJ commuter plane gracefully glided over the Potomac River and smoothly made it onto the runway. The flight only lasted about an hour and fifteen minutes, but Paula and I were able to sit next to one another, each enjoy a beverage and chat about some of the destinations we would see together, except that this time I would be taking her to my country's capitol city.

I booked us on a round-trip same-day excursion, which was plenty of time to see famous tourist attractions and government buildings, without being slowed down by carrying any luggage or other bulky items deemed admissible on a road trip. The only thing she carried was her black mini backpack and she just slung it comfortably on her shoulder most of the time. We were prepared for the cold temperatures as I wore a long black wool coat and a chestnut brown scarf, while she sported a black leather coat and leather gloves. We were ready for the elements of Winter.

Before we could conveniently take the Metro blue line from the terminal, we stopped off to investigate the sweet smell of cinnamon from one of my favorite destinations there – Cinnabon, for some coffee and a Classic Roll. DCA is one of the most efficient and noticeably clean airports I have ever been to, it is easy to navigate with clear signage and minimal clutter, and their security is professional. There is a great variety of restaurants and shopping opportunities and the staff is ready to respond to any questions a visitor may have. While waiting on the short line for a small black coffee, I noticed the ebb and flow of commuters and travelers walking with smiles and delightful anticipation along their journey.

Our first stop on the Metrorail, bypassing the Pentagon and Arlington Cemetery, was the Smithsonian and the Mall. We were, for the most part, above ground and checking out the sites of the neighborhoods as quick as we could according to the speed we were traveling, but we eventually went underground. When the doors opened at the Smithsonian stop, I couldn't help but notice the high-tubed chamber we were in, unlike the subway system I am more accustomed to in New York City. One of the signs read "MALL" with arrows pointing onward and I thought it was odd that they would build a shopping center in this area and advertise it in their transportation system. I didn't feel as confined and claustrophobic and at the end of the walkway were a pair of long escalators going up to a set of exiting turnstiles unto another set of upward escalators which lead to the surface street level and sunlight. An older woman handed out free pocket maps.

The overcast sky impressed a bleak overtone when I reached the brisk top, but it was that time of the year and we weren't in an amusement park. An open courtyard and field allowed us enough space to walk in between and admire the architecture of both sides. The short cut sap green and yellow grass contrasted to the non-cemented, non-asphalted gravel walkway along the sides of the periphery welcoming anyone who wished to sit and rest on the sturdy forest green benches.

Facing west in the near distance was a very tall obelisk, standing erect and presenting itself as a great landmark in the event we got lost. We stopped to take a couple of photographs with my Nikon F70, in front of several red-bricked and marble-faced buildings that were temples, warehouses, and museums of some of the most important historical artifacts known to man, such as the Smithsonian National Museum of Natural History, the Freer Gallery of Art, the Smithsonian Castle, and the United States Department of Agriculture. We could spend an entire day visiting all the buildings along this promenade and still not see everything it had to offer. I held the cup of her remaining coffee while she leaned and posed on a single chain-linked fence, as leafless trees and fallen multi-colored leaves draped the grassy grounds behind her.

As there weren't too many people walking about on this weekday, we took deep breaths and continued our trek towards an openness throughout the landscape. The Washington Monument, upon close inspection and examination, turned a different shade of white about a third of the way from the bottom.

"Did you know that James Madison started the Washington National Monument Society in the early 1800s and came up with the idea for a tribute to the first US President?"

I looked over to her in surprise and confusion as to how, and why, she would know that piece of trivial history.

"I only heard that it was the world's tallest building when it was dedicated, then the Eiffel Tower soon surpassed it," I chimed in.

It was cool to see and look up at its splendor, even though it wasn't entirely inimitable, and as we walked past it, two older men were also discussing its origins.

"Freemasons were involved in the cornerstone ceremony and they used Washington's masonic symbols in the ceremony," the one with the handle-bar moustache said. "Wasn't Abraham Lincoln at the ceremony in 1848?" his buddy asked.

To our right, to the North, was the White House, and it was surely a place we wanted to see, so we walked along what appeared to be a nature trail, the Ellipse, on grass and further away from the busy bustle and traffic of 15th and 17th Streets. We reached the perimeter fence of 1600 Pennsylvania Ave. with a small handful of other tourists looking beyond the boundary of iron rods with what appeared to be a cross between an arrow tip and the Fleur De Lis. Spiritually, the Fleur de Lis represents an iris, a beautiful purple bloom that symbolizes the holy Trinity, and although there are multitudes of symbolism throughout the District, I'm sure that this fence top is pointy to deter persons from climbing over.

Security wasn't visible or apparent. There were no trained dogs, secret service agents, or even fixed cameras on any of the nearby trees, none that I could see anyway, but there in the arm's throw distance was the White House – the living quarters of President George W. Bush and his family. I politely asked another capable and responsible tourist if they wouldn't mind taking our picture, and they obliged, but beforehand I quickly showed them the proper way I wanted them to hold my expensive camera and of course wear the neck strap. I then took one of Paula. *I love her smile. Click.*

"Welcome to the White House," I cordially stated, "and that's probably as close as we're going to get to it without a dozen helicopters and tanks storming us if we hop the gate and make a run for it." I was being way too melodramatic because my imagination got the best of me.

"No. No. We're good."

"Yeah. Yeah."

I took another photograph of her but this time I stood with my back to the South Lawn and the obelisk was behind her. To her left was the National Christmas Tree, which had already been modestly decorated and had a strange ten-pointed star with silver in the middle outlined by a crimson border. It took a long time before the Christmas tree became an integral part of American life. President Franklin Pierce arranged to have the first Christmas tree in the White House, during the mid-1850s, and President Calvin Coolidge started the *National Christmas Tree Lighting Ceremony* on the White House lawn in 1923. After I took the pic, I pointed to her backdrop because I knew she appreciated the tree due to its pagan origins.

"This one is nice but wait until you see the tree at Rockefeller Center. It's so beautiful to witness in person."

We walked along 17th St NW towards the Washington Monument Grounds by some construction, an unfinished project of an ovular forum and columns, and at the foot of the Lincoln Memorial Reflecting Pool there were only a few puddles. We strolled in the waterless pathway towards the Lincoln Memorial, along with some ducks, and the monument became bigger and more monumental as we approached it. Like Moses parting the Red Sea, the waters were cleared for us to walk towards a symbol of emancipated freedom, and when we arrived at the steps of the marbled marvel of the Lincoln Memorial, in a Greek temple fashion, I paused in awe of the symmetry and Henry Bacon's architecture that housed a statue of the 16th US President.

He was still hidden behind twelve Doric columns, and in between the center four columns I could catch a slight glimpse of his sitting pose in the inner chamber of the memorial, within the one hundred-foot tall monument. Before we would walk the inclination of several groups of steps, we decided to take a restroom break which I remembered was off to the left in a separate facility, by the vendors and park security.

I was finished before she was and while I waited, I took out the small map from my back pocket and surveyed the layout, and as I kept turning it clockwise to gauge the directional bearing of North, images of reality and geometry came into illumination.

"Wait a minute… the mall is not a shopping center, with carts and consumers, but a National Mall which was undoubtedly the promenade. Wow. Ok. From east to west is the US Capitol, Washington Monument, Lincoln Memorial, cross-sectioned by the Thomas Jefferson Memorial, The White House..." I said to myself as I rotated the map. "Strikingly familiar! What are these three circles up here in the north? Nah!" I wondered aloud.

Could it be? Was it possible that certain structures and buildings were constructed and placed in locations that represented... the Kabbalah – the Tree of Life that Paula showed me at her place? I'm sure it was just a coincidence.

Upon her return, we two-stepped it unto the next memorial chamber where it had two rows of four Ionic columns and, of course, the replica of the man himself – Abraham Lincoln. We admired the detail and held pensive thoughts through our temporary lull of silence. He sits on a chair, resting his arms in what appears to be a column on each side, and looks outward as if he is stern on greeting each guest. Behind him there is an inscription –

IN THIS TEMPLE
AS IN THE HEARTS OF THE PEOPLE
FOR WHOM HE SAVED THE UNION
THE MEMORY OF ABRAHAM LINCOLN
IS ENSHRINED FOREVER

"I love it here. This is my favorite place, and not because of the *Planet of the Apes*[7] movie from a couple of years ago. I remember it

---

[7] *Planet of the Apes*, a 2001 American science fiction film directed by Tim Burton and starring Mark Wahlberg, Tim Roth, Helena Bonham Carter, Michael Clarke

from another film years ago, not sure. It might have been from the Charlton Heston one, or maybe another older film. Wow – it triggers an old memory of climbing these steps that I can't quite figure out. Hahaha!"

I laughed at myself for not remembering. It was at this stark moment where I pondered my past and my existence. Rebecca had thrown all my things out, so I had minimal possessions or much to show for since my baby photographs and albums, collections and memorabilia I acquired throughout the years, and evidence of me were long gone. I was in a master chamber of memory, in memoriam, where in a Mandela Effect moment, time and space were questioned. I had to take a couple of pics to capture my new memories, of my new life, with my new love. She slightly leaned her head to the right, just as she did at the Purple Onion, first captured in my oil portrait of her and now in the image captured on 35mm film, which hopefully will be properly developed.

"I am having such a great time. Thank you for taking me here!" she said in such a comforting tone.

We looked outward, from the inner darkness to the silhouettes of grand columns and out into the light, as the Washington Monument and Reflection Pool were in tandem with our gaze. We held hands walking out, ready to leave and conquer our next attraction, and although it has been just a day trip, its impact will be more than ephemeral. Standing on the top step, I put my arm around her shoulder, she wrapped her arm around my waist and drew me closer

---

Duncan, Paul Giamatti, and Estella Warren.

to the hip, then we slowly turned to face each other. We kissed so warmly and lovingly, nothing else mattered and if I could remember an important moment in my life it was this one, here, where history is made and manifested.

Chapter XV – New Year, New Me

The brakes were running towards a shrieking halt. I told her that it was the last stop and that we should be ready to get off and exit, as the conductor made his announcement.

"Dirty-third Street… last stop. Last stop… dirty-third."

Sometimes, on the train, I come across a couple – a man and a woman who talk in a foreign tongue to each other, one that I can't exactly make out if it's Belgian or Dutch, or Croatian. I am not entirely sure, but I will periodically engage in silence in their language, mannerisms, or tone of voice as it relates to the differences to the others in the same cabin and myself. They are slightly different in their appearance, culture, and vibrancy and yet accepted among us as fellow urban dwellers, although this city welcomes the world through its diversity. Today was no different – the couple was us, except we spoke English but somehow drew subtle attention to ourselves. Perhaps it was our body language – our sexy vibe, or maybe I was just paranoid.

The doors on one side of the PATH train opened to allow the current passengers to disembark and as soon as they did, we walked off closely together to avoid splitting up. This was Paula's first time in New York City and the subway system is a labyrinth of different corridors and other transferring and connecting passageways to trains. I was extremely confident in my ability to guide us out of there, as I have been visiting this great city nearly all my life. In the back of my mind, I was pleased that she hadn't been approached by a healthy-sized rat.

I had reminded her, prior to entering this vast mode of mass transit, to limit where her hands would touch because of the seen and unseen filth and grime of the innumerable germs passed on by the faceless public, and to avoid speaking to strangers because they often have a tendency to be brusque. The indigenous people here are strong and resilient but do not favor the milquetoast, and it is only the beginning of building her tolerance for the potential kerfuffle and animosity of the New Yorker. If she could make it here, she could make it anywhere.

After a couple of stairway twists and turns, since there wasn't a direct straight line to exit, we finally reached the 6th Ave street level and were welcomed by the fantastic energy of Manhattan. We not only had to integrate into the fast-paced path of walkers like having to leap into a double-dutch jump rope, but she caught her first glimpse of street vendors and solicitors other than those from an organized fair or festival.

"Five dollars! Five dollars!" one man shouted while vending cell phone accessories.

Another was selling DVDs and cassettes in between the NY deco art table and a homeless person holding a hand-ripped and rough-edged cardboard sign asking for donations.

"I love it here," I told Paula. "C'mon… this way."

We strolled along Broadway, stopping and gawking at the Macy's front windows showcasing their annual Christmas displays, and soon after kept it moving cutting across Herald Square on 35th to 6th Avenue, because there was so much more to see, and there would be less people traffic. With no sense of urgency, we scurried along until we came upon the Winter Village in Bryant Park – a charming market square with pop-up shops, and a lit-up Christmas tree near the base of a skating rink.

"I've never ice-skated before and somehow it feels more fitting to try it out on the Rideau Canal. Am I right? With maybe a hockey stick and a puck?"

"Hahaha. You're more than welcome to try, the next time you come up. It would be nice to see you fall on your bum," she chuckled.

"Yeah. Yeah," I laughed.

We gave each other a kiss by the water fountain and held hands while we enjoyed the festive atmosphere that had lingered on for nearly another week. A subtle wind change captivated us with a warm scent, and we looked at each other.

"Hot chocolate," we simultaneously blurted out.

I lead her, or rather, we followed the scent that lead us to a quaint stand that sold hot chocolate and crepes and made our selections. I suggested we take a sneak peek while we snacked on our treats.

On 42nd, we went to take a quick glimpse of all the reveling people occupying the area, taking pictures, and trying to stay warm. I pointed to the shiny glimmering ball that was proudly and temporarily affixed to the top of the building but not yet climbed to the top of the pole with the year "2004", unlit and underneath it. It wouldn't be activated for another five hours but we were all ready.

"Welcome to Times Square!" I greeted her.

Within time we walked towards Bryant Park, along 42nd, and stopped off at a fortified granite building with some cool architecture on the outside, immediately past the two light columns that served as guideposts to another entrance to the park. The structure had a large doorway to accommodate the two lines leading to the appropriate restrooms, although the women's line was a bit longer, but once inside I felt relieved and cleaner – better than any city portable toilet. It was a necessary and secret landmark to notate, and truly a hidden gem in plain sight.

On 5th and 44th, there was an ornate black clock on the sidewalk that stood about nine feet tall, resembling a sphere resting on top of a column. She stood in front of it so I could take a picture of her, and quick enough that we didn't impede any pedestrians from their paths. To go with the flow of traffic, we took 44th to 6th Ave and when we reached 50th, the Christmas Spectacular neon lights at Radio City Music Hall were lit and she stood and posed in front of it so that I could take a picture. What wasn't immediately apparent to her was the attraction that was lurking along 50th St towards 5th Ave, past the neon lights of the NBC Studio Rainbow Room and Observation Deck entrance.

Crowds started to form into peaceful cliques about midway of the block towards the intersection and when we reached them, we were both amazed on how beautiful the Rockefeller Center Christmas Tree looked. The decorations reminded me of the rainbow sprinkles I usually get when I order a vanilla ice cream cone, and the multi-pointed star on the top was golden.

"Welcome to the Rockefeller Center Christmas Tree!"

I thought of how this was an outstanding Pagan symbol gawked at and appreciated by many of the masses, including myself.

Long before Christianity, evergreen plants were used in the Northern Hemisphere to decorate their homes, especially the doors, to celebrate the Winter Solstice, which on December 21st or 22nd is the shortest day and the longest night. The ancient Romans celebrated the Winter Solstice in honor of Saturn, with a feast called Saturnalia, where they decorated their homes and temples with evergreen boughs, like the wreaths used today. The Christmas tree tradition started in the 16th century by Germans who decorated fir trees inside their homes and bearing gifts around the fir tree became a custom around the time of Queen Victoria.

"What do you think? Spectacular, no?"

"It's so tall and beautiful," she commented in amazement.

We did the touristy thing and had our pictures taken together with the help of some kind and friendly visiting strangers, and to me this was a checkpoint and a must-see in New York City during the holidays. We circled around and walked along the area enjoyed the liveliness of the people and the continued spirit of today, especially around the skating rink.

"More ice-skating fun. Someday I'll do an axel, but first I'll need to work on my swizzles and twizzles," I wholeheartedly stated, but also joked.

"I'll rub your bum, honey."

"Hahaha."

I held her hand and we continued onward, admiring the Neo-Gothic Roman Catholic St. Patrick's Cathedral from the Atlas statue across the street, and from there we perused the shops, architecture, and even the people until we arrived on 59th, making sure we weren't struck by any yellow taxi cabs along the way while crossing intersections, to avoid staying in one spot for an extended period of time.

Toys, toys, and more toys from the oldest toy store in the United States – FAO Schwarz. I had to take her up the escalator to check out the dance-on piano I first saw on *Big*[8], and soon after we slowly passed Zoltan the Fortune Teller on the ground floor. She then stopped me, put her hand on my chest, over my heart, and gently rubbed it while looking into my eyes.

"You would make a great Zoltan… a great shaman who will invoke the deities for wisdom, knowledge, and to heal others," she commanded.

"Yeah. Yeah," I laughed it off. "And I could wear a cool chapeau."

We were but a stone's throw from one of our prime destinations, and one of my favorite places in the world – Central Park. Paula had taken me to one of her favorite places a couple of weeks ago, and I oddly enjoyed it very much. Mer Bleue is the largest bog and natural area in Canada's Capital Region and the second-largest bog in southern Ontario, and it provides a habitat for many species of regionally rare and significant plants, birds and other wildlife. We walked along its boardwalks and I found tranquility and stillness in the air and nature it provided, also feeling life within the seemingly stark forest of leafless trees and perched silhouettes of birds. This was my first time at a bog, and I felt comfortably naked, yet much closer to Paula.

---

[8] *BIG*, a 1988 American fantasy comedy film directed by Penny Marshall, and stars Tom Hanks

At the intersection of 59th and 5th, at about one o'clock from where the William Tecumseh Sherman Monument is permanently gazed, is one of the filthiest streetlights I have ever witnessed. At least thirty pigeons are resting on the arm that extends the directional lighting for vehicle traffic or on the four-sided, slightly yellow, feces-ridden, light itself. It is also at this corner of the park where we saw the first signs of horse-drawn carriages and an overpopulation of street vendors selling Sabrett hot dogs, roasted peanuts, salted pretzels, touristy photos of New York memorabilia, and shish kebabs. We bypassed all of them to visit the "The Pond" and although most of the leaves had already fallen, some glistened with their yellow and orange foliage. The pond was not frozen, and in the northeast section we caught a better glimpse while crossing the beautiful and schist Gapstow Bridge which offered one of the best skyline views of the city.

The sounds of laughter, joyful screams, and music were in a short distance at the Wollman Rink – another skating rink that attracted many well-balanced enthusiasts and the daring and scintillating gliders of the ice. We smiled throughout our walk mainly because we were ebullient and enjoying each other's company, breathing in the fresh prana. We found a large smooth rock to lounge on and took a short break. It looked like it had been there for at least a century and was part of a good foundation to decide which direction we would be headed next.

"Let me take you down somewhere I want to show you," I suggested. The view of the rink, its leafless tree line, and the sideview of Central Park West were all so breathtaking that I decided to take some photos of her, in the foreground.

I saw the Essex House behind her in the distance and was elated to see her grin as she sat there amazed in our current surroundings. She lit up a smoke and was taking it all in while I walked around taking snapshots of the different angles of her to capture this moment in time. Her black leather coat kept her warm and her black and white striped scarf was snug around her neck. At times I put the camera down so that I could witness and capture her beauty with my own eyes and without the help of a lens. She was majestic, confident, and ready for anything and although I could not confirm, without asking her, what was on her mind, I knew she was happy and that was all that mattered to me.

We took a trail that lead to a horse carousel that appeared to be hand-carved and folkish but were soon after engulfed by a promenade of trees from both sides. We made a left towards Sheep Meadow where some people were tossing footballs around while others walked their dogs or just cut across. There was non-stop energy and motion throughout the athletic fields while we took a trail that would ultimately lead us to 72nd Street, where I wanted to check out The Dakota – John Lennon's last residence before he was shot and killed there. When we came to a fork in the road, I asked her which way she'd like to go. She said *right*, and that's how I noticed the Daniel Webster Monument. I stopped over to check out the inscription:

LIBERTY AND UNION,

NOW AND FOREVER,

ONE AND INSEPARABLE

"Ok… next. Go left, or right? Both lead to the same place? You have free will. What will it be?"

"Let's stay to the right," she said. It was as if Terrace Rd and West Rd were at the center of an infinity symbol, but we kept our saunter down the path as the sun was quickly fading away.

There was a small green sign hanging on the fence and if were jogging or running, we may have missed *Strawberry Fields*, a Central Park memorial to John Lennon. During his career with the Beatles and in his solo work, Lennon's music gave hope and inspiration for world peace and his memory and mission lives on in Strawberry Fields.

"Strawberry Fields Forever" is one of my favorite tunes by The Beatles. It was released in February of '67, but I also like it because it's near 72nd Street – the year I was born, plus I love strawberries."

"Such a modest field and I don't think they grow strawberries here, but still… cool," she said.

The memorial is a triangular piece of land falling away on the two sides of the park, and its focal point is a circular pathway mosaic of inlaid stones, with a single word, the title of Lennon's famous song - "Imagine".

"Come," I lead her by hand, "Check this out."

We drew near to an already small crowd, gathered around the mosaic, singing to an acoustic guitar cover of "Here Today", and when the song was over, we waited for the light to cross Central Park West.

Three women with strollers were also waiting at the red light, and in one of the strollers was one of those Magic 8 Ball novelty toys, and a yellow balloon was attached to one of the handles. They were probably part of a meet-up group or neighbors because they were all chatting with each other, but when the light turned green, we walked behind them to let them go ahead of us since we would be stopping shortly. The Dakota was a nostalgic pitstop for me. I admired the building's high gables and deep roofs with an abundance of dormers, terracotta spandrels and many other triangular panels, that give it a German Renaissance character. At the archway of the building was where he was killed in 1980, and there is a column on each side with a big potted plant in each, that reached about nine feet tall. Guards protected the privacy of residents at the entranceway by deterring tourists from getting close to the historical attraction. I offered a bit of Americana history to Paula and provided an interesting tour of one of my favorite sites, but we were getting hungry and decided to get something to eat.

We could have gotten halal from any one of the neighboring food trucks, or visit a popular food chain establishment, but while we were living life to our fullest and were reaching pinnacle heights, we walked along West Drive and honored the reservations I made at the Tavern on the Green. It was so nice to sit, relax, and rest our legs from the active trotting and the way the lighting illuminated her eyes was a boost of refreshing energy. We started off with two glasses of champagne and between the appetizers and the main course, she mentioned that she was unable to have children but could reverse it with a surgery. I wasn't afraid of the conversation – I wanted children, but this was more of seed planting than committing to it. I was open to the concept and welcomed to revisit it at another time.

I thought about how natural and organic it is to connect with Paula on many levels, including physically, and providing a child wouldn't seem like a task or chore. She was solely on my mind, and before I began to sketch the "Study of Dulcinea III" while she was in bed wearing her glasses at the hotel last night, I noticed she had already, unbeknownst to me, finished a couple of her own drawings and renditions with the pad I left in her room, as I flipped to a new page. Her style was different and smooth, with minimal straight edges, and I appreciated her artistic abilities, as it was a neat surprise towards our collaborations. I envisioned her again, laying there with her soft skin, gorgeous smile, and ability to please me sexually. She is enticing and delicious as our dessert. We spoon-fed and shared the Crème brûlée and a bread pudding to each other from across the table, sharing in selflessness.

It was getting close to the witching hour so after dinner we lit up our after-meal smokes and strolled on West Drive to Center until we reached 59th and 6th Ave. From her pocket, she pulled out a small tube of salve and applied it on her hands. The streets were entirely crowded and there was no way we would be able to reach 42nd without bumping a few dozen shoulders and pushing our way through, so we hung out towards the entrance of the park by the Monumento General José de San Martín, then double-backed into the park over an archway, towards 7th hoping to get the best view towards Times Square.

Looking at my wristwatch, it was nearing midnight and pedestrians, bicyclists, and nature lovers began forming clusters of joining groups, like an amoeba destroying our chances of being in the front row, but we were content being together in nature. In synchronized tandem, we soon heard the chant of the countdown.

"Ten…Nine…Eight…Seven…Six," the collective pronounced.

Paula and I joined in. We held hands and looked down 7th Ave towards the projected New Year's Eve Ball at Times Square and trusted that it was happening since we couldn't physically see it.

"Five…Four…Three…Two…One…Happy New Year - 2004!!"

I pointed my camera towards us, in an extended left arms-length away, and took my very first "Selfie" in hopes that I had the right angle, focus, lighting, and that we didn't blink since it was film and I couldn't verify any of the results until I had it developed. We kissed, and hugged, and kissed again, and well… made out.

"Happy New Year, Honey!" she said with a smile.

"Happy New Year, Dulcinea!"

Chapter XVI - Dad

Dad was born on January 6th, a holiday known as Epiphany or Theophany or "Three Kings Day". It is also known as "Dia de los Reyes Magos" and is celebrated in many Latin American countries as part of the Christmas story. It commemorates the day the three kings, or "wise men" or magi, followed the star to Bethlehem and presented their gifts of gold, frankincense and myrrh. Although I celebrated that day as his birthday, I also recognized the Three Kings, as taught to me in my Puerto Rican culture.

It was always peculiar to me that the word "magi" was also part of the words: magic or magician, and so I was curious as to whether my father subliminally entered magic due to sharing the same celebrated day with the biblical text. It's the same speculation as the idea Carl Jung had when people are drawn to professions that fit their name. I was astounded to read about *nominative determinism* in the early nineties and the thought of having an unconscious preference for things people associate with themselves. I enjoyed my father's close-up performances with cards, and I learned a thing or two, and am sworn to secrecy. *Shhh!*

My father is a great entertainer and showman, and he focuses on the mechanics of his craft to delight the crowds. His slight-of-hand skills have always improved through persistent practice and it is this constant repetition that guides him through a natural movement of familiarity. Sometimes I drive to school and work, using the same route, timing the streetlights according to the required speed limits, and more often than not I don't even think about what I'm doing, and there are days I do not remember how I got to work because of the comfortabilities and recognitions my brain is accustomed to, without much deviation. Other than slight flairs or personal touches, my father's magic illusions are a well-timed act, without deeper contemplation or thought, and arrives at his conclusions at the end of his choreographed act.

There are some regions on the island of Puerto Rico where some of my parents' family live and it is so desolate and seldom visited by outsiders that they become accustomed to traditions and old ways of thinking from the lack of advancement, technology, or knowledge. The people of the mountains do not need all those things; they are satisfied with what they have and somehow the anxieties of life hardly pertain to them. Even the mosquitoes don't bother them. Most of the time we land on the island, we visit the family to check up on them and to see how they are doing, and the word ultimately gets out that "El Mago" is in town, but for those who live in higher elevations, the jíbaros, we come unannounced.

My father drove the three of us through never-ending winding one-lane roads where I shook my fists at the goats of the past for making them because of the erratic twists and turns that were affecting my stomach. Abuelita sat in the front and they were talking in Spanish about updates of relatives and of the family we were on our way to visit. Even though they were wrapped in plastic bags and on the floor behind the passenger seat, the smell of the baked chickens and fresh loaves of baked bread we picked up from a food vendor on the side of the road swayed its aromas from left to right, up and down with each movement of our journey to Sierra Alta in

Yauco, and just when I thought we were ascending high enough to be there we heard more car horns alerting us of their upcoming presence as we veered off to other dirt roads that served as shortcuts.

He was a good driver and enjoyed the journey. Often he would pull over so that he could take photos of livestock and the countryside, and we would have meaningful conversations about life, especially when a cow would defecate or when roosters would have sex with a chicken for those two seconds of happenstance, but not because he knew it was going to happen. He was ready for whatever nature insisted on displaying and just happened to have his camera ready to capture it. With grandma in tow, we had no time to gather data on farm animals. Besides, where we were going had enough to keep us busy and we were arriving up the steep incline to the crest of the property.

After chicken sandwiches and fresh roasted coffee and an hour of spending quality time and catching up with all the gossip one could obtain from people living in solace and minimal interactions with the world, my dad instructed all the children to gather around outside as he was announcing the great, if not the greatest, show to be witnessed in those parts. Willy and Wally ran through the woods and returned with neighbors who were also curious about the show. Some sat on flipped-over buckets, the elders sat on chairs, and the rest comfortably sat on the grass and cemented driveway.

Drake Youla was sometimes his stage name, whenever he went into character, but he didn't dress up as the Count that day – it was too hot and muggy, but it was stenciled in white letters on his black wooden box that concealed his props. To his delight, the younger children were elated to be randomly called up to be an assistant and be involved. He would turn a girl into a rabbit, or another wound up wearing a silly colorful hat, but in all, it was fun and humorous and innocent. It wasn't until after he pierced a balloon with a long needle causing it to pop and revealing glitter inside that he would perform the next set of tricks – cards.

His manipulation and misdirection with the cards alarmed and frightened some of the older teens and an aunt. They couldn't comprehend what they were witnessing and seeing with their own eyes.

"Aye, no!" a couple got up and walked away.

Seeing this, he assured them that it was all right, that is was only an illusion. They perceived him as a demon, even a devil, who was working in the supernatural. It was a good thing he didn't wear his cape, or else they would have really thought the Prince of Darkness was upon them. A mild crosswind blew past rustling branches supporting hanging mangoes and bananas. Suliana, the small dachshund, strolled to the front row and just laid down to rest. Short of showing them how the trick was done, they eventually came back under the assurance that nothing bad was going to happen to them. I understood their concern and their naivety, but I felt there was something more going on behind the curtain.

After the final thunderous applause, it was explained to him that there are some Seers in the mountains that predict the future using Spanish playing cards that have four suits and a deck is usually made up of forty to forty-eight cards. It is the same deck of cards my abuela has in her top drawer in the dining room, that she uses to play

Brisca. Cards are a powerful medium used to speak to the spirits and thus was the reason why most were fearful of my father's card handlings.

"Todo está dentro." That is what my grandmother's aunt said to me as she gently placed her finger on my chest plate, while we were saying our farewells. *Intuition*.

His use of playing cards and misdirection are an integral part of the illusionary process. It is my belief that his performance is graded on how great he's able to fool the spectator, and perhaps the real reason why he correlated trickery in the use of cards. Even great Westerns he was so accustomed to watch throughout his childhood sometimes delved on the Poker player, and the many who were shot or injured because of the cheating in the wild west. The Ace up the sleeve was a secret advantage and the use of cards for him are a game of folly and manipulation.

He was a member of the International Brotherhood of Magicians – Ring 106, the same number as his birthdate, and for years he would volunteer at local hospitals and rest homes to entertain the weak, old, or frail to remind them all how it is to be in wonderment, as in the times in their youth. I have been surrounded by magic and have often assisted him in those endeavors either as a stagehand, an assistant on stage, or just videotaping his performances and the audience. Throughout his magic career, I have been involved and open to the power it creates.

I was about four or five when I remember witnessing my first magic trick. We were at my grandparents' brownstone house on York Street when my father called me in to the parlor and showed me a shiny penny. I attentively sat on the plastic-covered cushions on their couch to see what the attraction was. He put it in his clasped hands and shook it around, put them behind his head, then returned them to the front for full disclosure, and in a tossing nature he simultaneously opened his hands and appeared to throw the penny somewhere towards me but it had already vanished.

"Where did it go?" he asked me.

I looked at his hands in wonderment, and I hadn't heard it drop where he motioned.

"Check under your seat."

I had been sitting there the entire time of his short performance and hadn't moved until I stood up and checked under the sofa, and when I didn't even see a dust bunny, I picked up the seat cushion and there was the penny. For the next couple of days, he would do the same illusion and I would either find the penny under an end-table doily or maybe in my abuelito's black shoe. Every time I visited them at their house, I felt it was magical place.

Any demons and monsters whom I've encountered come from people, folklore, or the power of imagination. Alfred Hitchcock became popular because he allowed the mind to construct the scary scenario or horror, and it was far worse than anything he portrayed in his films. When the lights and power went out one evening in Puerto Rico, due to a terrible rainstorm, my aunt and father suggested that I go to bed before the "Cuco" came.

"The Cuco?!" I asked.

"Yes. He comes in the night and eats children if they don't go to bed early," Titi Liz said.

My mental image and interpretation of this deadly monster was of the "Bogeymen"[9] in *March of the Wooden Soldiers*, where they were furry creatures with big eyes, ears, and a projected snout with sharp and pointy teeth. I was terrified, because I trusted my family members and what they told me. I was only seven. And then came the Chupacabra – the "goat-sucker", who attacked and drank the blood of livestock, including goats. It was initially reported that the killings were committed by a Satanic cult. These creatures were more real than ghosts or spirits since I never saw any of them but were vouched by different family members on the island. I think my father thinks it's all "ridicu-lie" – our plural form for information that's more than ridiculous, that it must be a lie.

I have determined that he is not a believer nor an advocate for Tarot cards, and he rejects the notion that it is a real thing. There is a science to the way he creates his illusions with the help of the use of cards, and not by way of the supernatural. He regarded the Divine speaking through the cards as poppycock and nonsensical, and I understood him to be firm and abhorred in those beliefs. It became taboo and we agreed to disagree and so out of respect for not beating the dead horse, I never discussed it in front of him and went underground with my curiosities to avoid unnecessary conflict.

---

[9] *Babes in Toyland* is a Laurel and Hardy musical Christmas film released on November 30, 1934. The film is also known by the alternative titles *Laurel and Hardy in Toyland, Revenge Is Sweet* (the 1948 European reissue title), and *March of the Wooden Soldiers* (in the United States).

Chapter XVII – Pisces Season

I stood looking out her balcony window at the colorful landscape of buildings comprised of houses and apartments and the snow-covered roofs, beyond the leafless tree branches. The sky came in different shades of dismal and bleak greys, but it stopped snowing a couple of days ago and the streets were already shoveled and filled with life once again. While Paula is at work on this Friday, I will be joining up with Richard at his gallery on Bank Street, so that we could discuss and collaborate on future projects.

Paula had already declared that she would be making dinner and that it would be ready by six, so I was certainly looking forward to her home-cooking. Aside from the very few sidewalk areas that weren't fully shoveled or had a lot of slush on them, the path was quite clear to the art gallery. I only slipped and pretended I was surfing, once – to immediately regain my balance, but otherwise the walk was enjoyable.

Within the glass storefront, different styles of paintings were featured from three different artists, and a 24"x20" desert landscape with an array of earth tones was proudly displayed on an easel. Above me, next to the RAG Art Gallery sign was a strange and peculiar artistic cutout of a green sea creature that, because of the number of legs it had, I assumed to be an octopus. I walked up the three green steps to the left, wiped my feet on the *Welcome* mat, then opened the door.

"Hi. Richard? I'm Coronado – a friend of Roxanne's and Paula.

"Hello. Yes. Welcome. Nice to meet you," he greeted me as we shook hands.

"Interesting sea creature you have hanging in the front."

"That's what she said. Oh! You mean my octopus? Yes... I was reading a book by Victor Hugo – *Les Travailleurs de la Mer*... *Toilers of the Sea*, and Gilliatt – the main character, battles with an octopus, and that's my rendition. Anyway, please sit. Have a seat. I'm just rearranging inventory in the basement. So, Roxy tells me you're from New York?"

"New Jersey. Right across the Hudson River from it."

"Cool. How long will you be in town?"

"I leave in a couple of days. I'm checking out the art scene around here. There doesn't seem to be many galleries."

"It's a shame, too, because there are a lot of creative artists that come into the shop and we just hang out here for hours.

A young professional woman dressed in charcoal grey pants and a black overcoat with mittens walked in the door with a covered package and seemed a bit nervous, or cold, because she was slightly shivering. She looked like a government official about to serve Richard some legal papers, but he didn't seem worried.

"Hi. I'm Stephanie. Can you please look at one of my paintings and let me know what you think?" she asked as she pulled it out of a brown paper bag, already wrapped in paper.

Richard turned and looked at me.

"Check it out and help her. I'll be downstairs for a moment, moving things around."

"Hi, Stephanie. I'm Coronado. Let's check it out."

It was a 16" x 20" painting on canvas, and I held it on its sides carefully to give her my honest opinion on it.

"I work at the Parliament and I came here on my lunch break. I only have an hour, and I came quickly so no one would see me."

"You're left-handed," I blurted.

"Yes. How did you know?"

"It's nice. Have you been painting long?"

"That one is my first one. I wasn't going to do more unless I was any good at it."

I was certainly not going to discourage anyone from not doing something, especially after the first time. I turned the painting upside down and held it further away so I could get a different perspective on it.

"You should definitely keep at it. Do more!"

She smiled in appreciation, and I suspected that because of her profession she was unable to freely express herself and cannot get honest feedback from her peers.

"Your brushstrokes... sometimes you hold yourself back, right? Let it flow. Don't doubt yourself. I'm glad you started with acrylic. Soon you will master oils. Nice choice of colors."

"Thank you, Coronado."

"The only thing I would do differently is to create a grisaille. Use a dollop of black and white and mix them into a light grey. Then wet your brush and thin out the paint on your canvas so there's a light layer of grey color but the important thing is that you cover the whole canvas. This will prevent any small white spots on the canvas to come through. See here where there's white spots? The grisaille will help eliminate that. They don't teach that, so it's a secret technique I use. Try it!"

Richard walked up the stairs with a 4' x 2' painting and began to enter the main room.

"A couple of more paintings later, you're bound to be on these walls."

I handed her back her painting.

"What do you call it?"

"I haven't titled it yet. It's just an abstract for now."

"'Good to the Core'," I suggested.

"I'm so glad I came here today. I must go. Thank you so much!"

"Take care, Stephanie!"

"See you soon," Richard added.

"You've done this before, eh?" he asked me when she left.

"It's what I do. I represent artists and I can get your artwork seen in numerous galleries in New York, starting in SOHO. You can stay with me in Jersey for a month."

I looked at my watch and it was nearing six. I had dinner plans at Paula's, but at least she would know I was at the art gallery because of the note I left her on the kitchen counter, to remind her. The business discussion that Richard and I were having regarding getting his art showcased, not only in the United States but to also capture on film and document the entire process, as in a reality series or documentary, extended to about 6:45. I would project, premier, and broadcast the movie on the side of a red-bricked building in the Glebe, not too far from the diner, after necessary permissions, from the City and the building owner, to do so. The word would get out that art was alive and thriving by one of their very own. I sold us on the vision, as it was solid, and I was all-in to make it happen. I pulled out a contract I had worked on to define the details of my representation and he signed it with a pen that was in between two empty Heineken bottles and a Molson.

"Here's my card."

I handed him my business information for *Infinito Art*, and he gave me one with his gallery info.

"What an interesting logo. A small 'I' with the dot on top and an infinity sign in between, makes it look like an angel. Interesting."

I had to haul ass back to the apartment since I did not call Paula to let her know I was running late, plus I was hungry, and I had to do it carefully so I wouldn't slip on the wet pavements. When I walked into the apartment using my key, she had waited for me then started serving our plates after I entered. She had already changed out of her work clothes and her hair was up in a bun. She cooked an Asian stir fry with fresh peppers and vegetables, and noodles, that smelled so good.

"Hi, Babe. I'm so sorry I'm late. I got caught up at the art gallery and tried to come sooner."

My father instilled punctuality in me so much that I am more often always on time for an appointment or a rendezvous. This stems from him picking me up after school, or after a sports practice or game, or any school event that I attended where I needed a ride home. It was to ensure my safety – not lost or kidnapped. The last time I wasn't at the time and place for a pick-up, my father yelled and scolded me. Looking back, I realize he did it because he was concerned and loved me.

"I represent Richard as his Agent, and now he's my first international client."

I pulled out the signed contract to confirm my whereabouts and the possible justification for my tardiness and placed it on the nearby table behind the couch, while she was carving the meat. Although I believe she doesn't see me as picaresque or mendacious, I felt that I needed to assure that she was indeed important and that I value her efforts and time. I wasn't out there with another woman, drinking, partying, or involved in any negative vices. I was late and I probably should have let her known beforehand. This was the first time I felt that I truly disappointed her and violated her trust, but that is rooted from my past regressions.

"It's ok. It's just stuff from my past that reminds me that I've gone through this before. Congratulations, Corey. Now you have more reason to come to Ottawa."

She looked at me, in a moment of happiness, and smiled. I hugged her while she was holding both of our plates and gave her a big smooch on the lips.

"It looks and smells great! What's your secret? Again, I'm sorry that I'm late."

"You're just in time. And it's fresh ingredients, some TLC, and a splash of fish sauce."

She lit some candles, poured some red wine into our glasses, and we feasted on a great meal filled with laughter and filling our bellies. She didn't have dining room chairs, or a dining room, and so we spent most of our time eating in the parlor, sitting on the floor sometimes using pillows for cushions. It didn't matter except that while she sat on the floor tonight I utilized the couch and it was awkward for me because I considered her my equal and at the same level, so I casually sat back down on the floor, using the couch as a backrest. Clyde didn't care either way. He hung out with us and lounged wherever he wanted, without a care in the world. *Meow.*

After volunteering to do the dishes, but not until after we tasted some of the rhubarb cheesecake desserts I brought back from a local bakery, she lit two of the tall white candles positioned in their own candelabras on the altar table by the balcony.

"Tonight, we're going to do a ritual together," she suggested.

"Great. Finally. Sounds cool."

"Let's get changed and put on our robes."

She handed me a black robe and asked that I remove all my clothing, excluding my undergarments but including socks, and to try it on. It had a sash so that I could tie it around my waist, and when I put it on, it was a great length, as if it were tailored just for me. It wasn't anything fancy that included a hood or even pockets, but it was comfortable for whatever we were about to engage in. Her robe was more stylish and was made of cotton, versus my polyester window curtain material, but it was less important than the ritual itself. She asked me to relax on the couch, while she lit a charcoal.

Her beautiful long dark hair flowed down to her chest and she picked up the sage stick to begin smudging the apartment. Sage is a healing herb used to benefit physical, mental, and emotional well-being. It belongs to the Salvia plant family that is derived from the

Latin word *salvere*, which means "to heal." She said that First Nations people used the ancient practice of burning dried sage for cleansing, where it was thought to promote healing, wisdom, and longevity. Paula walked along the entire apartment chanting at each point of direction, starting from the North.

"Spirits of the North... Spirits of the East..." until she covered all six primary points including up and down.

I walked with and behind her every step of the way, ending at the opened balcony window to allow those negative energies to release. When she was finished, she lit sweetgrass in the same manner, to bring and promote the positivity after the negative was thwarted from the sage.

"It smells nice in here." *Almost as good as the stir fry.*

We gathered in the parlor and she placed some crystal incense on top of the already-burning charcoal piece, and smoke began to plume upward. She used a feather to spread the smoke and scent throughout the room and in our lungs. We moved the couch back a few feet and moved the coffee table to the side to make room for floor work. I still wasn't sure what we would be doing and left it all up to her to direct, and when everything was in place and to her liking, she turned to me.

"In the spirit of today's manifestations and strengthening will, we will perform a "Blade and Chalice" ritual. I will perform most of it. You don't have to worry about anything. Ok?"

"Yeah. Yeah. Got it."

She brought out an ornate dagger and an equally impressive looking chalice and placed it on the table in front of us. The blade, or in this ceremony – an athame, is one of the essential tools of witchcraft and the double edges of the blade are considered to represent the dual nature of the Universe and symbolizes the dual nature of magic or intent such as good or evil, protection or malice, or healing and destroying. The other three essential tools of Wicca are the chalice, wand, and the pentacle. In many Wiccan traditions, the use of athame is considered a metaphorical symbol of cutting out or killing the old, unpleasant, and unwanted emotions and memories. The word "athame" may have originated from the Latin word "artavus" mentioned in the old manuscripts of "The Key of Solomon"[10] as a quill knife, like a dull letter or envelope opener that TSA confiscated from my luggage at the security checkpoint in Newark.

I watched in wonderment as she chanted the words. I bowed when cued to do so and paid attention and reverence to what she was doing. In the end, she lightly gripped the blade upside down and dipped it into the chalice, summoning fruitful wishes and desired manifestations. To me it represented sexual intercourse and the union of male and female and thought that maybe this was to increase our possibilities of having a child, but we never spoke of it and I hadn't believed for her to be malicious and deceitful. Whatever her desired intent, I went along with it because I never believed or suspected that she was out to harm me in any way. When she

---

[10]*The Key of Solomon*, a pseudepigrapha grimoire (also known as a book of spells) attributed to King Solomon. It presents a typical example of Renaissance magic, dating back to the 14th or 15th century Italian Renaissance

finished, she asked me to extinguish the flames of the candles with a candle snuffer.

Afterwards, we moved things back, cleaned up, and slipped into our pajamas like nothing happened. From my drawer, I pulled out a small box of chocolates in a red heart-shaped box and a card I spent nearly thirties minutes trying to pick out and handed it to her.

"Happy belated Valentine's Day!"

It was only six days ago but I surprised her.

"Oh, Coronado. You are amazing. You know that?"

"I love you, Paula," I confessed as I looked into her eyes.

It wasn't the first time I said those three words to her, but I used them sparingly and when I truly meant it. I didn't just casually throw it around at the end of a conversation or when she made a great meal, or even as an obligatory statement during sex. She gave me a long and meaningful kiss, then looked into my eyes.

"I love you too, Coronado."

On Sunday, we went to Roxanne's so I could get better acquainted with the future mastermind of art development in the community, and because she rocks.

"What do you call her again?" Paula asked me.

"Roxy, because she rocks!" I joked with her.

"Don't tell her I said that because I don't want to offend her. Some people freak out with nicknames. What if I called Richard - 'Dick'? He might take it the wrong way. Hahaha… I just made a joke."

"C'mon. Let's go up. The elevator is right over here," she sneered.

Although Roxy and I had only met up a couple of times, we have been corresponding via email. The last one she sent me was a month ago, dated January 21, 2004:

Hola Señor,

So, you would like me to do a little designing for you eh? I would LOVE to help you with your website.
Here is one obstacle – I don't have a computer. I do, however, have a friend, Ryan, who lives in my building with a computer and I have asked him if he could "lease" computer time to me (I can set-up a Hotmail account to receive the images). He'll get back to me, but I think he won't have a problem. By the way – he designs websites too. Funny how that works out. I think he may want a C. Borgia original in return for this. He has NO art on his walls. As for my payback – I would rather you just owed me a favor that I can recoup later on. Does that make you nervous? Payback's a bitch baby. But you know that it will have something to do with the Urban Art Project.
So, were you thinking of a layout like your last site, or something a little different? I really like the idea of a black or dark background. Is this for Infinito or is it something brand new? Please give me any/all details that you have and if you want to call to discuss this on the phone, I will be at your girlfriend's tonight.
I am honored that you asked me to help you do this.
Well, asked Paula to ask me. Coronado, if you ever need anything please do not be afraid to ask. Sincerely. I feel that you are my good friend too and friends help out friends. Always. OK? Smarten up.

Later mang…
Roxy

Paula walked in first when the door opened but it was a gradual insertion because we needed to take off our shoes, from the melting snow, so I waited for her to slide off her boots. I was slightly concerned if I had on matching socks or if I had any holes in them, but I when I removed them, I was deemed safe. Roxanne was just as lovely in person, and we hugged as if we had known each other for years.

"Hey, Ro," Paula said to her.

"Hi, Coronado! Nice to see you again."

"Hi, Roxanne! Nice to see you, as well."

"Come on in. Please… make yourselves comfortable. Mi casa es tu casa."

"Merci."

"Coronado, this is Monica."

Monica had on a friendly smile, wore glasses, and her brown straight hair was in a bob.

"Hello, Monica."

The immediate entrance walls were of a mustard color, and the next set of walls were crimson. Her apartment was very colorful and delightful to be in and her sofa was draped with a tangerine orange colored sheet with throw pillows that matched it very similarly. Roxanne is a ginger and her straight hair seemed to curl a little towards the bottom as they reached down below her shoulders. While she was in the kitchen, I sat on her couch admiring the view she had of a different part of the city. Six 2'x4' windows lined the bottom row and three larger windows made up the top row, and altogether there was much light coming in and at the same time allowing for an interesting view of a now snow-covered village. Rows of red-bricked two-story houses lined the streets and every other block accommodated a row of bare trees.

Four empty mug glasses were on her living room table along with a copy of *The Alchemist*. I had already finished reading my copy during plane rides and airport waits. I considered the concept of traveling to find what I was missing and contemplated on my interpretation of the book's message and meaning. Furthermore, I felt connected and comfortable here, and when Paula returned from the kitchen with two glasses of red wine, I stood up and accepted one.

"Thank you."

Roxanne walked in wearing a leopard print sweater with comfortable black slacks. A black and white domestic shorthaired cat sat comfortably on the beige sofa across the room and had no intention of coming over, rubbing its body on my legs and shedding any fur on my black jeans, or wanting any attention from me, for now.

"Nice place you have here. I like your cat."

"Oh. Thanks. That's Gerald. He likes to bother me and enter my space, when I least expect it."

"Manipulates boundaries? Like a gerrymander. That's funny."

"Yeah. I never thought of it like that," she chuckled.

"My other cat is hanging out on one of the chairs over there."

She pointed to her dining room table that displayed several of her original works of paintings. I walked over to check them out and to say hi to her feline.

"Hi," I said to the cat as I pet her on the back of the neck area. She was thinner than Gerald, and perhaps younger with a couple of hints of brown streaks along the back.

"That's Jillian."

"Cool. Hey, Monica, do you have a cat?"

"Yes. Her name is Monique."

Paula came over and put her arm around my waist.

"All witches have cats. The three of us are in the same coven."

I looked at all three of them and there was a stunning lull. There was no hint of a joke and I think that they were more curious about my reaction than mine of theirs. I thought of the three witches in *Clash of the Titans*[11], the Stygian Witches, who were blind but shared one eye to see, but these three ladies were so young and attractive that they were far from looking like conventional witches. Not all pagans are witches and not all witches are pagan, and although Wicca is a pagan religion, not all witches are Wicca, as was the case with Jeanette, so I was still trying to figure out what types of witches they all are. It was like Dorothy meeting Glinda the "Good Witch" in *The Wonderful Wizard of Oz*[12]. Which Witch is which? – who was good or bad, and what should they look like?

"Yes. Of course," I agreed as I raised my glass of wine and cheered.

The seat cushions to her dining chairs were red with Asian lettering on them. I could only guess what they said, but they were tucked under the table only creating a hideout for Jillian who was hiding from the sunlight. I turned to Roxanne.

"Did you paint all of these?"

"Yes. And I have more of them over there, along the wall and on the bookcase."

---

[11] *Clash of the Titans*, a 1981 British-American heroic fantasy adventure film directed by Desmond Davis and written by Beverley Cross which retells the Greek mythological story of Perseus.

[12] *The Wonderful Wizard of Oz*, an American children's novel written by author L. Frank Baum and illustrated by W.W. Denslow, originally published by the George M. Hill Company in Chicago on May 17, 1900.

Each painted canvas was unique and colorful and spoke to me in different ways. In its abstract and playful combinations, it was vibrant and eligible on anyone's walls for display. I liked her loose rendition of a four-winged butterfly, ovular yet symmetrical, yet after further contemplation it also resembled a feminine goddess. She was new to painting but open to creating and expressing herself. I saw it in the 16" x 20" red painting of a white flower displaying the seventeen open petals, with one hiding in the background, and the yellow disc florets. It was the beginning of something bigger than she was, perhaps bigger than all of us.

I lit up a smoke and walked over to the shelves of her bookcase and appreciated the opportunity to view interesting books, pottery, and personal photographs taken of family members. The doorbell rang and it was her friend Jennifer, a contact and fellow artist who is willing to bridge the gap from art to venue, since she was part of a cultural affairs personnel for a small grass-roots organization. She was a young single mother who brought her six-year-old daughter, so I automatically extinguished my cigarette. Our youngest guest wore a cute pink dress with white and red trim and had big brown eyes. Jennifer looked the youngest of all the adults and was also the tallest. Wearing a white headband, white dangling ball earrings, and glasses she may have been the most stylish and had enough self-confidence to exude ambition and drive. She was perfect for administration, and after we each had a drink in hand, we started our first informal meeting.

Roxanne lit a purple candle that was surrounded by a dozen smooth and different colored rocks, placed in the center of another table. We tossed around great ideas of logistics, demographics, investment capital, supplies, and especially location of venues. Roxanne was adamant to leap into bold territory with aggressive and calculated purpose. A true fireball - *Foxy Roxy with Moxie.*

Jennifer took detailed notes – Minutes, and it was exciting to be a part of this. Towards the end, after tremendous strides, I daydreamed for a moment. I looked within realizing that I did not need those past possessions. I had a woman who loved me, and I loved her, a new perspective and location, and a sense of belonging, and in this case – artists and an art community who accepted me and made me feel like I belonged. What else could I ever ask for?

"Mommy, I'm thirsty," Jennifer's daughter said as she grabbed an unopened bottle of wine. The ladies laughed due to her drink of choice. *Children.*

Some of the ladies left to go to the kitchen, and I sat contemplating my future. Paula walked in carrying a white cream-frosted layered cake with a lit candle on top, and they all joined in unison, singing a familiar song:

... happy birthday, dear Coronado. Happy birthday to you!

"Close your eyes. Make a wish!" shouted Roxanne.

I closed my eyes, made a wish, and blew out the candle.

"Happy Birthday, Honey," Paula said to me in a soft and sexy voice.

"Thank you."

I winked at her then gave her a kiss. My thirty-second birthday was on the twenty-seventh.

"It's not for another five days, you know."

"You won't be here."

"You really surprised me. Love you."

She smiled at me, assuring me that everything was all right, even though I oddly considered what we just went through as a ritual solely on its complexity, their performance as a group, and it's long-lasting intention and the involvement with a candle.

"Thank you, everybody. Who wants cake?"

I just stared at Paula as she cut me the first slice and handed me the plate, taking care of me. I hope my wish comes true.

February 24, 2004

Subject: Hello Group of 5 Members...

Below are some articles I found out about the lack of studio space and what the city intended to do about it. Which basically translates into "nothing". Just a little bee in everyone's bonnet.

Thank you all for joining me in my home on Sunday. It was a great vibe and amazing energy and I appreciated being around those of like mind. I think we have something powerful individually and collectively and we should seriously consider focusing our energies together to assist and promote artists (including us!).

We need a catchy name though for our group. Please add your ideas and we will vote as we are a shining example of community and democracy!

Take care all. And could someone please forward this to Monica? I didn't get her email address (and then could you c.c. me on it!) Much Gracias!

Chapter XVIII - Tulip Festival

Paula invited me to meet her in May 2004 for their annual tulip festival. It was so great to be able to see her again, especially in the Spring, where I felt comfortable just wearing a pair of dark-blue slacks, a black polo shirt, and black laced shoes suitable enough to wear in first-class without airline and company-policy scrutiny. She asked me to meet her at Major's Hill Park, by St. Patrick's Street and Mackenzie Avenue, as soon as my flight came in and by now, I was confident that I was familiar and welcomed enough to find my way around her city. The park stands above the Rideau Canal at the point where it enters the Ottawa River. Across the canal to the west are the parliament buildings, to the north of the park is the National Gallery of Canada, and to the east are the US embassy and the Byward Market.

During World War II, the Dutch royal family came to Canada to seek asylum, and in 1943, Princess Juliana, who was nine months pregnant, was about to give birth. This posed a problem to both Canada and Netherlands because according to Canadian law, all babies born in Canada will automatically become a Canadian citizen and according to the Dutch royal succession law, a prince or princess must be born on Netherlands soil in order to be recognized as a royal member. Because of this situation, the Canadian government passed a special bill that placed the sovereignty of a maternity ward in Ottawa Civic Hospital under the Government of the Netherlands. On January 19, 1942, Princess Juliana gave birth to her third daughter, Margaret, on "Dutch land".

In May 1945, with the help of the Canadian Forces, Netherlands gained its victory and liberation, and the royal family returned to their homeland after several years of separation, and in the Fall, the Dutch government presented one hundred thousand tulip bulbs to Canada to express their respect and gratitude. The following year, Princess Juliana presented twenty-thousand tulip bulbs in her own name and requested them to be planted at the Ottawa Civic Hospital. Since then, Ottawa receives thousands of tulip bulbs from the Netherlands royal family every year, and in recognition, the first Ottawa Tulip Festival was held in 1953.

When I arrived at our rendezvous, I noticed the event sign whereby it was written in English first, then in Canadian French. If I were in the Province of Quebec it would have been dictated with French above English. Quebec is the second-most populous province of Canada, after Ontario, and it is the only one to have a predominantly French-speaking population, with French as the sole provincial official language. Because I was in Ottawa, it read: *Canadian Tulip Festival – Festival canadien des tulipes*. To the right was a smaller sign indicating a concert venue line: *Evening Concert Ticket, Billet – concert individuel*; to the left lead to a different classification: *All Concert Pass – passe concerts*.

I packed light for this weekend trip, so I carried a duffel bag with some clean clothes and accompanied it with my camera bag which housed my Nikon F70. I really enjoyed taking photographs with that camera because it had a distinct panoramic option and capability, and although I hadn't learned to develop my own film it allowed me to sharpen my artistic eye so I could focus on taking my desired photo without the possibility of seeing my intended subject, through instant gratification. I attached a zoom lens, that allowed me to magnify beyond the silver barricades that protected the prized flowers and the grass they were planted on, from the public, so I could take pictures of the most beautiful and rich-colored orange, yellow, and red tulips I had ever seen.

Amid the well-manicured green fields of grass, in fresh-tilled dirt, were planted rows of vibrant-colored tulips, grouped in like hues, in rows of ten. The pink ones were the first to be contrasted against the forest green bushes along the perimeter while the rosy assortments were next to them. Rather than a linear display, they were more in an s-shaped formation, throughout parts in the park, with the next grouping having an orange and red symbiosis.

In the distance I could see the light green spire that hosted the country's red and white flag on its tip and glancing downward my eyes fixated on the tower clock which coincided with the time on my watch, as I looked to confirm – 4pm. The Peace Tower, also known as the Tower of Victory and Peace, is over three-hundred feet tall with an arrangement of stone carvings consisting of gargoyles, friezes, and grotesques in Victorian High Gothic style. The architecture of the Parliament pierced above the tree line and below, on the near meadow grounds, small crowds were forming and drawn to the outstanding and engaging petals of color. I took a conservative number of pictures, since the 35mm color print film only allowed me to take thirty-six on the roll I purchased. Kodak began to struggle financially in the late 1990s, as a result of the decline in sales of photographic film and its slowness in transitioning to digital photography, but I wasn't ready for the change yet.

I slowly turned the lens with my left hand to focus as I firmly held the camera with my right, ready to press the button with my index finger. *Click*. The Nikon strap was around my neck to support the weight of my camera obscura and to ensure that it would not fall or slip out of my hands and break. When I stood up, satisfied that I captured the depiction I wanted, another image of beauty captured my vision.

"Hi, Honey," she said as she also smiled at me.

I quickly smiled back as we instantly gave each other a warm and inviting hug. I hugged her again, tighter, and held her close with my left arm around her waist, pulling her closer, while I placed my other arm behind her upper left back. We kissed then held hands as we walked along and through fields of tulips, while making small talk of pleasantries, each word eliminating stress or worry from our everyday perceived troubles.

"You want to grab a cup of coffee? How's *Second Cup*? I see them all around. Any good?" I asked.

"Yeah. I'm not into having a second cup. After my first cup, I usually have tea. Did you want to check out a shawarma place?"

"Shawarma? What's that? Sounds like that bee thing problem you guys have."

"No. No. Shawarma is a Middle Eastern dish consisting of meat and they cut it into thin slices, put it into a cone-like stack, and roast it on a rotisserie. They have lamb, chicken, turkey, beef, or veal."

"Sounds like a gyro. I tried that once years ago. It was pretty good. Ok," I agreed.

Ottawa is a significant point of entry into Canada for immigrants from around the world and receives the highest percentage of refugees and family-related immigration of any major Canadian region. Because of the influx of the West Indian and Middle Eastern population, their culture and cuisines have invitingly increased and accepted, and their presence is less ersatz and are just as much a part of Canada, which increased my desire to try it.

During our walk, I thought of how often I heard many people say that Paris in the Spring was very romantic, but I think they got the wrong French-speaking country, as this moment was the epitome of a love stroll with great history and flowers, and a great woman by my side, not to mention that I have never been to the "City of Light", or France, for that matter. I asked her about her day, and she asked about my flight with a couple of lulls in between, none of which were uncomfortable.

It didn't matter where we dined, but as soon as we opened the front door and the burst of aromatic spices awakened my senses, I was ready to order one of everything but settled on a mixed shawarma pita wrap, and we shared a small order of falafels and poutine. It was a suitable place to unwind and catch up on the latest news and to continue our playful banter. These new experiences were fresh and flavorful, and it was nothing short of sharing them with each other and rolling with the punches. Soon after, we lit our cigarettes and walked back to her place, to also feed Clyde.

The next morning, unlike my last encounter with Rebecca and the bogus robbery, Paula and I had a cohesive and comprehensive discussion as to where my allegiance was, but she directed it with a sense of urgency and immediate decision. It felt like an ultimatum, because that's what it was. It was the "talk" that ultimately needs to happen in any relationship where one seeks growth and stability with one another. It was the dialogue that propelled us to determine and define who we were as a couple and if we would remain together, moving forward.

I wasn't officially divorced, neither one of us officially filed for one, and although Rebecca and I were separated and hadn't cohabitated for months, I felt the process to dissolve was taking too long for Paula. To be honest, I was deeply confused and unaware of the severity I was in. According to the Catholic Church, divorce was shunned and unheard of. I was thinking about how all those family members, friends, and guests who attended our wedding would be disappointed in our current circumstance – that it wasn't fair that such a couple would be divorcing, especially after having an amazing wedding ceremony and reception. I also felt shame. I didn't know anyone else who had gone through the divorce process, my parents were still married to each other, and I wasn't sure how to proceed. I was sickened about thinking of all my things that were destroyed and gone. I was subconsciously overwhelmed with anxiety and stress, and it was slowly coming out and no longer being suppressed.

I can see how Paula might think that there was a possibility that I was just using her as the mistress, the other woman, with no intention of leaving my wife, if she had insecurities. There was no commitment, no joint bank account or roommate situation, or even the serious talk about having children together. Because this was new to me, I didn't know how to proceed. I loved Paula.

"Coronado, I love being with you and the time we spend together. This long-distance relationship we have... I wish we could be together more, but you needed to make a decision."

"We're only a country apart, a short flight away, or just a seven-hour drive from each other, but I understand what you mean because I want to spend more time with you. It's just that I can't right now... with my job, with major transitions, plus I'm still married."

"It's too late for me to have children. I was at a crossroads when you came into my life and had a choice between you and someone else. I think I made the wrong choice."

"You made the right choice. I made that same decision and we're here now," I interjected.

She began doubting her decision even though, in my mind, what we were having was very real and worth experiencing. I was honored and sad at the same time – like I let her down, wasted her time, and maybe it was my fault. I didn't have all the answers, nor did I pretend to have cosmic clues. All I had was love and it was fleeting.

"Corey, I have all of your things gathered. I haven't taken anything of yours. I'm not like that. I even took your easel apart so that you can take it with you."

She packed up the easel she gave to me, but I encouraged her to keep it and to paint, since I no longer had the willingness, or room, to create anymore. My inspiration and desire to create artwork seemed fruitless, since it ultimately seems to dissolve.

"No. That's your easel. You use it to paint and create!" I insisted.

"If you need someone to protect your paintings, I will be more than willing to be its guardian!"

"Thank you! If there's a moment where my remaining paintings are in danger, I will ship them to you to protect. Keep all the artwork, I had already given you, here. They're yours!"

In a bag was "The Secret" painting and another still-life titled "Reflections". She also packed and gave me a tin Pisces capsule that had an image of two fishes on its top cover. I shook it and asked her what was inside.

"The leftover benzoin resin, since you loved it so much."

It was more like ashes after a cremation.

"I love you so much. Why don't you come with me?"

We hugged one last time.

I wasn't prepared to be taking any of my things back with me. I didn't suspect that this would be the end of us, but who I had become was metamorphosing into another form – heartbroken and betrayed. I didn't know what was expected of me, what I was supposed to say or do, but I wasn't going to continue a relationship with someone who doesn't want to wait for me any longer. Out of respect, she didn't want to live a lie or to continue being with a man who was still married, I walked the long dark corridor of her hallway towards the front door.

"When you walk out that door, I no longer want to see you again."

I hesitated. My hand slowly grabbed the knob and turned it. I looked back to see her once more. Everything I loved was in front of me. Despite my empty drawer, the collapsed easel and any physical thing that existed between us, it no longer mattered. I'm not entirely sure what was happening nor why, but she was clear with her words and I had to respect that *no* meant *no*. I held firmer grips on my bags and opened the door, took the step forward, and without looking back I closed the door behind me. I put the bags down on the carpet and breathed in a big sigh. At no point during my stall did I feel her come towards me, or the door, or feel like she wanted to resolve it in a different way. Perhaps I could have done more to persuade and convince her that we should be together. Maybe this and maybe that, but it was too late. Once in the hallway leading to the elevator, pressing the button, and patiently waiting for it, I sang an excerpt of "Save Me", to myself:

"... I will go so far away. I will always love you, but you knew..."

Chapter XIX – Crateful for Art

There are thinkers and there are doers, and most of the time I am both. In order to get merchandise and artwork to and from requires a reliable vehicle and space and I had neither – not for this project. Starting all over with no adequate funding for investments meant that I had to be resourceful and be more hands-on to be more cost-effective. I need to store valuable commodities of my clients to protect their original state of intention as no one is going to accept or purchase damaged goods, especially a canvased painting that is torn or warped in shape or a broken arm of a sculpture. I was in the business of safe handling and selling one-of-a-kind masterpieces.

I couldn't just cut stapled canvas paintings off from its wooden frames and roll them up in tubes and there aren't big enough bubble wrapped mailer envelopes to protect the integrity from bumps and dings, not with all the hands and machinery that it takes to process the package from one point to another, so I obviously needed a stronger barrier. With my extended experience working in warehouses and cargo facilities, there was only one plausible solution – wood.

I measured the measurements of Richard's twenty-seven paintings I intended to transport to Newark from Ottawa for its debut gallery showing, sizes from 8" x 10" to 20" x 24", and I applied all my mathematical applications to make sure I got it right. On July 7, 2004, I shipped the empty wooden crate I built and retrieved it at the cargo facility near the airport. Richard picked me up with his hand-painted and colorful van and off we went to his place.

Although I was successful in transporting his paintings and getting every one of them sold at a New York gallery, the journey just wasn't the same without being able to see Paula. It was strictly business and Rebecca made sure that my enterprise was shut down and dissolved, by cutting my funds and resources from the joint bank accounts we had, since she closed them all and kept it all. My contracts were fulfilled with Richard, and with the other artists I represented, but my trips to Canada soon ceased and I no longer had the drive nor desire to involve myself in creative endeavors again. I forgo the inspiration to make something only for it to be taken away or destroyed, like blowing bubbles in the wind – it eventually bursts, and no wand can immediately fix it. I allowed myself to be victimized and stripped of any power.

I was grateful for the opportunities to have been able to snap and take photographs, to have applied a brush and painted on canvas, and the ability to express myself freely – maybe too freely – for the sake of self-discovery and evolvement. I dared to venture off in foreign lands, to see the possibility of greener pastures and the other side of the fence, and the fortitude to try new things. I was a creator and somewhat of a maintainer, but not a great sustainer. As I walked up the steps to the US Post Office, on 69 Montgomery St, in Jersey City, to pick up the last of my company mail before I closed out the mailbox, I heard Cher's "Believe" playing from a car as it was waiting for the light to change. I didn't know what to believe anymore. I whistled the tune and it echoed inside the great chamber of the edifice, and when I finally opened PO Box 282, there was but one parcel – a card from Ottawa, Canada. A card from her.

Chapter XX – State of Mind

In self-preservation and to minimize mental anguish, I needed to get away not only from the low-vibrational anxieties and thoughts, but from my environment. A co-worker had recently brought in a real estate magazine from a recent trip, one found on an exit rack of a supermarket, and I flipped through its pages to see the different styles of houses in Houston, Texas. Some were very spacious with a selection of amenities, and when I looked at the prices, I was a bit confused.

"Greg, there's something wrong with this book. They're missing some zeroes. It's too cheap."

"The cost of living there is lower. They're building and developing everywhere and so there's a lot of competition. My wife and I were furniture shopping and they had a free BBQ in the parking lot. It's like they're giving everything away."

"Wow. Good promotions and marketing. Why isn't everyone moving to Houston?" I asked.

"It's too damn hot, but we loved it. We're thinking about moving there."

I had been passed up a couple of times for a promotion at my job. Employed at a major airline for five years, I worked hard and applied for a leadership role as a supervisor. The only two people who put in for it was me and a guy from Boston, and so they gave it to him. Later, I found out he was a brother-in-law of the director of our department. Such is life – I put in a transfer request to Houston,

TX, and the proposed answer to my prayers were underway for possible advancement.

When I returned from Ottawa, that May in 2004, I met with Rebecca at our old apartment to tell her that I was going to file for a divorce so that we could move on with our lives, but she had other plans. She pleaded and begged that she wanted children, and I told her that children would not save our marriage. She started to cry and get melodramatically emotional, but seemingly sincere.

"Please! I want children. I want your children! I don't want them from anyone else. Please!"

She went down on her knees, clasping her hands in a prayer-like fashion. My love for love and being able to provide and help someone superseded my ability to think that she was being insincere. We were already married, and it was a precursor to having children, according to our traditional faiths, so I obliged, and we tried to work things out.

Rebecca and I had then reconciled and when I requested to work at our main hub at the George Bush Intercontinental Airport location in 2005, our daughter was already a little over three months old. The paperwork, from what I had been told by others who transferred from our Newark Airport location, should have taken about two months to process and complete, so it was an immense shock to hear from Administration two weeks later that I only had two days to respond because they needed employees to fill their vacant positions due to steady growth and company needs.

Sacrificing nurturing time with my family, I accepted the transfer and got my foot in the door on the entry level, working my way up from the bottom again. After several months I applied for the then-posted supervisor position and was fortunate enough to get the role and finalize that ambition. Using my flight benefits, I was able to visit and travel every other weekend back to Jersey and a couple of times, my wife came to visit me at the apartment I was renting. I was gaining the momentum and stability expected of me and I was looking to provide, in my marriage and for my family. I was focused on our current values and for the most part it was halcyon without distraction, until I met the next messenger on my spiritual journey.

Theresa was a veteran supervisor who worked the graveyard shift and so I hadn't much, if any, interaction with her. She was filling in for Tom, who went on vacation to Mexico for a week, but she had no problem maintaining the operation considering she was very knowledgeable and well-respected by all team members, especially those employees who benefitted from her generous gestures of hosting Friday evening pot-lucks. She even purchased a couple of frozen whole turkeys and donated them to agents who were less fortunate during the Thanksgiving holiday.

Theresa walked into the cargo facility from inspecting the backyard and approached me while I accessed the nearest computer in the warehouse to verify the manifest for a full-capacity flight to the Charles De Gaulle airport in Paris.

"Howdy. You came down here to meet me. I'm Theresa."

I wasn't entirely sure what she meant by that, so I just listened and waited for clarification since first impressions were considered critical and long-lasting, and we just met as colleagues in a professional setting. The conversations we had were not considered popular and perhaps due to our proximity within the Bible belt and its unwillingness to bend on their own beliefs, our topics were ineffable to avoid scrutiny.

"That was the message I'm supposed to give you. It's nice to finally meet you. Welcome," she continued. It was still slightly vague, but I was pretty sure I knew what she meant.

Over time, she revealed to me that she was also a Reiki healer and I felt her energy whenever she poised her hands around me, transferring and guiding her vibrations and frequency, until the minor aches and tension on my shoulders were dispelled. She told me about an instance where she was on a full flight to Seattle and felt intuitively, or from an inner voice, that she needed to give the man sitting next to her, in the tight middle seat, a message. They periodically rubbed shoulders together especially when he dozed off for minutes at a time. For the entire three-hour flight, she was conflicted with speaking to this stranger, especially with the specific message she had for him. When they landed and he got up to get his luggage from the overhead compartment, she was compelled to tell him.

"Hey. You need to have your heart checked out immediately. Your left ventricle is blocked, and a heart attack is most probable."

"Thank you. It's been weighing on my mind whether to see my doctor, or not. I will."

It wasn't the response she expected but apparently, she learned to trust her instinct and be the messenger, when she is called to do so. Even though she was forty years older than me, we got along rather well. She was a very strong and focused woman, determined to live positively and in the present, and our spirits and energy were somehow connected on the same life path and journey.

She attracted positivity and practiced what she professed and introduced me to Rhonda Byrne's "The Secret", in 2006. I tried to read it three times but kept falling asleep throughout. While she continued lending me the book, she also talked to me about Sylvia Browne, the psychic who made television appearances and episodes on *The Montel Williams Show*. As a visual person, these books and shows were a good way for me to stay actively engaged in these spiritual matters.

On a weekend, she invited me over for coffee and homemade banana bread, and when she gave me the "nickel-tour" of her one-story house, I noticed the geodes, her massive collection of coffee mugs on tops of her kitchen cabinets and some stocked in their shelves, and a 16" x 20" painting of an interesting Native American man on the wall in the living room.

"Who is that?"

"That's Remzem. He's my Spirit Guide."

"Whoa! That's amazing. I wish I had one, and if I did, I'd like to meet him."

"You have three, and they just wait around for you to ask them something. One of them taps their foot, with patience. I met an artist in New Mexico who painted him for me."

"New Mexico, huh? Never been."

"That's where you're going to find your Healing Center. You'll love it. Ruidoso is beautiful."

"Where do you get your information from, Theresa? Does it just flow?"

"Yeah. Sometimes I don't know what I'm saying because the message needs to come out, you see. Stay in the now. Be present. Don't worry about the future and forgive the past. All we have is now. Trust in the Universe. In my past life I was Thaddeus – a disciple of Jesus, and in another life, I was a famous Opera singer and you were my brother."

Theresa didn't seem delusional at all to me. She was a respected leader at work, was in great physical shape, and consistent with her teachings. I didn't doubt her, but I also couldn't prove her statements either way, so I took it at face-value and accepted her messages. I sort of envied her ability to know these things about herself, if they were indeed true, because if I knew it to be true about myself, then it would provide an organon towards my origin story.

One evening, towards the end of my shift, I went upstairs to the offices, and my cubicle, to prepare a shift report to send via email to the rest of the team. Theresa walked in to begin her evening a few cubes down.

"Here's a couple of more books you need to read," she said when she walked over and handed them to me in a brown paper bag.

"I'm gonna need to get some more book markers," I laughed as I took them out of the bag, until I read its titles and then author name. I was flabbergasted, then I read them aloud.

"*Way of the Peaceful Warrior* and *The Life You Were Born to Live*, both by Dan Millman. Thank you so much!"

I never told her about my visit to Minneapolis or of JJ and her book recommendations, so I just took it as a cool coincidence maybe due to the popularity of these publications, and for good measure when I made it to my car to head back home that night, I pulled out the card from the wallet to confirm that they were the remaining two books written on the back of the card.

One afternoon after conducting a Shift Briefing, Pedro approached me to the side and asked me if I was a Master Mason. Although he was integral part of the team, I didn't know him personally or what his affiliations were outside of the job, so his question confused me. I noticed he was wearing a gold chain with a "G" symbol I had randomly seen on men and some of their rings.

"No, sorry. I'm not."

"Oh, because some of the ways you stand or move your hands are familiar," he explained.

He, by no means, was soliciting my membership, and I thought about how I sometimes talk with my hands in a form of creative expression. We shook hands and he went off to his department.

A short couple of months after that, Theresa asked me if I would like to go to Sedona, to check out the landscape. She was stationed in Arizona at a nearby base when she was in the military, so she was familiar with the climate and comfortable dry heat, compared to Houston's humidity. We planned the trip around our mutual time off and the flight was only less than three hours away to Phoenix. When we landed, we rented a car and drove the forty-five minutes to one of the most scenic and earthy regions this country had to offer.

Passing majestic crests of ascending and descending colorful rock formations, I was enamored by its beauty and arrays of red sandstone. The steadily rising sun illuminated the brilliant orange and red formations and appeared to be as smooth as the road Theresa was driving us through, sometimes winding around in a snake-like formation. Random Kokopelli art images were perfectly scattered along the way, some just dancing but most were playing their flutes. A helicopter slowly hovered and navigated above while its passengers soaked in aerial views on their scenic tour.

"Sedona is a magical place. Do you feel it?" she asked me.

"Yes. Unlike any other," I responded.

"Houston is not your final-destination. It's just a stepping-stone," she revealed.

I felt less committed after hearing that. I didn't want to plant strong roots if it was only temporary, hang any photos or paintings on the wall if I would just be taking them down, and I wondered where I would be going next. We passed through small shops along the road, mostly those selling original artwork of southwest and Native American culture.

"Sedona picks and chooses who stays and goes, according to the energy. Some of these shops have been here a long time. Others have gone; they didn't fit – didn't belong."

Less than an hour later, she pulled into a parking lot of a small strip mall that occupied three quaint stores. Surrounding trees supplied ample cover for shade from the sun and the first thing I heard when I opened the passenger car door were the sounds of wind chimes, activated by a calming breeze, neatly hung under the canopy near the front entrance door to a mystical shop – *The Mystic Eye.*

"I love this place. Let's check it out."

I was taking it all in, unaware and unafraid of the unknown in a new place and State. I was out of my element, or was I always in it but never fully aware? I followed her lead as she was my guide.

Theresa and I had a four-thirty appointment with Margaret. She read Theresa's cards the last time she was here and was accurate over a year ago, enough to recommend and convince me to fly to Arizona to reveal hidden truths. It was only a few minutes past four, so she and I split up after being greeted by an employee at the front entrance register, and I started to peruse the shop in all its wonder. It contained every type of item I usually find in a gem and mineral store, and more.

Two ladies were looking at the jewelry section where the rings and birthstones were colorfully combined in their showcase enclosed glass. I walked towards a three-foot tall geode that was illuminating in purple and white amethyst crystals, in the corner, and placed my hand near it to feel its warmth and energy, and it recharged me giving me strength and vitality like plugging into a battery to recapitulate my cells. The smell of frankincense from the nearby cone incense soothed me, giving me a sense of calm and peace.

"Let me know if you need anything," a young helpful woman with her hair in a unique gem-crafted barrette stated. Although she didn't wear a name tag or uniform, I was certain she was an employee there. I just smiled at her in affirmation.

There was a vast variety of incense sticks and cones, and their holders, and I picked a few of them up to sniff and figure out which ones would appeal to my senses, and although I enjoyed most of them I only automatically picked one out for purchase – benzoin. I took in a deep inhalation whilst closing my eyes. *Whiff.*

"Hey... check out this beauty, huh?"

Theresa showed me the clear quartz she just purchased. Cylindrical in shape, it was approximately three inches long and looked majestic.

"Pretty neat, right? I can't let you touch it because I don't want to mix the energies. They cleansed it for me – put it in sea salt and it was already smudged."

I was already familiar with smudging. She told me that it was practiced by some Native Americans and it involves the burning of scared herbs, like sage or sweet grass, in some cases for spiritual cleansing or blessing.

"Quartz is the most powerful healing stone, helps relieve pain, and this one is a stone of power and radiates energy," she continued.

"Nice! I should go and check out their crystal collection."

The first thought of crystals reminds me of a television show in the early seventies when Marshall, Will, and Holly went on a "routine expedition" and plunged down a thousand feet below to the *Land of the Lost*[13]. Reptilian and humanoid beings – the Sleestak, and dinosaurs prevent the family from accessing the crystals found in caves, that would help them go back home. Interestingly, different

---

[13] *Land of The Lost*, (1974–1976) is a children's adventure television series produced by Sid and Marty Krofft

colored crystals emit and cause various reactions when brought in contact with each other. The television series came on once a week on Saturday mornings and it was the first time I was introduced to the idea and concept that crystals had supernatural powers. An image of a Kokopelli creature flashed in my mind and I asked myself if I entered the land of the lost, as I am here in search of truths because, perhaps, I am lost.

Soon after being exposed to that concept, a movie came out in 1978 and introduced a dying planet where a crystal is prominently seen in the beginning, and Jor-El plucks the mythical green crystal from a nest of hollow crystals and places it in the infant Kal-El's pod before jettisoning his son away from danger, into space and ultimately to the safety of Earth. This kryptonite is an alien material that has the capability of depriving Superman of his powers, but further lead me to believe that crystals had great powers and significance.

"Black obsidian helps to reveal truth. It's smooth and it blocks negativity. I carry one in my pocket all the time. It helps to relieve mental stress and tension."

"I'll check it out. I can't have too many things in my pocket. My pants will fall down," I joked.

"Better to release weight off your shoulders than to put all of that weight in your pants. I'll buy you a new belt."

There were so many things to look at. They had a good selection of angelic figurines, tarot cards, incense, and literature, and it was interesting to browse the aisles.

"Have you ever had your aura taken? C'mon."

We had another ten minutes before our readings, so we asked for a photographer to assist us on taking my photo, in another room, and when the woman with the barrette came, I was excited but didn't really know why. I saw images on the wall, of previous photos of people surrounded by different colors of light, along with Chakra charts.

"Do you use different filters for the colors?" I genuinely asked.

"This camera will take a photo of your electromagnetic field, like a pic of your inner self."

"Like a mood ring?"

"Better. This deals with your chakras, and each one reveals a particular aspect of your personality specific to you."

"Cool. Let's do it!"

When it was over and the film was developed, Theresa helped to break down what it meant for me.

"It's really dark, Coronado. You really need to lighten up," she said with a smile. She knew how to put me at ease, especially when things aren't so hunky-dory.

"Pink denotes the energy of love and passion, and all the positivity that comes with it. Red is connected to your first chakra – the root of your being that establishes your deepest connections with your body and the Earth. You're not yet grounded enough with all the things you've been through. Things like shelter, safety, food and letting go of any fear. You don't have those colors here. You have a lot of dark greens and some yellow. No blue means communication is nil and is connected to your throat chakra."

Margaret's door opened and when she saw Theresa and me, she greeted us.

"Hi! Good to see you. I'll be back in a moment."

Off she went to the Ladies room, and Theresa handed me the aura depiction and was thrilled for me that I had it done.

"We can talk about it some more after the readings and I can show you mine when we get back to Houston."

"Sounds good. Thanks. I'm a little nervous about the reading."

"It'll be fine. She's really good."

Chapter XXI – Jack of Clubs

I have been surrounded by many mystics throughout my life, all of whom were part of my underground experiences since my belief in mysticism, especially in Catholicism, and was verboten or at least shunned. I had already heard about the Salem witch trials in the 1690s where women were hanged or burned during Colonial America's mass hysteria, concerning religious extremism, false accusations, and isolationism. There is usually one mystic that may be involved in an art festival or a venue where open-mindedness is encouraged, but for the most part, it just isn't a common mainstream practice.

Without an appointment and as a walk-in, I took my chances on the waiting time since I was already in the general area, so it was opportune to take advantage and test my luck. I opened the door to the *Sabio Botanica*, in Houston, and trusted that my Spanish would get me in the next set of doors. The storefront was in the middle of a block in a residential neighborhood, and if I drove by it fast enough, I might miss it. I was referred and recommended to this place by my friend, Felicia, who lived in a vicinal town and is bilingual, but translators were not permitted because the energies of other people in the room might mix, plus the concept of privacy was regarded, so I came and ventured in alone.

There was a bell above the front door and it chimed when I opened it, and although the chairs to my left were empty and there was no one behind the counter, a large ceramic statue of the St. Michael Archangel with his raised sword about to smote Lucifer, somehow was all the security they initially needed if an employee wasn't present to greet a customer. Behind the counter, on a strong shelf, were other large statuettes of religious and saintly representatives.

"Buenas dias," a woman said as she was coming from a back room.

"Buenas dias," I replied.

"¿Cómo puedo ayudarte?"

"Quiero saber si hay alguien que pueda leer mis cartas."

Asking for a fortune teller to read my cards isn't illegal but she gave me this look of apprehension and discernment that almost had me doubt myself whether I said something offensive, unconventional, or just plain inappropriate. There isn't an extreme difference between Mexican and Puerto Rican dialect, granted I don't fit any mold of categorizing myself as looking Hispanic, or maybe I was juxtaposed to her reality. She excused herself and went to the back room but this time, upon returning, she was accompanied by an older woman.

"Hola. Buenas. How can I help you?"

"Hi. I'm looking for someone to read my cards."

I don't refer to them as Tarot Cards since there are so many different decks, and Tarot refers to a particular type of cards that were primarily used from the fifteenth century in various parts of Europe to play games such as Italian tarocchini, French tarot, and Austrian Königrufen. My preferred method for gaining insight into the realm of mysticism, as a method of communication, is the use of cards and I find the artwork to be stunning and creative.

She invited me to the back room where she does conduct her readings, and it wasn't a showroom of two lit candles and a crystal ball such as the setting found in the presence of Professor Marvel[14] in his traveling coach. She asked me to kindly sit on the other side of her wooden table as she answered a quick phone call. I looked around and scanned the room, and although it was bright and clean like an operating room, I wasn't nervous. It was solely a consultation, and there was always room for a second, third, or a fifth opinion if I didn't believe or like what I heard. Only time will tell if she is a charlatan as the Professor was, so with many of my readers, I do not divulge much personal information about myself, to prevent possibly having it used to manipulate me.

When she hung up the call, she apologized and asked me what I had questions about, but I didn't specifically have one. When I remained pensive and silent, she carried the conversation.

"¿De dónde eres?"

"Nueva Jersey."

"Ah. Soy de allí – North Bergen. But my English isn't that great, but I'll do my best to help you understand."

"Thank you!" I said in relief.

She shuffled a deck I have never seen before, simpler with cartoonish figures, then cut the deck and started to flip them over.

"What kind of business do you do? What's your job?"

---

[14] *Professor Marvel*, a character portrayed by Frank Morgan in the 1939 film – *The Wizard of Oz*

I somewhat felt a wee bit interrogated and that my answers would taint the validity of an honest read, but at this point I just went along with it to see where it would go.

"Me botaron, after ten years with the airlines. Now I own a coffee company."

With her forefinger, she rubbed her left arm up and down a couple of times, so that I wouldn't lose much in translation.

"You are going to meet a man with your same skin color."

I naturally tan and have somewhat of olive color skin. She paused and looked at me, puzzled, wondering how she should proceed.

"Are you into anything else? It's ok to be open and honest about it."

"No. That's it."

You are safe here. There's only the three of us in this room."

The three of us? There was only the two of us that I could see.

"Tu, yo, y El," she explained.

She nudged her chin behind me to my left and there was a bust of the head of Jesus Christ staring at us. I was relieved, amused, and concerned all at the same time.

"I'm innocent. I haven't done anything wrong," I confirmed.

"This man wants to put something in your coffee. I think it's something illegal, and he's going to use the help from a darker-skin man – un moreno."

I immediately thought of how coffee was used to disguise the smell of drugs and perhaps I would be shipping large quantities of my product, along with their cargo, but also be in cahoots with these mystery men.

"No. I don't think so. I don't know anyone like that. Don't know."

She rattled off a couple of more scenarios and story lines that didn't make sense or seem important enough for me to remember. She collected the card spread and regrouped them to reshuffle and start a new reading.

"Are you married?"

Again, it was too much info to divulge but I had to go with it.

"Divorced."

"You have two beautiful daughters."

That was a hit. She looked at me and stopped to gather her thoughts, as if there would be no other in my life as good as Rebecca.

"You don't really care about new relationships. Why don't you just go back with your ex-wife? Woman are just about all the same, so just stick with her."

I had already gone back to my ex-wife after leaving Paula, and it didn't last long after that, hence her becoming an ex-wife. I got the feeling that she saw no hope for someone new in my life, not anyone better than Rebecca, but I knew she wasn't an option. I took her reading in stride and went on my way, and as usual I went over the questions and answers, statements, and recommendations in my head repeatedly in case I missed something.

About three or four months later, I joined a multi-level marketing (MLM) team that also sold coffee. Being mentored by Geraldo and Bernard, I soon learned that what separated this brand of coffee from all the others is that it was infused with Ganoderma, a genus of polypore fungi used in traditional Asian medicines, into the blend of the product, so in essence it was mixed with the coffee. Were these the two that she saw putting something into the coffee? In my naivety, although my business was lucrative in the beginning, it was short-lived because I didn't believe in the ethics of the pyramid scheme, and as far as reconciling with Rebecca, I felt those days are long gone, and that three was a crowd.

In another instance, a co-worker wanted to visit a local Tarot reader that resided in a trailer park off the side of a main road but didn't want to go alone. With all the issues and challenges that she was facing in her life, I recommended that she go and hear what they have to say, however since I've never been there myself, I was vouching for readings, in general. Like a car mechanic, it is hard to find a great card reader. She smoked a Marlboro Red in the parking lot before we walked in, and because she was nervous and apprehensive, I assured her that it would be fine and that it could only help and not hurt to go.

Once inside, we were led through someone's living room into a den area where there was a wooden table and two chairs. Before I could take a seat, I was asked to leave because she was ready to get read, and when she was finished she hinted that I should go next but the reader said that it wasn't necessary because I already knew the answers to my questions. My dilemma was that I don't follow my intuition more and persist on needing to hear the answers I seek for confirmation and affirmation. I knew what she meant so I decided to leave and save myself the money I would have spent on the consultation.

"How did it go?" I asked her.

"Good. She told me a lot of specific stuff that no one else knows. It was like she knew my story."

"Cool. So, it was worth it?"

"Yes. She told me to light this candle and wash myself in this oil to cleanse all my bad energies away."

Maybe that's why she insisted that I leave and why she separated us – so that I wouldn't discourage her from being upsold to buy all these extra products of protection she probably didn't need. If it helps her and gives her peace of mind – fine! I never really met a card reader who I thought was deceiving me or making things up. Unlike clairvoyants, readers are looking at the cards and somehow you can follow along and see where they could be getting their predictions, but with clairvoyants they would either need to exactly or specifically tell me something from my past or I would need to wait for their prediction to come true later on, for me to truly believe them.

My favorites are the ones that have been counseling or guiding my close friends or family members for a long time, and they are referred and vouched by them, such as with Julia. Julia is a family friend who often attends our family functions and get-togethers. She is a wonderful woman who enjoys life and the simple pleasures that are bestowed to her through gratitude and humility. I had no idea that she read cards for years, until a good neighbor of ours went through a difficult and challenging time and was mentioned that she was confiding with Julia for guidance.

Since then, I would periodically trek into Julia's neighborhood without an appointment, ring the bell of the multi-family apartment building and hope that she is there to consult me in some grey areas or curiosities that I might have. When I was buzzed in, I could smell fried pork chops from the main hallway lobby and could hear crying children from the stairwell that led upstairs. Luckily, Julia lived on the first floor and she opened the door.

"Mira quién está allí," she said with a welcoming smile, "Entre. Entre."

She was adorable at 4'10" tall and she had a short buzz haircut and a grand smile. She only spoke Spanish, but I had to trust that the messages that I needed to hear, I would understand. I sat in the living for about ten minutes until she finished with a previous guest in her room, so I entertained myself by watching a Spanish talk show that was already in progress on her television. Down a long corridor, at the end of her hallway, was the room where she operated out of, and I like it because it was her dedicated office, and not a common thru-room area.

It had a gold metal twin day bed to the left as soon as I walked in and the main fold-out table was by the window straight ahead. There were statutes of Saint Lazarus, a couple of the Virgin Mary, Saint Raphael, and other figurines I didn't recognize. I wasn't intimidated because she was detailed on her readings in the past, but the more I went to see her I felt that she sometimes used what information she already knew of me to build on the story. She would often refer other close friends' scenarios and how it could concern me, as if we were all playing out a novela that only she was watching, because the others would also see her.

She used the brisca cards, just like my grandmother's deck, so it also brought a sense of familiarity – an indication of old school methods, since I admired the artwork on them, especially the coins.

The spread was different from a Celtic Cross formation. She laid them out in four rows of six and crisscrossed and picked and chose from all over the place relaying a story that made sense to me every time. Whenever she mentioned my parents' involvement it would almost always come true. As a bonus, in the end, should would give me a three-digit number to consider playing in the lottery. I would never play because I do not gamble, and the number would eventually come out within three days.

So now, with all the different decks I have had Readers use throughout my lifetime, and with all the new ones in production that I have seen on shelves of mystic shops like this one, I was curious to see Margaret's choice of cards and to witness her interpretation. Teresa didn't mind that I sat next to her during her reading. We sat in separate chairs next to each other facing Margaret behind her big wooden desk. She had a small clutter of gems, stones, books, and stationery, but our views weren't obstructed.

She was an older woman with flowing blonde hair and eyeglasses that had chain lanyard attachments on each side, perhaps to prevent her from losing or misplacing them since they wouldn't leave her neck. She wore a royal blue blazer with slacks and looked like an ordinary woman who was casually dressed in business attire. She held on to a pen, or a type of writing tool that also served as a pointer, in her right hand, and interpreted many of Theresa's scenarios with her left. None of my co-worker's story lines made sense to me, as it didn't pertain to me, but I wasn't confused with her insightful messages according to the cards, I was simply perplexed that she was using a normal deck of playing cards.

When they were finished, and it was finally my turn, she asked me what my birthday was and after I revealed it she quickly flipped some pages of a thick yellow book that displayed different colorful patterns of the four suits on its cover. Unfortunately, I couldn't see the title since she closely guarded its contents and secrets.

"You are a Jack of Clubs," she revealed.

"Hi, Jack!" Theresa said, "I'm a Queen of Clubs."

"Great! What does that mean?" I asked them both, whereby Margaret began to explain.

"Cards weren't just an instrument for Jesters of the Court to amuse Kings and Queens, hundreds of years ago. They were used by astrologers to calculate and decipher a blueprint for the solar calendar. Fifty-two cards equates with the fifty-two weeks in a year, the four suits equates to the four seasons, and if you add up all the cards in the deck you get three hundred sixty-four, plus the Joker is three hundred sixty-five – the number of days in a year."

"Fascinating," I blurted.

"Now, depending on the day you were born, you are a specific card in the deck. According to your birthday, you are the Jack of Clubs."

"Ok, so, what does that mean?" I naturally asked.

"Jacks of Clubs are creative and youthful energies and are one of the most mentally creative cards in the deck. All Jacks are creative and persuasive but can also be irresponsible or plainly dishonest. I can decipher and tell you what tests you were going through, throughout your youth and what you will be facing in your future."

"Wow. How can you know all of that?"

"Every fifty-two days, and there are seven a year, we all go through a theme or a test. Did you ever have a winning streak or a period when something was consistent? Most people don't realize that there is a common thread that occurs. Anyway, there are seven fixed days where each person's life cycle changes – the first one starts on your birthday, but your Birth Card is and will always be the Jack of Clubs."

Margaret gave me a weekly reading and further explained that, according to the card, I will either experience an event with a person who is that specific card, or experience the energy equated with the card, on each day. For example, if a Queen of Clubs is drawn on the sixth row, Friday – since the reading begins on a Sunday, I will most likely be in contact with Theresa more than any of the other days, because she is a Queen of Clubs. If I do not meet her, I will most likely be organizing, nurturing, or being intuitive because that is the nature of that card. Because I was just being exposed to this esoteric knowledge, anything further would be an overload to digest.

I was mesmerized with my reading, even though I couldn't see the title of that mysterious book. I didn't understand whose card was what, but I was certainly intrigued, and it further elevated my quest for knowledge. It had me thinking that there was an outlined path, or set of things I must go through, in specific times in some sort of mystical pattern, and that maybe I never had a choice in my decisions. That's where my next conundrum occurred. Do I really have free will, or is my life ordained for a processed purpose?

Chapter XXII – Proposal

Because I was two years older than my sister and we attended one of the best private Catholic schools in our urban city, it was a bit lucky and convenient for me to get along with some of her friends. I once asked her classmate Veronica, who lived about twenty minutes away in the Heights, out on a date and we went to the opening showing of *Goodfellas* in Secaucus, NJ. I remember waiting in a long line outside the theater booth surrounded by couples in suits and dresses as if we were going to a party or a family gathering. I leaned over to her and thanked her for coming out with me to a crowded venue like this. When we finally got our seats, we sat near the left rear corner of the theater, and when the lights dimmed out, there was a strong sense of excitement because I heard the applause when the show was about to begin. As I looked at the left row floor in front of me towards the screen, I could see a couple of tall brown bags. They weren't the ones for cans of coke or beer but taller, for wine. About thirty minutes into the show cigars were lit but somehow it didn't bother anyone. This was a non-smoking theater, yet no one seemed disrupted or inconvenienced by the subtle puffs of smoke.

Lastly, in one of the great scenes in the film before Henry laughs at Tommy during the "How am I funny" scene, Pesci's character mentions being in the middle of the weeds while on a bank job in Secaucus. There was a thunderous roar, laugh, and appreciation that he mentioned the city in which we were currently in. I felt connected, involved and in a culture that I belonged. That was the best-ever hands-down opening to a memorable film I had ever attended, and I don't think Veronica would ever forget it either.

Joanne also lived in the Heights, about two blocks north of her friend Veronica, and she was fun to be with too. We would often walk over to Leonard Gordon Park on Manhattan Ave and play tennis. That was actively fun, different for me, and energetic. Afterward, at times, I enjoyed walking with her around the buffalo and bear sculptures and along the hilly and shady walking paths. We would walk back to her house and see her younger brother and sister playing on the front porch, her mom would be cooking dinner inside and we would hang outside until her father came home. He was a Sergeant of the Jersey City police force and was rather cool with me since he didn't act surprised or overly concerned with me being around his daughter. He even offered me a beer a couple of times but I'm sure it was just a trick. We would all come in and relax on the couch in the living room and just hang out. I enjoyed and respected this family unit because they welcomed and respected me.

My sister was on the high school basketball team and I would often go to her games and check them out, but that's when I started to get interested in her friend Eva. She was probably one of the very few on the team that had "poofy" curly hair on her head, as what seemed to be the style with all the girls in Jersey, during our current time in the 80s. Eva was athletic and had a nice firm body, but around this time I started to really think about my relationships with girls. I did not want my sister to think that the only reason her friends started to hang out with her was because of me. I enjoyed being with them and discovering my unique attractions to each of them, but I realized that I couldn't be with all three of my sister's friends, also because they were friends with each other as well. I decided that I couldn't continue dating or even seek boyfriend/girlfriend status with either one of them because it would hurt the friendships we already had. My commitment issues were coming into fruition again and, unfortunately, it became worse than that when I ignorantly started to ignore them and the girls stopped talking to my sister, as well.

I have not been the best brother and have ruined relationships with my sister and her friends. Out of the five of her friends that I had dated, she is still friends with one. Twenty percent is better than zero, but I must admit I need to work on being a better brother and a better person to my sister. I love Gloria, and I don't tell her enough. *Love you, Sis.*

I noticed another one of my sister's friends from her high school. She had long brown hair, wore a burgundy dress and a nice sweater. I think her name was Rebecca. She came to the house once to visit my sister for something, and when she left, I asked Gloria who she was, but she told me that she had a boyfriend and that she wouldn't be interested in me. That was her way of involving herself and not allowing me the opportunity to do any more damage with her friends. I professed to Gloria that "she was the one I was going to marry."

I let it go and hadn't seen her visit the house for a long while, but then one fine afternoon the doorbell rang, and it was her – Rebecca. I opened the door and welcomed her to come in, but she didn't even look at me; she just hurriedly walked in and spoke to my sister, who was in the kitchen and already on her way to the door. She asked Gloria if she knew any places that installed tinting for car windows, and she told her that I knew a few places and that she should ask me. Well, she did and we were off to Union City in her car to get it tinted, and on our way there she took JFK Blvd which wasn't the quickest route there but it gave us a chance to listen to the *3rd Bass* song – "Brooklyn Queens", on the radio. I saw the car repair shop designated on a triangular island in front of Roosevelt Stadium, and they were open for business. It hadn't taken more than an hour for the job to be completed by two Dominicans I knew, but in the meantime, she and I just talked and got to know each other a little bit in their waiting area. That was the first time we ever had a real conversation, and I was rather sad that her car was completed and that it was time for her to go, but we dated exclusively for a couple of years since then, and even lived in the same building in the illustrious and historical Paulus Hook section in Downtown, Jersey City.

We couldn't wait to be seated at Zesti's to hear the daily specials later that evening. It had only been three in the afternoon, and I wanted to tour parts of the city before we became more comfortable throughout dinner and beyond. Rebecca had no idea about my wanting to venture off with her; I just wanted to do something different, and we weren't doing anything around the apartment anyway.

The doorbell rang, and it was one of her friends, Stacey. Her grandmother, Ms. Wasniewski, had been living next door to us in her apartment for nearly thirty years, and she carried her groceries herself every week up two flights of stairs. She was a very strong-willed woman despite that just a few years back, she was struck by an ambulance and did not sustain any permanent injuries. Stacey was visiting her grandmother but decided to say hello to us for a few.

We were celebrating our anniversary date on Tuesday, August 8, 1995, and we wanted to spend as much time together as we could, but it seemed that we couldn't escape from our bustles until a quarter to five. After saying goodbye to Stacey, we met at the top of the steps and when we reached the bottom of our ten-step descent, she veered to the right in the direction of the restaurant, but I dissuaded her.

"We still have time. Let's go for a walk along the waterfront."
We walked along the shady street until we saw the back of the Colgate clock, proceeded to walk along the paved path along Greene Street that lead us to the Waterway Ferry which would in turn take us across the Hudson River into Battery Park. The ferry was coming towards the Jersey side so I suggested we walk a little quicker so we could check it out.

"Since we're here we might as well take a ferry ride. It shouldn't take long."
I ran into the trailer which served as the ticket sales office, and immediately purchased two round-trip tickets. The passengers had disembarked, and we boarded and climbed the stairs to get a topside view of the Hudson and the two skylines. A gentle breeze patted our faces as we held hands and enjoyed the view of the Statue of Liberty and Ellis Island off in the not-so-distant horizon. Other boats and its passengers were enjoying the warm, August evening and within ten

minutes we had reached the shore and disembarked unto Battery Park.

She knew that we were in New York, but she had never been in this part of town. Cobblestone steps welcomed us to a distinct, yet warm landscape with light posts, trees, benches and a small boat yard. Skaters and those rolling blading brought a vibrant feel to the environment, and executives and their office personnel had been enjoying the open bar advantages outside in their designated café tables. A professional businesswoman had been enjoying herself with her colleagues, and I could hear her laughing in the background. She wore a nice red dress with gold jewelry which complimented her skin and brown hair. A flock of gregarious men gathered around her, and each of them were wearing tailored suits and looked uncanny.

"So, this is how the other side lives," I joked.

Rebecca and I walked around and along the rail, to keep a view of the water and to notice everyday life as with the grandmother and granddaughter feeding bread to the pigeons from their black wrought-iron bench, next to the *Please do not Feed the Wildlife* sign. We continued to hold hands as we approached a large statue of what looked to be of a bull. It probably had to do with the markets since being bullish meant being optimistic. We ventured on further into the unknown and two blocks away from us were the "Twin Towers".

"Since we're here we should stop and check out the World Trade Center. C'mon."

It had only been about five twenty, and we were working up our appetites. Black limousines and car service vehicles were becoming prevalent, and the mood altogether suggested that this area was congested. After crossing a freeway and a short distance afterwards, we came upon the World Trade Center. When I opened the lobby doors, the refreshing air conditioning hit us, and we didn't mind it. One of the security guards had a tape playing from his cassette player which I recognized to be Beethoven's "Pathetique" Sonata, a classical piano piece which I enjoyed immensely. The ivory keys cleverly jolted feeling into my soul and precluded my surreal visit to this famous building and further uplifted my mood.

"Let's walk around. Maybe we could find the way to the top?"

"That sounds good. Let's try this way," she agreed.

It felt good to be with her, because she also allowed herself to be in the moment. We rarely shared in spontaneous events, and more rarely took trips into the city. I became overwhelmed in a perpetual feeling of love and awe. She brought warmth into these cold and hollow walls, and I was just happy to be next to her.

"Here we go. There's a sign for the observation deck. Let's do it," she demanded.

We rode the escalator to the upstairs level and agreed to have our bags scanned for any weapons or explosive devices before we had the chance to pay the fare to the upper deck. There was a semi-long maze of a line, but we were determined to stay and see where it took us. Although we lived ten minutes away from here, technically, we were tourists, and that meant that everyone on the line had to also have been a tourist, because basically no one spoke English. Families and couples from different parts of the world gathered for this chance to view a great scene from the observation deck and came at a great time because sundown would be coming in about an hour. They let a certain amount of people at a time to ride the elevator, and we were part of the next group.

The usher signaled for us to come in, and upon entering there was another short line inside.

"Becky?" One of the female attendants asked her.

"Oh, hi."

She was in a surprised and good mood to see her friend from College, who incidentally was a Biology Major. We were introduced, but they tried to get as much information they could before the next elevator came for us. Rebecca and I had our game that if we ventured off together to a new place, and if anyone of us saw someone we knew, we lost a point in the game. It was just a game I made up so that we could just be together and not spend time talking to others. Anyway, she lost this round. The doors opened and we said our good-byes. It was time for us to get uplifted.

When we reached the top, we slowly walked around and looked outside the windows which were designed for onlookers to check out the city. We tried to find our apartment and it wasn't hard because all we had to do was to find the Colgate clock and look left. Our eyes were gazing along the Hudson River and we could see the Statue along with Ellis Island again. We continued to walk along the floor, and we passed the gift shop and the food court, as many, if not all, tourist attractions have. I started to check out the other tall buildings and tried to spot any penthouses but found myself entranced with being up so high above the ground.

"I really can't get a true feel with all these people and different columns. Let's go the very top."

"Lead the way," she said.

We found another escalator and this one took us to the top. Our stomachs had to have been growling at this point, and we wanted to make it quick before the sun went down. There was nothing but tourists up there, and most of them had cameras in hand snapping away shots to capture the moment. It was cooler up there, and I got a better view of the Empire State Building, and the other buildings to the North. I was feeling strong and on top of the world for once. We spotted our apartment again, and then Zesti's. We already walked around once when I suggested that she sit and relax for a moment, or at least I had to because of my fear of falling. I looked around and the crowds had somewhat dissipated from our romantic view. *Breathtaking.*

I turned towards her and pulled out the black velvet case from my pocket, that was a mere sign of my love for her and I bent on one knee, as I was taught that it was customary and traditional to do so, but I wasn't sure why. I believed in the sanctity of marriage as it related to it being a Holy Sacrament through the Catholic church, and through this everlasting respect for God, I knelt to express my devoted service. I had also seen and read about this act in medieval paintings and literature as a sign of honor and respect, to express eternal servitude and admiration.

"Rebecca, I love you. I want to spend the rest of my life with you. Will you marry me?"

"Oh, my God...Yes," she said excitedly as she looked inside the box and saw the two-carat diamond marquis ring. She was so excited, and some of the Japanese tourists upon seeing what had transpired started taking photographs. Rebecca rose to the occasion to give me a big hug.

"I love you too. Let's eat."

"Let's go."

I had so much of an intense sensation over me when she accepted my proposal, and it seemed as everything made sense in my life. I wasn't nervous or focused on detailed exact words or how is was going to happen, other executing the goal. We took the same route back as we did there, and when she saw her friend from school again, she hadn't mentioned a word of the engagement because she was still in shock.

We reached Zesti's a little before six-fifteen. I had already reserved the table next to the window, and Brian was our waiter. Rebecca and Brian worked together at the restaurant to gain some extra money on the side and she told him about the engagement and showed him the ring. He congratulated us and after listening to the specials, we decided on the Veal Saltimbocca with glasses of wine and although it was certainly delicious, she hadn't finished her meal from being excited and in shock, so she took hers home.

The next morning, we met at the front steps and just sat there together holding hands and enjoying the moment. The neighborhood wino and homeless man, Bobby, came around and struck up a conversation with us. He was a skinny, elderly man who was never clean-shaven and always had something interesting to say. He lived across the street with Frankie, the neighborhood Historical Observer. After Bobby left to get some food from the Church pantry, Rebecca and I looked at each other, and wondered if we could really make it last together and forever. It was better than being alone, and we would have plenty of time to figure it out, I thought.

Chapter XXIII – Close Call

From the second-floor balcony, I gauged the almost-full can below and let go of the heavy trash bag I filled from purging useless items from my recently moved-in apartment. I was being lazy and tired from moving loads of the only remaining possessions and belongings I had, since being evicted from my own house. It was the final straw and bag, and all I could think about was going for a walk and checking out the amenities and the lake, to get some fresh air.

Three years prior, after transferring to Houston in June 2005, for the major airline position, Rebecca visited me once to check Texas out, and we utilized that time together to search for houses. Out of the six or seven we viewed it was determined that we liked the first one we saw, and so we made an offer. After that, I experienced Hurricanes Rita and Katrina in September and was tasked with securing our cargo equipment and other major assets from the storm surges, with much success. I survived nature's fury and it made me stronger for a better foundation.

In October, she came back down and attended the "closing" fun of signing thirty pages of paperwork, when the seller accepted our offer. There were about six other people in attendance around a long table in a conference room. Midway, she stalled, and I noticed her eyes starting to tear up.

"Hey. What's wrong?" I asked her softly.

She just sat there motionless, and emotionally disturbed. I held her hand and asked her to come outside with me to get some air, and she nodded her head in affirmation.

"Excuse us. We'll be right back. We're just headed outside," I addressed the room.

Their heads all went up, and they all stopped fumbling and organizing documents, as if we stole something and were about to run away with the goods, and perhaps, in a slight panic, they were thinking that we would be backing out of this deal at the last second.

"Ok," our real estate agent attested.

Once outside, we walked along the strip mall exterior and even around the parking lot, certainly panicking real estate and Title officials inside, if they were peering through the window blinds.

"Are you all right? I know this is a big deal; one of the biggest purchases we'll probably make in our lives but it's a great and affordable price. It's a great Public-School system for our daughter and they're building a new Elementary school that'll be finished by the time she's five, and in first grade. It's a great investment and the perfect opportunity to start over, right?"

I rubbed her back and held her hand to comfort her no matter what she decided. She was feeling overwhelmed and finding it hard to breathe, until she finally released her emotions and cried for a minute. I held her close to my chest as I hugged her.

"You want to forget about all of this? It's not too late, but now is the time," I asked.

Rebecca regained composure and wiped her tears. We went back inside, signed the mound of paperwork, and became the newest homeowners in a suburban community.

Unfortunately, I was living in that empty house, with just a queen-sized mattress on the master bedroom floor and very minimal furniture, for two years. During that time, I flew up to see them every other weekend and stayed at her parents' place. She gave birth to our second daughter and stayed with her parents in New Jersey while I lived alone in our new four-bedroom, three and a half bath, two-car garage house. When I filed and was granted a divorce in 2007 for her not living with me in Texas, she then decided to move with our two daughters and after six months of us living together, she became a Texan resident.

Two months later, towards the end of my shift, Theresa and I were working on saving an employee's job because he refused to wear a safety vest while operating company equipment on the ramp. Consequently, I was buried in paperwork in the process, so I arrived home over an hour late, and when I did, Rebecca accused me of hanging out, possibly with other women. I smelled wine on her breath and noticed an empty bottle of *Yellow Tail* on the dining room table, in the shadows. A discussion ensued and she was quick to call the Sheriff's Office, after she splashed water from a glass she was drinking, on my face. She already knew the phone number and didn't hesitate to dial it which was mildly peculiar and suspicious.

"Yes... Hispanic male... assault."

Flashbacks of her animosity triggered me to leave the house and wait outside, so I waited for the cavalry to arrive. After ten minutes they pulled up with their lights and started to interrogate me, and after they concluded that there was no domestic violence or any signs of assault, they advised me to leave the premises until things cooled down, to make things easier. I was embarrassed that the neighbors would be watching and judging us with the unnecessary commotion on our front driveway and thankfully, the girls were asleep in their bedroom.

For the sake of sanity and to be the adult, I naturally complied, so I stayed at a hotel for a few days, and when I returned at the end of the week, she continued with her negative attitude. Living out of a hotel for nearly three weeks, I sought to find an apartment with a monthly lease option to minimize cost and expenses. Every time I went back to the house to gain access to my domain, she raised hell and denied it. She changed the locks, and four months later, I received a letter from the Attorney General's Office to begin the Child Support process for "abandonment".

I remembered all of that, while I was circling the lake that was in the center of my new wooded residential apartment complex. I was once again thrusted into the world of law enforcement – marshals, sheriffs, bailiffs, judges, lawyers, and how I didn't ask for them to dictate and control my life, especially when I am able to see my children. A trail led to a flock of yellow-billed ducks with a few ducklings, and I stopped to think of my children. According to the Divorce Decree, I was able to have my girls every Thursday, from 6-8pm, and every other weekend, as per my visitation rights. My wages were garnished, and I only have fifteen more years of child support to go, not to mention that my lawyer rooked me and was just as deceitful in this entire process.

One evening after another late-night shift, I went to my two-bedroom apartment to make dinner and grilled some chicken and vegetables, boiled white rice, and made a side pot of red kidney beans with potatoes. When it was all ready, I took a few steps to the living room and pulled up one of my two chairs and faced it towards the television. I placed my plate of food, napkin, and fork on the tall empty box I used as a side table, and finally sat. I didn't reach for the remote control yet. I just sat and closed my eyes, then I decided to pray aloud.

"Lord, thank you for everything I have. I am very grateful. Thank you for this meal, as I will use it to nourish my body for thy will. I don't have much of anything. I have my wonderful girls and I love them very much. Lord, can you please give me a sign of direction? What will you have me to do? What is the key to my happiness, so I don't continue wasting any time or efforts in the wrong direction? Thank you. Amen."

I clicked the remote and watched a late-night show, for entertainment, and finished my meal.

The next day, I was terminated from my job, after being with the company for ten years. The airline was merging with another airline, and unfortunately, I was on the wrong side of the management team. I wasn't bitter. I wasn't angry. My life was already numb to the ridiculousness of it all. I recognized that my life was a lie. I was sold on a path to happiness, but it was "ridicu-lie". Working for a company, towards a career, was old news and discarded from my mind so I turned my back on working for someone else, and focused on gaining control of my life, on being happy, under my terms. I gave it a go towards entrepreneurialism because the only person I could believe in is myself.

Chapter XXIV – Café Fantástico

I was working on the Business Plan for my new LLC coffee company I created. The template offered me guidance and posed very interesting points and concepts that I had not considered before, and because this was going to be my primary source of income, I needed to fully engage and understand at least the basics of product business, versus the service I once provided as an Art Representative. I sat at one of the round tables, at the apartment complex's Clubhouse, with a notepad and a pen, and my willingness to survive on my own.

Dusk was approaching and the families with their children, by the pool, were packing it up. At times, I would look out the big windows overlooking the well-manicured landscape, pondering tranquility and my natural inclination to question life and my role in it. My reason, my "why", was clear – my children, and so I focused on family and my decision to embrace the coffee industry. I had brewed about four cups of it, utilizing their pot and kitchenware, anticipating a long evening of brainstorming and masterminding.

When my services were no longer needed at the airline, I wasn't sure what next to do as far as an occupation. I questioned my skill sets and how to apply them and thought about it some more. I sacrificed a lot just to risk transferring and living a new life in a new State and considered what I had lost – family. My marriage, whether it ever recuperated from 2003, was over. The house that we bought and is reflective in my Credit Score is six miles away and about a fifteen-minute drive, so I wasn't too far away from the girls, but I no longer had access to live there. I was sixteen hundred miles from my parents and sister, in New Jersey, so here I was – alone with my thoughts.

I decided to take a trip to Puerto Rico to visit the elders with the help of my aunts and uncles who live there, to get reacquainted with my family and roots, so that I could try to recover who I am and whatever I lost in myself. My uncle Lenny and aunt Nydia drove me up through the mountainside to visit my mother's uncle – Don Luisinio. He didn't know we were on our way because he had no phone and if he had a mailbox it would have been designated in the town's Post Office, but no letter was written. Instead, we drove the thirty minutes through winding dirt roads, chose correct forks in the road, and scaled steep passageways to his house that would be restricted if it were raining, due to the loose gravel and mud slide vulnerabilities and possibilities. Today, the weather was an enjoyable eighty degrees and the route was unobstructed.

"One of the key things in life is to forgive," Aunt Nydia added to one of our many inspirational talks that we always seem to have.

These two are the ones that go in-depth with me and expand my consciousness, and some of the topics have included Nostradamus, The Bible and prophesy, and the End Times. They focused on morality, astronomy, and they're how I heard about Scientology. They challenged me to think.

"There is a disease on this island that is far greater than the Aids epidemic or any other catastrophe – ignorance. You need to educate yourself to gain higher knowledge about the world and yourself," uncle Lenny added. They weren't "bible-thumpers" but used verses to assist them in showing examples of moral behavior through parables. I was able to freely have discussions with them without persecution, and I loved them for caring enough to engage in less than mundane pursuits.

She added, "You need to get to the core of a situation in order to figure out the real problem. It's in the roots. And in order to grow, you need to learn, accept, and forgive."

My second uncle, Don Luisinio, must have heard the car's motor as we got closer because he met us outside his front door before we could fully pull in and park in his cleared driveway. The elevated latched cages that housed six rabbits allegedly killed by the Chupacabra, several years ago, was still there next to his goat pen. He had found his rabbits one fateful morning with their blood drained and their internal organs removed with no trace of blood or evidence other than the two puncture wounds in their bodies. He was distraught and mystified in the murder of his animals.

Chickens scurried to lower level slopes behind the pig pen, and his dog, Juan, also came out to greet us. He wore a white T-shirt, light blue pants, and sturdy sandals. The sun hadn't burned or damaged his late seventy-year-old skin as it was a well-tanned and golden-brown color. Juan just circled around me, wagging his tail, then went off to find something else to do.

"Hi, Tio. La bendición."

"Dios te bendiga."

My aunt and uncle brought over a rotisserie chicken, a half-gallon of milk and a couple of loaves of pan sobao, which was so soft and sweet with a crunchy outside that my favorite way to enjoy it is to toast it with butter with a cup of coffee.

Don Luisinio lived off the land, he didn't drive a car, and wasn't stressed over too many things. After lunch, he asked me to walk the land with him to help pick vegetation. We trekked down a gorge pulling yucca roots from the ground, but we set off primarily to pick red coffee cherries, the fruit or berries from the coffee trees, he was growing.

"Sólo los rojos," he told me.

"How many trees do you have?"

"Our family owns one of the oldest coffee plantations on the island. Many years ago, when Spain invaded Puerto Rico, we fled to the hills and mountains and concentrated on farming and agriculture. We worked the land so well that the Queen of Spain loved and drank our coffee. These trees here are just a few on the six hundred acres that our family owns."

"Wow, Tio. That's a lot of coffee. What do you do with it all?"

"I come and pick what I need. That's it."

"Amazing history. I had no idea," I told him in amazement.

Only the red ones are ripe enough to pick. I had been down this trail, numerous times throughout my life, over a creek, all of which was unseen from overhead due to the overgrowth of vegetation and trees, but one man can only do so much. He bartered with neighbors, exchanging plantains and yellow bananas for whatever he needed. Money wasn't a commodity as much as livestock or fruits and vegetables, and he was happy.

When we returned to his steady and old wooden house, we brought our baskets of picked coffees to his shed. The shed itself was somewhat hidden and tucked away near his cemented and unpainted front porch, which to him was his castle. I could see the deep, small cavernous grooves in the dirt of where the water flows from heavy rains on this unpaved, but well swept, property. It was on a pier and beam system and three cinder blocks served as steps to the shed's front doors. He unlocked the combination lock and pushed the doors open to let it breathe since it contained no windows or vent for fresh air to circulate.

It was extremely dark inside except for a peering beam of sunlight coming through a side wooden wall from a quarter-sized hole. Still outside, looking in, I could see an image from the focused beam on a shelf he secured with three large rusty nails and a two-foot wooden block. I took a step closer, and on the shelf, was a picture of the Virgin Mary wearing a blue robe.

"Come. Help me lift this bag to weigh it."

There was an old scale with a hook at the end and we placed the burlap sack handle on the hook, and it weighed nearly fifty pounds.

"What's in it?"

"Coffee beans."

Upon closer inspection of the shelf, there was another photo next to her. I blinked, took a step back, then took two steps forward and couldn't believe what I saw – an eighth-grade photo of me, in my light blue cap and gown, smiling with my braces. I thought that it was either strange or an omen that of all the things stored in this shed, deep in the mountains of Puerto Rico, there would be a wallet-sized photo of me. Once outside, he opened the bag and it contained shells, or hulls, of coffee beans. I asked him if I could purchase or compensate him for the bag and its contents, and after some convincing and a lot of ambitious inspiration on my part, we had a deal.

My aunt had been walking around picking beautiful and colorful flowers throughout the general area, and my uncle helped her gather some medicinal plants such as aloe, peppermint, and lavender.

"Your grandmother grows a lot of these plants and makes medicines. She's an herbalist who uses plants to heal, like for teas, or even to reduce a fever," Titi said.

"Like a witch doctor, or voodoo," Tio added.

She playfully hit him in the arm so that he wouldn't continue portraying my grandmother as an alchemist of spells. Their stashes were modest and were radiantly green.

"What's a 'muere-vivir'?" I asked.

"You've seen one?" he asked.

"Yeah. Years ago, at my grandmother's house, outside by her washing machine, in Aibonito."

"It's a plant that looks dead but when you water it, it blooms open to life. She's had that one for years. They're pretty neat," my uncle explained.

"I have a lot to learn about nature and how it works, but now, instead of teas I'm learning about coffee."

"We used to lay the coffee cherries out here in the sun for hours until they dried up and then we were left with the shell. Then we had to crack open the shell and take out the bean. It's a long process, like two weeks long, from the moment we pick it to when we pour it in to a cup when we do it that way. You should see when we roast it in a pan. The entire house smells like fresh roasted coffee," uncle Lenny explained.

From that fateful day, I learned how uncle Luisinio roasts his own coffee from his yard to his taza, but also how to properly pick, de-pulp, de-hull, and sort and graded similar-sized coffee beans before I had it taken to my Master Roaster in Houston. From that day, I worked with him and local farmers, and provided jobs for willing workers, to sustain the process and manufacturing while I handled the exportation and sales distribution within the contiguous US. We didn't use pesticides or harmful chemicals and I enjoyed the grass roots and organic routes I was taking to manifest vitality, growth, and health through nature. Café Fantástico was born.

Chapter XXV - Ramona

I needed the assistance of investors for growth, since I had close to nothing, so I continued to work on the business plan when I heard a noise in the kitchen. It was an employee of the complex and she was cleaning and tidying up the facility before she would leave for the day.

"Hi. Sorry if I made a mess in there. I'll clean it up."

"Hiya. It's smells like fresh-roasted coffee from somewhere in Latin America. Costa Rica?"

"No. Close. Puerto Rico. I'm Coronado. Nice to meet you."

"I'm going to call you 'Rico', for short. I'm Ramona."

"Hi, Ramona. Make yourself a cup. There's plenty. I'm gonna call you 'Dahling', for short."

Ramona wore a matching light brown shirt and shorts, as her uniform would entail, and her blonde zany hair came down to about her shoulders. She grabbed a mug from an overhead cabinet and poured herself a half cup of my "Executive Blend" and added a dollop of milk, before coming over.

"If I drink this any later than now, I won't be able to sleep, and I need to go to Church tomorrow."

"Oh yeah? Which church? There are so many around here."

"The Church of Jesus Christ of Latter-Day Saints."

"That's a mouthful. Where is it?"

"I think it's in Ward Two."

"Ward Two? Off which street?"

"A couple of miles down the road from here."

"Like those two guys that ride around in bikes, with white shirts and striped ties? They should probably start wearing helmets, even though we have that 'No Helmet' law here in Houston. So, you're a Mormon? I've never talked to one before."

"Yeah. Tada. In the flesh. Those young men are probably on a Mission. They do that after they're eighteen, either because they want to make their mom or dad happy or they truly want to make a difference and change the world. Most believe that this is their calling – to 'preach the gospel to every creature' and to help the people where they're going. They reach out to single mothers, teach English to some, and participate in social activities to bring members together."

"That's great. I wish I knew what my calling was. At least they're aware of their purpose," I said.

"I felt your energy when I entered the room. I didn't see you at first, but I acknowledged a presence, and even now, I feel and recognize that you are going places and that you are going to accomplish something."

"You're an empath?"

"We both are. I must skedaddle. Busy day tomorrow."

"Twenty-three skidoo. Anyway… skedaddle. Nice meeting you, Dahling."

"Nice meeting you too, Rico. And thanks for the coffee. It was good. We'll talk more."

"See you."

I did, indeed, occasionally see Ramona as I adjusted to my newer surroundings at the complex and we often met and spoke about life and its curveballs, and I was thankful for the opportunity to learn more about her when she invited me to her place for dinner one evening. Vibrant plants and exquisitely ornate terra cotta planters adorned her ground-floor apartment doorway. After knocking three times, the door opened, and her dog came out to greet me first.

I was only bitten by a dog once, when I was about seven or eight, by a beautiful tan and dark brown German Shepard while walking home after school one day. The canine and I stared at each other intensely for a few seconds, and I calculated in my mind that the house was only a few doors away and that I could outrun him to my front steps. I only went as far as five feet before he leapt at my left leg and bit me. I made it to the house soon after that – terrified that my parents would be mad at the puncture marks in my gray uniform pants. The matter was escalated when neighbors saw what happened and rang the bell to see if I survived the attack. Maybe it was love at first bite or I'm half animal, but the German Shepard is still my favorite dog breed.

The only other animal that had ever bitten me was a rabbit that my grandfather brought home for that evening's dinner. I was terrified when he first entered the room with the bunny in his grips. The entire family in the room was aware of my apprehension and fear, slightly due to my immediate yelping. He squirmed so much that he jumped out of my grandfather's arms and headed towards my left forearm with his enormous buckteeth. A few years, I wasn't sure how I felt about my father giving me a rabbit's foot for good luck, but I graciously accepted it and thus exposed to my first superstition.

Ramona's dog, Bolt, was a mix between an Italian Greyhound and a Husky, and he seemed playful enough. After she and he let me in, I handed her a bottle of red wine suitable for our meal.

"Dahling, so this is what a first-floor apartment looks like around here. Nice!"

"Thank you for the wine. Oh yeah. Come and see how the other half lives," she joked.

Bolt pranced back and forth, excited to see me, I guessed, but he seemed happy with the interaction. On the other side of the living room and dining room was a nice view of the nearby lake, and trees covered the sides of the back patio to somewhat block its rays and harbor shade from the everyday brutal Texan sun. Her furniture wasn't modern or nouveau. It didn't have fake wood or faux anything. The sofa was Victorian, with ornate hardwood carvings, and was also noticeable in its multiple sturdy legs. Her end tables had white marble tops and the lamps that complimented them had laced jewels trimming their shades. A tissue box was readily available on the one closest to the black piano. It almost felt like I was in an exquisite and staged funeral home. We stopped the mini-tour half-way to check on the oven.

"And here's the kitchen," she said, "Voila!"

Her kitchen wasn't as cozy as the rest of the place. It was under construction or in the process of getting organized, stemming from the glassware and plates that were scattered throughout the beige countertop or what was left to be seen and exposed. In one of the opened two-tiered cabinet doors, matching dishes that I would never put in the microwave because of their delicate gold-trimmed designs that would probably spark, were stacked high from top to bottom, from small to large. The lighting was bright from the four uncovered fluorescent bulbs just a couple of feet above our heads. She popped the cork and poured two glasses.

"Please have a seat."

I sat on a large wooden table, resembling a picnic bench, and listened intently on how she was still unpacking and putting things away. Bolt came over and his head lifted my resting right arm, signaling for me to pet him.

"Bolt. Leave him alone," she said in a loving way.

I took another swig while she was setting the table. I motioned to get up and asked her where the restroom was so I could wash my hands, and when I returned, she was about to carve the bird.

"Smells delicious."

"Thank you. I have my own recipe for the potatoes and added some extra herbs."

"Great. Sounds delish."

Dinner was enjoyable, and light-hearted. Bolt ate with us too but from his own bowl. One of my biggest pet peeves are animals that are fed from the table, sitting there staring and waiting for their next hand-out. He had his own serving, I'm sure, of the most nutritional mix of vittles in his big blue plastic bowl.

Continuing with the tour, she showed me a bedroom in the back room that housed her massage table, aromatherapy oils and other aromatic materials, and remnants of her healing practice – stalled until her will and desire picked up again.

"Looks like you have all the tools you need to perform a massage. How did you choose that profession?"

"When I was young, I gave massages to my parents and my siblings. I could feel their pain when I touched them, and it became natural over time, but more importantly, their pains would go away. When I was fifteen, my parents took in a foster child who came from a Navajo family. She called me a name in her native tongue, but I didn't understand what it was. She said it meant the 'one who heals with her hands'. She knew that I could perform that healing aspect to people just from the use of my hands."

"Cool. You knew back then?"

"Yeah. It was amazing. I was at a supermarket and my intuition kept telling me to touch this guy's shoulder – 'Touch his shoulder', but I was conflicted because I didn't know this man and I wasn't just about to touch him. His back was turned, and something said to 'touch his shoulder', so I did. He turned around and rubbed his shoulder, then looked at me."

"Did you run away, like a ring and run at a random house? If I touch a random woman, there's a strong possibility that she would either scream or try to slap me, and then I would have either fled or been arrested."

"He said, 'I don't know what you did but thank you! The pain I've been having for a few days is gone. My arthritis is gone.' Years later, when my first son was older, he was going through physical therapy for treating his difficulties with clubfeet. They were sideways and stiff and not as flexible, so I rubbed his legs and hips, and feet, and the doctors said that he recovered sooner than normal patients. So, I went to Therapy school and the teacher brings in a video about chakras. Then I'm learning about feeling energy and neuropathy."

"That's rather intense training. I thought you just slap some oil on the person and give them a happy ending," I snickered, "but it's quite interesting on your abilities to heal. That's some power."

"It is intense. When the video was over the students told me that they could feel my energy just from walking by me. I use the higher power of light to heal, and for those who are in tune, can see the light around me. Although the 'New Age' had already been around since the 70s, the other students recognized that I was involved in the belief in some sort of spiritualism through holistic approaches to health and ecology. Now I'm a level-two Reiki healer."

"Do you need help setting up this room?"

"No. I'm going to paint it first. I just needed to get this stuff in here, out of the way, then work on it later. You can help me paint it, but not today. Thank you."

"Yeah. Sure. Just let me know."

We continued talking in the living room where it was more comfortable, and we didn't have to stand in an unfinished office. I sat back in her love seat and allowed myself to relax, while she sat diagonally from me on her couch ready to engage in further contemplative reasoning and discernment.

"Sorry this place is a mess. I haven't fully unpacked yet."

"It's ok. It's nice."

"Years ago, I stayed in the Church to get married in the Temple, and so we did. Years later, I started seeing symbols, visions, and geometric shapes... Chakras, Sanskrit, and flower power relating to sacred geometry. Then I got into Tarot and that's when the Church disciplined me."

"Flogged and tried as a witch?"

"Yeah. Right? I couldn't partake in any more of the fellowship, or able to take a sacrament or any church positions. I was pretty much ousted. I was considered an 'exmo'."

"Exmo? You had irritating blisters on your skin?"

"Not eczema, you goof. Ex-Mormon. I had a collapse in my belief systems. When I spoke to a therapist, who was a former member of the Church, she told me I was considered a 'cognitive dissonant' – a person who holds two or more contradictory beliefs, ideas, or values. I just turned fifty, and I divorced last year. I'm also diabetic and on top of my parents being a root cause of my stress, I got acidosis. My kidneys, heart, and liver were severely affected. I lost part of my left kidney. And now I'm here until I figure out what's next."

"So, we're living in a half-way house? In a place where people transition and try to figure it out? Sounds like we share similar circumstances – the same story. Now what?"

For the short duration I knew her, I would never have guessed that she was in a bad place. Despite, knowing that everyone has their own issues, we hadn't discussed real passed events, we never judged each other, and we individually recognized that it was an opportunity to start anew.

"In Mormonism, I was taught to be a lady and you have treated me like one, but you've also allowed me to be myself with no preconceived rules, while still being proper. I mean, you often make me feel like it's ok to break my own boundaries. Thank you, Rico."

We connected with each other through our true selves with no physical boundaries or sexual tension, we found common ground, and even though we had our own baggage we didn't throw it in the other's face. Hitting below the belt was always too extreme for me – a cop out, and a quick way to inflict pain and try to stun your opponent. Having literally been hit below the belt with either a knee, a fist, or a projectile, it takes a while to recover but shouldn't be the first course of action. We were having an incredible friendship dynamic and were healing each other.

One afternoon, I sat relaxed at the edge of my made twin bed, while she positioned herself behind me, on her knees, rubbing her clasped hands together, so she could perform a reiki healing on me. Ramona placed her hands, starting on my left shoulder, and worked her way down the left side of my back and then coming back up the right side and out the right shoulder.

"I'm taking all the negative energy from one side and releasing it out the other."

It felt like she was siphoning all my ailments and soothing my body at the same time. I breathed in deeply through the nose and released slowly out my mouth. After a few minutes she stopped and blurted sentences and ideas that didn't make sense to me.

Her touching me was somehow merging with her mind purely by using specialized contact with her palms and fingertips, similarly to Spock using his Vulcan mind meld technique on a targeted partner's skull temples. While the mind melds can also allow more than one mind to experience memories and sensations, and sometimes even interact with the memories, I could not see what she was experiencing.

"You have a dark spot, in a watermelon shape encapsulation inside of you... but it's not your fault. It's in your mid-chest area, between your Heart Chakra and the Solar Plexus Chakra. You inherited it from a relative."

I concentrated on my breathing and didn't interrupt. I stayed silent to allow the message to come through, however disturbing or strange it sounded. I was curious. Her breathing was getting heavier, perhaps from extracting my heavy burdens and quickly releasing them from my body.

"There is a woman at a train station... she's wearing white gloves. She's standing on one side of the tracks, and behind her are two tall red-bricked buildings... under her right arm she is carrying a 5-7lb. bundle, like a brown paper package."

She started to rub my back again in that methodical behavior, but also trying to focus on the details.

"The lettering on one of the buildings is white... '& Sons', it says... there are two, no wait... four train tracks and in the background, there is a stone bridge where you could walk to the other side of the tracks. The stones are in different shapes. All I keep hearing now is 'I will take this on and clear it.'"

"Take this on and clear it? What do you think that means?" I asked.

"I'm not sure but it's like I'm there watching this. It's in black and white. Ok... There is a gunman and instead of her running on the bridge to escape, she jumped down and ran across the train tracks to get to the other side. She was shot because somebody didn't show up when they were supposed to, and she was caught in the crossfire. I'm at the train station watching all of this. There is a park nearby with lots of trees. I'm not normally in the vision, so this is extremely weird for me. Wait! Before you came here, you knew what happened. You said that in order to stop and it, you said 'I will take this on and clear it.' I keep hearing that, over and over. But you have an encapsulated brown spot, a little foggy one, between your nipples and navel area, and not because of something that you did. It's from your dad's side of the family."

I thanked her so much for the extra vision. It reminded me of my guided meditation, with Paula, where I went into a sleep or trance and saw things that didn't make sense at the time. I wasn't sure where to begin to investigate Ramona's findings, other than asking my father if he knew anyone from our family who was shot and killed, but I had to present it in a way non-affiliated with out-of-body experiences or mystics.

I began further researching the spiritual powers of the Chakras and how I could align myself with its teachings and understandings of how I am able to better myself and to compensate for those inchoate things I am lacking. Building on the basics I learned from Paula and Theresa, I took an active interest in studying the seven chakras, each of the centers of spiritual power in the human body – their order, colors, and attributes.

I automatically thought of "Cha-ka", one of my favorite characters from *Land of the Lost*, because of the name resemblance, then thinking on how he was a young adolescent hominid learning and conforming towards civility, from the Marshall family he just met. Primitive beginnings, crystals, and temples, this television show may have been the introductory stepping-stone to my awareness into the occult.

I delved into the two chakras that Ramona spoke of regarding my internal abnormality. The Solar Plexus chakra is the third one and it focuses on willpower, identity, ego, projection, and motivation. Whatever I learned from my parents was influential in my direction, and perhaps worked for them in their time and circumstances, but with my current situation I have developed more of a "go with the flow" attitude. The chakra deals with focusing on purpose, and on what matters, and to go after it. I am still trying to figure out that purpose, the Higher Purpose so as not to waste much valuable time and effort, I thought, but instead I am allowing it to happen instead of forcing it. I stopped caring what other people thought of me. In my rigid upbringing, I listened to my parents, to authority, upheld The Law, doubted nothing and believed everything they told me. I trusted the people around me. At some point, that was all skewed and I am left here to fend for myself, but I am not yellow or afraid to find out who I am to be.

The Heart Chakra speaks of loving for others, love for God, love for self, community, and forgiveness. It is the center of unconditional love and compassion and is in the center of the human energy system. Although I am a giving and nurturing person, I have always been challenged with receiving. Yes, it was great opening presents on Christmas or on my birthday, and for the most part those were the only days I would have a gift presented to me, so I didn't expect much else. Working on a job and getting a paycheck was a reciprocated contract, a quid pro quo that did not come from generosity, but from a requirement. I was more aware with being gratuitous and appreciative with those around me whom I cared about, and so I managed to deplete myself and, in the process, loved myself less. According to the "Golden Rule", referenced in The Bible, I should do unto others as I would have them do unto me. I focused and put others first.

While I was strong in some areas of my life and within the chakra system, I was weak and unbalanced in others, so I began to recognize those strengths and weaknesses and began to take control of my own life, self, and purpose. I was solely responsible for my own happiness and I needn't be afraid to receive and accept those faults and tribulations, along with the rewards and victories that may also come from it. I am worthy to receive.

Chapter XXVI - Bethany

I first met Bethany in 2007 while working at the Service Center when I was planning and strategizing weight loads and cargo facilitations for a major airline in Houston, TX. She was in a nearby department answering phone calls for freight reservations and I would see her from across the large room because our cubicles had little or no walls separating most. We hadn't much interaction, maybe the occasional greetings, but in our global company, as large as it was – 40,000 employees, we somehow all knew and recognized each other.

I enjoyed my position and I shared the space with three other Agents in our department. Our area was in the center of the room and when anyone stepped on to the floor, they would have passed by us since we were also by the main entrance doors. Occasionally, whenever someone wandered around my area I would stop and say hello especially to Cindy and Kim, who were both single but were about ten years apart from each other. Cindy and I got along well, and we wound up dating and spending quality time together. She gave me a Spessartite garnet ring, as a gift. Kim, in her early twenties who was married with a couple of children already, was having marital problems and she heard that I read Tarot cards.

She would come over once in a while to my work area for a reading but we had to keep it discreet since the dark arts was something that was shunned by most of society, especially at the workplace, so I would read her energies, with my dark orange mystic ring, and report back to her during lunch, outside while smoking our cigarettes. Since I was a fledgling to the Tarot, I used the small book that came in the deck box as a reference and guide, and less of my intuition. Kim was really my first subject and she had a lot of questions in life, and I trust that the messages that came through helped her remain positive especially within her marriage.

After working there a year, I transferred back near the George Bush International Airport of Houston accepting and transporting boxes and crates that were destined to travel all over the world via the almost near-congested air spaces, and after my sudden retirement from the airlines in 2010, I went off to decide what I was going to do for work, since my desires for a career were skewed.

On August 3rd, 2012, I was working as a secret shopper and conducting a survey outside of a movie theater exit at the local mall when I saw a familiar face – Bethany. She just finished watching "Total Recall" starring Colin Farrell. I had only seen the Schwarzenegger version at the time. I approached her and asked her a set of questions to meet my job quota and requirements, and afterwards we exchanged phone information to keep in touch, and we did. A month and a half later, in September, she invited me over for dinner at her place and it was delicious, but oddly, her ex-husband had been stalking her and eventually had the courage and audacity to ring her doorbell and question who I was, while I was there. It was a bit awkward, but I stayed at the dinner table waiting for her to return from having an extensive conversation at her front door with him and continued to savor her baked chicken, roasted potatoes and grilled veggies for a second helping.

Another thing Bethany and I had in common was that we saw the same psychotherapist. To avoid a disruption or any possible complications in my job, and to help talk through the aftermath of my divorce, I sought counsel from the company psychologist. This was the first time I took advantage of clinical help to solve a problem, and it was unlike seeing a card reader or an intuit. I remember her trying to help me understand a situation about myself.

"Coronado, you have a physical responsibility on this plane, and that requires coming down from your clouds of fantasy."

She didn't accept the nature of the spiritual plane that I was enthralled in. Hopes and faith or fortune telling didn't equate with hard work, bills, and accepting the consequences of marriage. After my session was over, I saw Bethany sitting in the waiting room for a second time, but I never acknowledged her presence to her, for the sake of anonymity and privacy.

The more time we spent together, the more I introduced and influenced spirituality into her world. We painted together in her living room, while I lit incense resins or cones, even though she was more familiar with certain types of incense sticks. We alternated days of music. When it was her choice, she played soothing tunes of Indian music and it had me swaying at times. My go-to band was The Smashing Pumpkins, especially the *Gish* album, but *Oceania* just came out, so I rocked them. She was delighted to feel free enough to express herself through painting and gradually became very good at it. I spoke of self-love due to my losses, and even did readings for her. Bethany became my first pupil and is the Ten of Hearts.

Because of my constant thirst for knowledge in reading cards, I concluded that Margaret's secret knowledge of the Magi readings was referred to as *Metasymbology*[15]. Some think that Astrology is wrong because there is no way anyone could predict what is going on, like in the horoscopes, but what if people view the world differently because of when their birthday falls? Maybe celebrating the 4th of July has a different feeling to how close their birthday is celebrated to another event or a holiday? A Pisces acts a certain way, or a Leo acts a certain way because they were born on a specific time of the calendar year and their perspective of Spring is conducive to feeling more rain and being outdoors and not because the constellations are in Aries. Or perhaps, just maybe, it is because the stars are fixed that develops and determines the unique characteristics of a person's way of being.

All these things, and many more concepts, were constantly being explored because we sought answers to many of our flummoxed and cantankerous flows towards true happiness. We lit candles, bought stones and arranged them around her place, meditated, and supported each other in these creative endeavors. I learned a methodical way of performing a weekly reading, and it has been accurate more than ninety-five percent of the time. I was amazed on how I started to plan my week around its interpretations and used it to my advantage. This style and method were less about intuition, like reading the little tarot guidebook for clarification, and more about structured

---

[15] *Order of The Magi*, Olney H. Richmond – Grand Master, "The Mystic Test Book" 1893

extraction of information. I was able to pinpoint the specific seven days in the year when my fifty-two-day tests would begin, and the last one before my new yearly cycle is January 6th – 106, my father's birthday.

I needed to use my watch with the second hand on it, to precisely time when to cut the cards, for them to get magnetized and in tune with each other. Flipping seven cards over for the first row, one for each day of the week and for each planet if you exclude Earth, and Pluto – the now-considered dwarf planet, I was able to determine a primary factor for that day. Two more rows supported either the situation or the people involved.

The fourth row of cards I dealt has the three of spades, the seven of spades, and the ten of clubs. Rebecca is the three with a personality card of the seven, and our older daughter is the ten, according to their birth cards. According to metasymbology, one or two of them could be undergoing favorable expression through art, or an illness related to worry about money or work, or a success in any mind related activity such as publishing, speaking, or any of the communication fields, because it falls on Jupiter. I hoped that my girl aces her Math test on Thursday.

While I felt there was an increased awakening of spirituality, whether it came from the "11:11... make a wish" folks, or from the customers that would swarm the "Mystic Muse" shop, I became more aware, and more in tune, with other liked-minded individuals. As my interest in the occult grew, so did my willingness to connect to my increasing soul-tribe. Bethany and I took a trip into the small town of Old Town Spring and I was interested in purchasing an

Artist amulet for a chain I would wear. As soon as we walked in, there were multiple scented incense sticks hanging on the right side on peg boards and behind the nearby glass encasings were intricate miniature ceramic Japanese-themed incense holders. Naturally, I rummaged and sniffed some of the ones I never heard of, but they were too sweet for my tastes.

"Hi. Can I help you with anything?" a bald man dressed in black asked me.

"Yes. I'm looking for an amulet to wear around my neck."

"We have a selection right over here."

There was a great selection, next to the collection of mini daggers and sterling silver jewelry.

"I love to paint. I'm looking for one specifically as an artist."

"Why? You're a writer!" he stated without hesitation.

I hadn't written anything, except for essays in school but that was mandatory. He confused me but seeing as that I hadn't spotted one with a palette or paint brush symbol, I felt it wasn't meant to be. Trusting him to invest in an impulse item when I hadn't even fathomed the thought being a writer, I kept looking at other items in the store.

Bethany was interested in getting a Reading from one of the ladies in the backroom. He went to go get her and when she arrived, Lisa took off her glasses and asked which one of us needed guidance. She pointed to me and dismissed me quickly.

"It's not you. You already know."

She focused on Bethany and they went off to the back for about fifteen minutes. Max, the man in black, kept me company while I checked out the different sculptures of the "Green Man" on the wall. They each depicted the head of a man covered in leaves and vines, symmetrical and representational of growth and rebirth in accordance with the society of the Celts.

I was also admiring all the handcrafted woodwork of local artisans, in a different section. There were a few small boxes, some with golden latches to store items like rings and other jewelry, and several wands that looked cool and handy, but I had my eye on a wooden chalice that seemed simple enough yet magical.

"Is she Jennifer?"

"No. She's my friend from work. She has a daughter named Jennifer."

"Oh. I keep hearing the name *Jennifer*. Do you know a Jennifer, Jenny, or Jeanette?"

The backdoor opened and Bethany was smiling. It took me a long time to convince her to go see a card reader, and I was glad that it was a positive experience for her.

"She was shocked when I told her that I already knew I was the Ten of Hearts. She asked how I knew, and I ratted you out."

"Cool. Thanks. So, she used a normal deck of playing cards?"

"Yes, but I'll tell you later if my stuff comes out or not."

"Oh man. You can't do that! Give me something… a taste, a clue."

"Later. Did you get anything?"

"Nah. I was just looking."

"C'mon, I'll get you something. What would you like?"

"I was checking out this wooden handcrafted stuff over here."

"Pick something out."

I walked over, timid, and feeling undeserved of such a gift. I tapped on the glass above the wooden cup, and Max already knew which one. He wrapped it up in some circular newspaper to protect it during transport.

"Thank you, Bethany."

"You're welcome. Let's go. I need a treat."

Our visit to that shop was intriguing and mysterious, and by the time I realized who Max might have been referring to, the store had gone out of business and I hadn't seen them since.

We went to get soft ice cream, although *Blue Bell* would have been better, before we went back to her place, and at the strip-mall across the road someone in a mask ran out of the liquor store and sped off in their black F-150 truck.

"Dang! He didn't just rob that store, did he? It's too hot to wear a mask."

"Too far away to catch the plate info, and we don't really know what happened," she responded.

"Well I hope nothing happened, and he doesn't get in a wreck for speeding or driving recklessly. If that was Zorro, he would have worn a cooler mask and probably have driven away in a white, or silver, truck instead."

"Or a horse."

"Hahaha. Yeah. What a coward. He should have ridden off on a horse."

"'No good deed goes unpunished'. So, lucky we didn't try to stop him."

I took another lick of my vanilla with rainbow-sprinkles cone, contemplating the dualistic cosmology of good and evil, Ying and Yang, black and white, and how I am lactose intolerant.

Meanwhile, back at the ranch, she started clearing off her fireplace and mantle and started laying out her candles and stones instead. The coffee table used to have a couple of empty dishes and glasses but soon she cleared them off and replaced it with more gems, stones, and candles. Even the remote control went missing. She was staging and setting up an altar and a meditation arena. To get mentally prepared and stimulated, she lit some incense and played some of her Indian music again, but softly.

"Let's practice our breathing techniques. I need to relax and meditate," she said.

It took me a while, but I cleared my mind and let it go. Soon, I was brought back to the vision I had when I was in front of my parents' house, double-parked at night, in the driver's seat of a car. A woman came up to the window and yelled at me to 'Get out!' There were two children in the backseat, and as I now stood behind the car, she drove off with them. That woman I knew to be Rebecca, even then, since I recognized her clearly, but I could not have known that those two children would be my daughters. I must have been told to "get out" of Paula's world so these girls could manifest and come into fruition – to be born.

Bethany soon continued onward towards her spiritual journey, where she feels she has been chosen to assist the people in the time of an upcoming great flood, or a natural disaster, very soon. As a Virgo, and the complete opposite sign of Pisces, she is very intuitive and is undergoing serious preparation, including her willingness to learn the Hebrew language. She has spoken to me about the importance to health and fitness, and her connection with natural honey, and before she can heal the world, she must heal herself first.

Chapter XXVII – Bobazeb

Café Fantástico hasn't been easy to accomplish but I have taken great pride in creating something on my own, through hard work and determination. From the primary fifty-pound bag I used to start this endeavor, there was a lot to learn through trial and error on this roller coaster, but after finding the right Master Roaster, I was more confident that I was headed in the right direction. My first business meeting with the coffee roasting company was very educational and they were so impressed with my progress that a small handful of my first beans are displayed in their "cupping" room – as the worst batch of coffee beans they have ever seen. In its natural state, if not nurtured, picked, or processed at the most-ample times in their growth cycle, the beans will obviously not be at their best. My product was the "before" sample.

I took my first born to my first-ever roasting of the best amount of beans I could provide, and when it was complete, the freshest coffee smells saturated into our clothes, hair, and our bodies. The owners of the company were invited to join us to sample and "cup" its flavors, essence, and taste. Sips and slurps were the sounds of succulent success.

"Tastes like white chocolate with a hint of raspberry," one of them said.

After our meeting, my six-year-old and I walked out of there, happy and proud, and I was just grateful that she was by my side to share the moment with me, even though she was too young to like or even try coffee.

Researching and test-trialing commercial necessities such as bags, labels, and marketing tools, I was able to finally launch and take it to market. One of the main images of my Puerto Rican Blend labels is that of the endemic Puerto Rican bird – the Spindalis, while my Guatemalan Blend has the Quetzal bird on its label. One of the venues I wanted to distribute it in was a café in Jersey where I admired the owners so much for their story and their vision that is was a natural decision and selection. I met the two sisters when I bumped into my mother's cousin, Sammy, at a nearby barber shop in Downtown, Jersey City. He and I hadn't seen each other in years, and we took the opportunity to catch up at *Sonia's Café*.

We brought each other up to speed about the family. His father was responsible for giving me my first haircut and was well-respected throughout the community. Sammy was also involved in helping the community and I respected his willingness to help others when in need.

"What kind of ring is that? *G*? What does it stand for?"

"It's my Mason ring. I'm a freemason."

I was curious about it, but I didn't follow up since time was fleeting. We finished our espressos and he had to run off to a meeting.

"La bendición," I said as we shook hands.

"God bless you," he replied.

I stayed a while because I was enjoying the vibe. Not only did they sell coffee, but they also sold organic products and other healthy items. Cool indie music was playing from their cd player on the hardwood ledge by the window, and I walked over to check out their collection. The third track is what caught my sensory awareness

– "Ulysses" by Dead Can Dance, off their *A Passage in Time* album. Although they had been around for over twenty years, it was the first time I heard of them and I stayed to listen to a couple more of their songs before I left. Those ladies allowed me to display my original paintings and artwork on their walls, during the annual art show in the city, and I will always be thankful for their generosity and support. When I represented artists, they allowed me to display some of their artwork, including the few of Richard's paintings I sold.

Selling my coffee from *Sonia's Café* was a success, and it gained positive notoriety from a fan-base of local customers and coffee snobs throughout the community. Not only was our alliance a success, so was the trust and rapport we built over time. I told the ladies my story and were familiar with my past, so they knew about my spiritual growth and my willingness to overcome adversity. Evelysse, one of the sisters, was responsible for calling and involving me in that MLM Ganoderma coffee business, and even though I helped others become financially successful, I decided to eventually back away from it because I didn't feel it was a right fit for me.

Evelysse was also the one who introduced me to Antonio, an artist who painted an admirable 5' x 3' portrait of the Virgin Mary that was eventually displayed on the brick-faced wall inside the café, who was soft-spoken and seemed well-intentioned. His girlfriend, Elizabeth, was a regular customer who ordered her freshly squeezed organic juices with an occasional turkey on wheat sandwich, and she also tried and enjoyed the robust flavors of my Guatemalan blend coffee.

The three of them were talking at one of the tables about a man Elizabeth is in communication with who is a medium that receives messages not only from a spirit of the dead, but he speaks in a different voice when channeling.

"His name is Bobazeb and he used to be a priest in the Vatican. We're invited to go over his place next week, in Newark. Would you be interested in going?" Eve asked me.

"Sure. I'll check it out."

Eve and her sister, Nadia, were twins but had different personalities altogether, other than their commitment to their business. I took Eve to see Julia once, after I told her about an accurate card-reading she gave me, and she was so curious that I just had to pick her up and take her there. I listened in while Julia was specifically talking about a relationship, and something that happened in the past, but Evelysse kept nodding her head as if none of it was accurate or made sense. It was in Spanish so I may have lost some of it in translation, but I didn't know her well enough anyway to verify what was true or not. She seemed bummed out.

"So, what did you think of Julia?"

"I keep going over the things she said but they don't make sense."

"Oh man. Sorry. I just hope for the best when I go."

Back at the café, Nadia was cleaning up behind the counter and putting all the left-over dirty dishes in the double-sink so they could soak first.

"So how was it?" she asked Eve.

"It was a bust. She was talking about how years ago a girlfriend of mine stole something out of my purse and I didn't find out until later, but by then she already died. She said that she wanted to tell me she was sorry. And then another one about my ex, how he cheated on me with her. Crazy, right?"

A dish crashed to the floor – shattered and now broken. Nadia turned around with her eyes opened in disbelief.

"That's my story! You remember Lynda? I knew it. I almost caught them one day, but I couldn't prove it. She overdosed on drugs," Nadia revealed.

"Wait a minute. She crossed the two of you... you are twins. Probably picked up on your energy. Woah!" I exclaimed.

"That's probably why she went into your purse! Dinero por los drogas." Eve followed.

"I should be pissed, but I forgave my ex a long time ago. But now I have some closure about it. Wow. She's good."

"Now you need to go see Julia for your sister's reading," I joked.

That was the incident that increased my psychic cred out there to these ladies, and why Nadia was so open about inviting me to see Bobazeb – open-minded entertainment.

The following week I met up with Nydia as she was closing the shop and she drove us to Newark for the channeling. I was familiar with this route to "Brick Town" when I visited my Uncle Justin at the VA Hospital. He lived on a quiet two-story walk-up, and luckily, we found parking out front. She rang the bell, and when we were buzzed in, we walked into a dark hallway with crème-colored walls, some of which were covered with a trail of dirty smudges of handprints from those eerily wanderers feeling their way out to safety. Two of the six bronzed mailboxes affixed into the wall were missing covers, none of which had the names of their occupants, but I trusted Eve that we were at the right place.

A door opened and it was Antonio who had already arrived with Elizabeth.

"Hey, guys. Come on up."

I held on to the wooden bannister and climbed the twenty-five steps, or so, then the burst of fluorescent light from the kitchen illuminated the bakers in the oven. Elizabeth was whipping up some hors d'oeuvres and appetizers when the man of the hour approached and greeted us.

"Welcome. Good to meet you both. I'm Gregory."

He was an elderly man, perhaps in his early sixties, with a gray mustache and hair combed to his left side. Although his shirt and pants weren't completed ironed, his black sweater covered most of black button-downed shirt, and joined with his black pants and shoes, all he was missing was a priest's white collar.

The kitchen looked almost too clinical for me with the amount of light, four four-foot bulbs hung overhead the island in the center, but the rest of the place was cozy with adorned lamps. To my left was a painted-white fireplace with an area rug on the wooden floor. The inside of the fireplace was empty, without any logs or an ornamental black gate, just clean and clear. To the left, in the corner, was a small nook of a bookcase that had two literary works – a brown leather-bound Bible, and a copy of the *Lord of the Flies*. Two couches formed an L-shape to enclose and construct a close-quartered waiting area. Straight ahead was the living room that had an open floor concept, where it certainly could serve as a dance floor. On the right was a dining area that led to the kitchen behind it. All in all, his living quarters was rather spacious and comfortable for one person, maybe comfortable enough for others to help and prepare meals.

"Hi, Elizabeth," Eve said to her.

"Hi there. The mini raviolis are almost finished. Did you bring the chocolate?"

"No. I didn't have time. Sorry."

Eve was asked to bring an offering to Bobazeb, and he especially loves rich hot chocolate, but she didn't bring any to melt. I didn't know about any offerings or pot-luck dishes to bring, so I was out of the loop.

I sat at the dining room table, which oddly resembled Ramona's wooden picnic table, and several mini finger-food treats were set and ready for consumption. There were two bowls – one with dates and the other with marinated green olives with pimentos in them. Eve joined me shortly after and sat next to me. Gregory Rasputin sat across from me and popped a stuffed mushroom in his mouth, and I followed suit.

"Elizabeth mentioned the chocolate. I heard you make a delicious hot chocolate," he reiterated.

"Thank you. I was so busy at the store today, I forgot to make some," she responded.

Antonio was helping in the kitchen, moving about from here to there, and I was feeling uneasy about the whole thing. Just who is Gregory and if he was just an acquaintance, why would they be freely accessing his kitchen and making food? I've been in scarier situations, in more harmful environments and neighborhoods, but things weren't quite settling yet, so I was on my guard. Whenever I visited Julia, I never thought to make cookies or even change the channel on her television.

We finally gathered, sitting next to one another in a line, on fold-out chairs in the main parlor area. The four of us faced Gregory as he comfortably sat on his own seat, facing us, then practiced his breathing exercises. I wasn't entirely sure what to expect. There was no table, crystal ball, or the holding of hands like in a séance, but after he took his last strong breath, his tongue started to move about from side to side. It didn't slither or move quickly like a snake, but more of a drunk person either thirsty or trying to feel sensation in it because it was numb. His eyelids may have flickered, but his facial demeanor was beginning to change in a more jovial and positive manner.

"Greetings! Do we have an offering?" he said in a slightly raspy and flamboyant Rip Taylor voice. Elizabeth had already whipped up a hot chocolate drink in the kitchen to appease the requirement and placed it on an extra chair that separated us from him. He gripped the mug and took a big gulp, and when he was satisfied with its contents, he set the mug back down on the metal folding seat. His hands remained on his knees in efforts to relax and draw the entity forward, but I thought that he might roll up his pants to reveal John and Marcia in a skit I once saw at a Jerry Lewis Muscular Dystrophy Association marathon, back in the early 80s. I doubted whether this was an act or a one-man play.

"It is an honor and pleasure to meet you all. I am Bobazeb. My English isn't great, but I will do my best. For now, I will speak in my native tongue."

Being bilingual in English and some dialects of Spanish, I could not determine the official language he was speaking, but it sounded tribal in nature. Like watching a good Kung-Fu movie, and not being distracted by the sub-title verbiage underneath, I focused on the visual presentation and the choreography. I heard sounds and stressed syllables, all combinations were unrecognizable to my auditory records, until he quickly said the word "quetzal". I was familiar with that bird because I created a logo image of one on my Guatemala coffee label.

Listening more intently, concentrating and focusing on not being distracted, I didn't take my eyes off him, and then suddenly mid-sentence he spoke in English. Much like "story-time" around a campfire or a lesson given by a schoolteacher, he began speaking about a snake and God, and then I lost interest because I was already familiar with the Adam & Eve story in Genesis, but then he mentioned Quetzalcoatl – an Aztec god of wind, air, and learning, and how he became a feathered serpent. While researching and studying the Book of Mormon, it is said that the resurrected Christ descended from heaven and visited the people of the Americas, shortly after his resurrection, and that Quetzalcoatl closely resembles that of the Savior so much, they are believed to be the same being. Then again, I have heard many creation stories among other religious beliefs. Rip Taylor was also known as the "Prince of Pandemonium" and I wasn't clear or didn't understand the point or what Gregory was leading up to, and then he spoke of us as a collective.

"You all have met before in past lives. You are all connected. And you are here to meet again in this life to understand and work towards your purpose together. The transformation has already begun, and we are living in exciting times."

What now? I thought. He started with Antonio, who sat to my far left.

"You were a blacksmith and always worked well with your hands. Your creative endeavors are therapeutic and has helped many to feel at ease and peace. You continue to inspire through your works of creativity and will do well in art and design."

Evelysse was next and recognizing that he was going down the row and specifically pointing us out, I was getting nervous at the attention I would receiving in front of the crowd, especially being last.

"You were an apothecary in a past life. Knowing which medicines to prepare and dispense for the purpose of healing was your major focus. Villagers came to you to provide herbs and roots to make them stronger, also as an herbalist. It's no wonder you own a shop that sells products that benefit the people's general well-being through positive awareness of natural and organic foods, medicines, and other provisions."

He drank the remaining hot chocolate and made a content slurping sound. While taking a few deep breaths, I was curious what he would have to say about me since he didn't know much or anything about who I was, other than I like stuffed mushroom caps since I woofed down three of them earlier.

"You have done extremely well in organizing and accommodating those who needed shelter, as you helped with their comfort and basic needs through their difficult times. You were an Inn Keeper – providing security and guiding guests. You will continue facilitating the clerical and management of a business, administrating their needs."

I was next and I almost fainted.

"With each business you have started, even in those far off lands and regions, you created an opportunity for others to gain a job, money, and a sense of purpose. You have a vision for the bigger picture and have always encouraged people to embrace their passions and to pursue their goals. Many have benefited from your inspirational wisdoms, and your enigmatic presence allows anyone to approach you for further mentoring guidance. You will be the one to find and open a Healing Center and the four of you will be working together to finally make this happen. The time to reveal this information is now. That is all."

Antonio and Elizabeth were excited to hear the revelation, but I wasn't impressed with tonight's anti-climactic production. I certainly had my reservations and doubts and hid my skepticism from them. I remained thankful but I was more focused on another mushroom. Eve also didn't seem to look excited either, but maybe I just empathetically felt that. Bobazeb returned to being Gregory and asked how it went, since he hadn't concise recollection of the channeling.

Now, it was my turn to express my confusion about what we witnessed, on the ride back to the café. We hadn't said a word until at least halfway back to Jersey City, and even then, it was sketchy. I wondered if I was just paranoid or if everyone was involved in this deception. Mr. Rasputin was a charlatan – a fraud, and the entire evening was a setup to have me believe that we a part of a collaborate effort, but to what end? Was I being naïve in thinking there was something more, beyond this realm, this third dimension of thought and being, or is this the exception and an example that not all are true and just? My intuition, or Spidey-sense, was tingling.

"What did you make from all of that?" I asked Eve.

"I'm not really sure. He really didn't say anything that was concrete. They all know about the Café, they know about your coffee business, and he was talking in a different voice, right?"

I wasn't fully convinced on the reality, but how did they know that Theresa also said I was going to find a healing center? If he specifically told me where, then maybe there would have been a slight chance, otherwise, he was not wise. I felt misled and betrayed for following Eve on another alleged scheme, the first being that MLM coffee business, but a bigger part of me feels like she didn't know and wouldn't do anything to hurt me. When she pulled over to drop me off by my car, I quickly leaned over to her side and gave her a kiss on the cheek, the way Judas did to Jesus in the garden of Gethsemane. We never spoke of that evening again.

Chapter XXVIII - Forgiveness

Living in the present and "in the now", it is a challenge not to look back and dwell on mistakes, possible regrets, and not remain victimized from past hurts. To move forward, I must learn from those lessons of life and apply them in a more fruitful direction. Reflecting on those things I may have done differently, especially with past relationships, I considered reaching out and making amends for my immaturity or shortcomings. I wanted to get closure and get my own answers as to why things didn't work out and be able to fill in any questionable gaps of information. In the process, I sought forgiveness.

Parking in Hoboken could be a challenge with the overwhelming population of residents and car drivers, and the constant monitoring of authorized Permits, time limits, and meters. Real estate isn't cheap in the city, and to minimize the hassle of finding a legal spot to park, I decided to commute to our rendezvous using the PATH train, since the *Spa Diner* on Hudson Street was only two blocks away. She picked a good spot, it was one of her favorite diners, and the outside looked nouveau in its brilliant white and orange popsicle colors. Adorned with fresh green potted plants, it was as therapeutic and comforting to be around as an actual spa, and a contrast to the vintage and historical neighboring buildings.

We met outside at our scheduled agreed time of 8 a.m., and she looked the same as her social media pictures, but it wasn't easy to initially find her since she took her ex-husband's last name, and I didn't know anything about her relationship status. Throughout the years I was aware that Veronica joined the Jersey City Police Department and was an officer, since graduating from the Seton Hall University law program, but I only became aware of her current post as a Port Authority lieutenant or sergeant through a fellow officer and long-time friend of mine. Her occupation didn't matter to me – she could be the waitress of this diner or the Mayor of this city because, either way, she was cool and fun to hang out and be around with.

Her long straight and dark brown hair almost reached her waistline which was extremely different from the curly and poofy hairstyle she wore back in the 80s. She was fit and in shape. Her white jacket and blue skinny jeans helped define her slim figure and I recognized her trademark grin on her right side when she saw me, and it melted my heart because, in my experience, it indicated that she was willing to put up with my crap. Had she grinned on her left I would have been in immediate trouble.

We hugged at the entrance before I opened the door for her, always being a gentleman, always being good to the Jersey girls.

We grabbed a table for two and she sat facing the entrance, perhaps law enforcement training to assess civilians accessing entries and exits, but I was just comfortable sitting across from her. I thanked her for meeting me and complimented her on her earrings. Because of her active focus on health, she ordered the Greek Omelet and an orange juice, and I ordered my savory favorite of Taylor ham, egg and cheese, on a plain bagel with a coffee – black. We were both Pisces and we each were divorced with two children, except she had two sons. While the waiter placed our order, I got to the point.

"Veronica, I asked to see you because I wanted to say that I am sorry for the way I behaved when we were together. I was young and immature, and afraid of commitment. Looking back, I could have done things differently, but we went our separate ways and I never explained how I felt. So, I'm sorry."

She didn't know what to say, but she wasn't wearing a left grin, so I was still in good-standing, for now. From my backpack, I pulled out a card and a cd I purchased days ago in preparation for this moment, which compounded the level of surprise and maybe furthered more confusion.

"It's Gloria Estefan's greatest hits. I remember you wrote me a letter, a long time ago, saying that you couldn't really tell me how you felt because the words would only get in the way, so you referenced that song and said that you thought about me when you heard it. So, 'Words Get in the Way' is there and so are some of the other cool jams she did."

"Thank you," she said appreciatively. I loved when Veronica chuckled and she had a unique laugh, but I never told her so. She may have never been told, or appreciated for it, but I kept it to myself and just enjoyed listening and watching her. She read the card and smiled, because she understood that we would remain friends. Our plates came and we enjoyed our dishes, conversations, and company, but I started to realize that the more I ate the sooner we would be saying goodbye.

"Oh. I almost forgot," I said after taking the remaining gulp of my coffee.

I pulled out a creamed-colored rectangular jewelry box from my pocket, handed it to her, and watched her slowly open it.

"I wanted to give you a small something as a token of our friendship and so you can think of me whenever you decide to wear it. Don't pawn it!"

"This is beautiful, Corey. You didn't need to do this. Thank you so much."

I helped her hook the clasp to the sterling silver Aquamarine bracelet, around her wrist. That is the birthstone for March, and so I was happy she appreciated the thought and effort I put into it, plus I felt better for making amends and friends.

I tried contacting other past girlfriends but most of them were either married, in a serious relationship where they considered it to be inappropriate, and one or two of them that have either threatened my life or blocked me from ever seeing them again. Those Bayonne girls are tough, especially when your girlfriend finds out you were also messing around with two sisters and another friend of hers. I was good with not knowing any of them anymore; I valued my life and freedom too much to revisit the crazy ones, but I wanted to reach out to someone who made an impression and impact in my life.

I had to get my nerve up innumerable times to dial the last digit of her phone number. When it finally rang, I was extremely nervous and I started to pace around frantically, about three times, and then it stopped ringing.

"Hello," she said in her French-Canadian accent.

"Hi, Paula. It's me." I didn't say anything clever, nothing that I had thought to say to her within the past decade. I would periodically have mock phone conversations with myself, never knowing what the actual one would be like. My imagination got the best and worst of me, and I left no stone, or angle, unturned. There was a short silence.

"Coronado, how are you? What are you up to these days? Why are you calling?"

I told her that Rebecca and I finally divorced years ago and that I had two daughters, and although she remained on the line, she wasn't very talkative.

"How about you? Are you all right?"

"Yes. I'm living with Jean on a farm and we've been happily living together off the grid. I'm with him now. I don't understand why you're calling."

"I called to see how you were and I'm sorry for the way things ended. I didn't see you as a fling. I loved you, and what we had was real."

"I know it was real. I'll never deny that. I loved you too, but I'm with someone else now."

It was almost as if this Jean character was standing right next to her listening in on the conversation, that she needed to sound distant and aloof, but I pressed on sensing that this would be the last time I would ever hear her voice.

"How's Clyde?"

"Clyde passed away quietly in his sleep."

"I'm so sorry to hear that."

"Thank you. That means so much to me."

"So, we're good?" I asked.

"Yeah."

"Yeah. Yeah," I interjected.

"I'm just trying to figure out why, of all days, you're calling me on my father's death anniversary."

I didn't even know her father or that he had died, and like she, I often contemplated why things happen when they do. It was bitter-sweet. On one hand, two entities close to her passed away and I was able to offer my condolences, and two, I was able to converse and hear her voice one last time – knowing that she was happy, even if it was with someone else.

"Please don't call me again," she demanded. *Farewell, Dulcinea.*

Within a twenty-five-year span, since Jeanette and I broke up, I have periodically called her parents' house and left voice messages on their answering machine, at least a dozen of times. Mr. or Mrs. Kaminski sometimes picked up and assured me that they would relay the message, but I never received a call-back. Jeanette hadn't lived there and was extremely focused on college and her studies. I was able to obtain an email address from an internet search engine, and decided to write a quick message, and she responded once. I was thrilled, but the trail kept getting cold and I refrained from contacting her again.

I went to McLaughlin's Funeral Home because her father's death was a fantastic opportunity for me to see her again. I already paid my respects to her parents and most of her family had traveled from Ohio, but I would have preferred to have met all their acquaintance at our wedding instead of his funeral. Many parishioners from their church came and said a group prayer, but the three rosary-toting women were not present.

I heard clamoring voices by the entrance doorway. It has been a tense couple of days, not only for the family, but for the avid dog walkers and joggers, concerning the constant rain which hasn't let up for three days creating delays, visual obstructions, cabin fever, and it just being a wet mess outside. The couple was having a slight debate and were obviously disappointed and frustrated on their tardiness, judging by their tone and raised voice levels. Mrs. Kaminski came and greeted them.

"Jeanette, so glad you finally made it."

I didn't see her face. She was whisked away to meet and greet those visitors, friends and family members who needed to leave but stayed just long enough to see her. The man she was with had taken their coats and hung them on a portable closet.

I believe that people are either an *Elvis* fan or a fan of *The Beatles*, and since my preference is the latter, I never thought to go visit Graceland in Memphis, Tennessee. My perception of his home is of grandeur and nothing less than a "bigger than life" mansion suitable for the "King of Rock & Roll", but when some of my friends told me that it was just as plain as a modest house, I decided to keep my version ahead of its reality. Because I had unconditional love for Jeanette, perhaps because she was my "first", it would not change the way I felt for her or saw her. She was far from grace. She was hope.

My hands were clammy, and my throat was parched from the extreme nerves and uncertainty of rejection and fear. I looked around and there were many people here to honor her father's life and memory. No one noticed me slowly pacing around the main empty vestibule that lead to many other chapel viewing rooms, and I distracted myself by noticing some of the patterns in the wallpaper design. A large ornate mirror decorated the center of the wall and I took a closer look at the white-washed painted frame, and as I took a step towards the center of the glass I looked up and there she was – looking at me through the reflection as I slowly turned around to face her.

"Corey?"

"Hi, Jenny."

We walked towards each other and embraced our youthful flood of memories in that moment. We held each other tight, and she began to sob. I clutched her with my left arm, and although she slightly buried her head into my chest and I didn't want to mess up her hair, I gently cradled the back of her head with my right hand.

"I'm so sorry about your dad. My sincerest condolences to you and your family."

"Thank you so much. Have you seen my mom?"

"Yes… earlier. It was very nice seeing her, and so wonderful to see you again. I missed you guys. I missed you."

She looked up and I handed her a handkerchief but before she could use it, I brushed away a tear or two from her eye with my thumb. She lightly pounded my chest and broke away from this beast.

"Stay a while."

I looked up and her male companion friend started walking towards us from the other side of the room.

"No. Thank you. I've been here a while, and I must go. Sorry."

I looked her right in the eyes and lowered every internal defense system I had in me, eliminating my thoughts and ego with prevailing vulnerability, allowing my soul, spirit, and essence to guide me.

"I'm sorry for all the bad things I did, and how I treated you in the end. You always deserved the best and I didn't give it to you. Please forgive me."

She came towards me willingly, gave me a soft embrace, and softly kissed me on the cheek, whispering "I will always love you."

"Je t'aime, Jeanette."

CHAPTER XXIX - Rebirth

In the Tarot deck, there is a Death card which often gets misunderstood and misconstrued to portray an actual death, but it is a renewal card that which symbolizes the end of a major phase or aspect of your life that you realize is no longer serving you, opening up the possibility of something far more valuable and essential. Much like in *The Lion King*[16], when Rafiki tells Simba that he knows his father but goes and shows him who he is in Spirit within the "Circle of Life", or when Obi-Wan Kenobi tells Luke Skywalker that Darth Vader killed his father but he ultimately became another person after his "death", or that Jesus died on a cross and resurrected three days later through the power of the Holy Spirit, I have died many times and shed many skins in my years of growth and transformation but to what end?

In my quest for knowledge, I haven't found that one book that explains who I am – although The Bible makes a valiant attempt, where I come from, and what it all means. There is no encyclopedia that defines why things happen – outside the context of Science, and there is no guide ledger that takes me by the hand and leads me to direct euphoria, so I am here experiencing, and being, in the hopes that I survive and live a purposeful existence, including the possibility of reincarnation. My willingness and endurance are testimonies of my curiosities and love for life itself and finding beauty in the many perceived flaws of my universe.

---

[16] *The Lion King*, 1994 American animated musical film produced by Walt Disney Feature Animation and released by Walt Disney Pictures.

I equally want to explore possibilities of false narratives, and throughout my going against the grain of popular belief and consensus, and spoon-fed science, I am not entirely convinced things are what they appear to be, and have often been labeled as a "conspiracy theorist". My doubts through the inconsistencies and the effects of human error, where lies and deceit govern the greedy whether in monetary value or personal gain, and how society as a whole has not yet managed to live in utopia for the good of us all, shows that there are many angles, motives, and agendas to shed light to or darken the truths.

My thirst could only be fulfilled if I allow myself to see past the mundane and search for my truths through suppressed or hidden meanings or perhaps to find a pattern of why I do the things I do, and where those root causes stem from. I need to clear my mind of the unnecessary distractions that plague my everyday life and not only is it essential that I provide for my physical basic needs to include food, clothing, and shelter, but to understand that in this play we call life, what role I play in it. In the grandest scheme of it all, where I fit is still a mystery to me. I do not see myself as a cog in the wheel, conforming to any cookie-cut design, but in my uniqueness I am able to be one with a specific purpose on carrying out the master plan, except I haven't a clue, map, or blueprint.

While I have an interesting array of books in my private collection, it does entail the studies of multiple religions to include Hinduism, Christianity, Buddhism, and Islam to name a few but I have read the Quran, and The Holy Bible at least a dozen of times. I have an interest in learning Hebrew so I could read the Torah and the

Talmud. Belief is a powerful thing. At times, I've had interests in reading those texts that are not in the bible, that were decided for the canon of Scripture in the First Council of Nicaea. One of them is the Gnostic Gospel of Thomas, which was discovered in Egypt in 1945. I have found remarkable hidden truths in this gnostic literary work, and it has been troubling because it goes against most of what I have been taught. In one of the verses, Jesus said:

When you make the two one, you shall become sons of man,
and when you say: Mountain, be moved, it shall be moved.

If I can join thought and emotion into one potent force, that is when I will have the power to speak to the world. There are two other verses that share the same message, so it must be that important to understand, but what also intrigues me about this concept is that it is Verse 106. Perhaps the coincidences or idiosyncrasies I have with this number, whenever I periodically see it, is to highlight this message for that specific point of time? In the very least, I have become more aware of the information I receive, and I find it worth looking into. Combining these two factors also coincides with the theory of the "Law of Attraction" and rising vibrational levels – my vibe, to receive other matching vibes.

I know, and feel, that we are more than physical beings, that there is a spiritual entity within us – vibrational beings composed of energy. I first witnessed this when Abuela Marissa was there with Miguel's transition. As he laid there fading away, she comforted him and performed her ritual of safe passage to the other side, and I saw the imagery of a sprite, or light orb, leaving his body similar to that of a crystal ball, and her eyes also followed it upwards until it left the room. I have seen so many anomalies and incredible events, that many would call miracles, that are often automatically discounted as being true because of their inability to categorize it in the name of science or proof beyond the shadow of a doubt. The fear of blatherskite rhetoric promotes the concealment or pulling back from what can be shown, like a turtle or a shelled creature that hides to protect itself from an impending damage or from an unpleasant force that rears its head, a person who goes against the norm may be subject to psychological evaluation, or ridicule.

The Laws of the Universe are among us, yet scattered throughout experiences and fateful circumstances, to be seen when we choose to see them, deflected by trivial false pretenses of political ruses and the absurdity to project false images and perceptions. The guise to control the masses by deciding what knowledge the people have access to ensures that the media does not expose those truths that will allow us to gain control of our own lives. Simply put: the truth is out there... somewhere, but for those who seek it.

Many women in my life have been instrumental in my spiritual journey and there is much more to learn about myself through my interactions with them. I am excited to meet all the entities that will continue to divinely guide me on my quest of self-discovery and self-mastery, but since we are all androgynous energy, physical attributes aren't altogether relevant.

One thing I learned is that when a door closes – another opens, and an integral part is realizing what is a good opportunity and what is toxic. In order to move forward, I must leave the past behind, but still have the ability and pleasures to remember what once was, to enhance what is to come. The dogmatic and authoritative point of view without adequate grounds misleads in thinking that there isn't an alternate way of perceiving and existing, but there are still many questions yet to be answered, however all roads should lead to happiness.

I believe while we are all guilty of something, we should all strive towards innocence and recognize that there is goodness in everyone. People make mistakes which is an impetus that makes us human, and these mistakes are really lessons to be taught and learned to guide us in our future experiences and endeavors. The act of free-will gives us the ability to make choices, however volatile they appear to be at times, and character is built in those lessons but sometimes will-power is all we have to continue.

Personal relationships are a great battleground to test your very limits of dedication, desire, and fortitude. The ups and downs of togetherness can help strengthen or weaken your alliance with a significant other and it can become an emotional roller coaster, and even a tug-of-war, that tugs on your heart strings. It is through communication when one can at least get a glimpse and continue to gauge if someone's intent is mal.

I needed to get my life in order and prioritize and focus on what was truly important. On the top of my list was my daughters, whom I love with every being, but in order to do that I must first love myself. Before I could cast a life preserver to a novice or troubled swimmer, I must first know how to swim and wear my safety vest, to prevent drowning. I needed to remind myself that I didn't need anyone else to fulfill me, complete me, or be responsible for my happiness – that was my job. I took a break from wanting a relationship, and instead diverted to the pursuit towards my career, finances, and my happiness.

Education and meditation overruled fornication, so before I went to bed that evening I stopped to pray for spiritual guidance once again. I was grateful for the many opportunities I had, for the blessings I have received, and for the knowledge to understand why I needed to endure some of those lessons.

"Please guide me towards my true purpose. Show me the way. Please provide the answers I seek."

The next morning, I made hearty breakfast burritos consisting of scrambled eggs, diced red peppers and mushrooms. I propped a blank 16" x 20" canvas on the easel and opened my wooden paint box containing my oil tubes of paint, enjoying the smells of creativity and possibility, in the process preparing myself to regain my power and strength. My walls were decorated with earlier signs of days long ago, reminding me that things truly happened. "The Secret" hung next to "Reflections" in a colorful expression of still life. A business formation certificate was framed and displayed above my modest and uncluttered wooden desk designating my office area. I opened the front door and greeted the new day with prudence.

Instead of driving the distance, I planned on walking the mile to the local library to expand my knowledge in the esoteric and at the same time increase my health in the course of implementing a regimen of daily exercise. During my walk, I thought of how much I had changed and if the end of the Mayan Calendar prediction that occurred six months ago had anything to do with it. But first, I wanted to trade in my Nikon for an updated digital camera, so I went to Old Humble by the railroad tracks towards the nearby photography store.

Living in Humble, TX, I distanced myself from the bustling Downtown Houston city life and was still near the suburban community my girls lived in, plus the house I was now renting was in my budgeted price range. Humble became an oil boomtown in the early 1900s when oil was first produced there and hence there is a lot of history, and sustained growth. Walking along the wide two-way Main Street, one-story buildings aligned the clean and quiet path I was taking, and it somewhat resembled an old Western my father used to watch, except there were no dirt roads, wagons, or horses. The shops were quaint and were owned by individual business owners, and not by any corporations or popular chains.

Living in this old town helped me to start all over and be humble. The pace was slow enough to stop and smell the cacti and appreciate the Bluebonnets that periodically grew wildly among the brushes and bushes of abandoned yards. I was only a short block away from Humble Camera when a group of well-dressed men, mostly wearing boots with their suits, were carrying trays of food into a building.

"Howdy!" one of them said to me.

"Hi. What's the occasion?"

"We're having a charity event this afternoon. Join us."

I noticed he was wearing a similar ring to that of my cousin Sammy, who was a freemason. I looked up above the blue awning that covered the front entrance and there was the "G" shrouded by a Square and Compass.

"Is this a Masonic Lodge?" I asked him.

"Yes, it is, son. Can you please help me hold the door? Thank you."

I kindly held the door open and was amazed with the black and white checkered floor tiles and the amount of fellowship congregating inside. A sense of calling came over me, a hunger to be fulfilled, and a strong foundation for knowledge. I saw the sign.

"How does one become a Mason?"

"You're in luck. I happen to know the right men to help you."

The door closed behind me and the new saga of my transformation began, with a heightened sense of enlightenment, purpose, and light.